SHOT THROUGH THE HEARTH

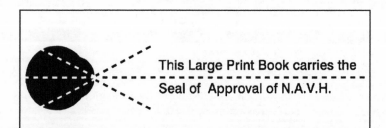

This Large Print Book carries the
Seal of Approval of N.A.V.H.

A FIXER-UPPER MYSTERY

SHOT THROUGH THE HEARTH

KATE CARLISLE

WHEELER PUBLISHING
A part of Gale, a Cengage Company

LIBRARY OF CONGRESS CIP DATA ON FILE.
CATALOGUING IN PUBLICATION FOR THIS BOOK
IS AVAILABLE FROM THE LIBRARY OF CONGRESS

ISBN-13: 978-1-4328-6813-0 (softcover alk. paper)

Published in 2020 by arrangement with Berkley, an imprint of Penguin Publishing Group, a division of Penguin Random House, LLC

Printed in Mexico
Print Number: 01   Print Year: 2020

This book is dedicated with love and affection to John and Courtney, with best wishes for a long and happy life together.

CHAPTER ONE

"Have you ever been to a barn raising?" I asked.

My foreman, Wade Chambers, chuckled. "No. But I've seen them in the movies." We strolled around the old Victorian farmhouse we were about to start renovating. Raphael Nash, the owner of the house and the acres of farmland surrounding it, wasn't here. He had been smart enough to rent one of our town's beautifully restored Victorian mansions until this rehab was completed.

"I've seen that movie, too," I said.

"Right?" Wade nodded, grinning. "Some city guy hides out in Amish country to avoid being killed by the bad guys. And sometime in the second act, everyone in the community comes out to help the Amish family build a barn. It looked pretty cool."

"Except for the part where the guy almost drowned in a corn silo."

"Oh, yeah." He made a face. "Ugh."

I sighed as we stepped gingerly on the badly warped planks of the rickety wraparound verandah. "Watching that movie probably doesn't count as actual job experience."

It was embarrassing to admit I'd never built a barn, especially since I'm a building contractor and I've been hanging out at my father's construction sites from the time I was eight years old. My name is Shannon Hammer, and ever since my dad retired five years ago, I've owned Hammer Construction all on my own. And even though we specialized in *Victorian* home reconstruction, I was proud of the fact that we had built or renovated almost every other style and type of structure out there. But in all my years of building and rehabbing, I had never taken part in a barn raising. In fact, I couldn't remember anyone in the Lighthouse Cove area ever building a new barn.

That might've been due to the fact that I was born and raised in this small coastal town in Northern California, not the first place that came to mind when you thought of farmland. But back in the eighteen fifties, the town was settled by dairy farmers, and to this day, outside the town limits, there are thousands of acres of rich farmland with a gazillion happy cows wherever

8

you look. And yet, I couldn't remember ever seeing a new barn go up. Apparently, the local farmers had managed to get by with the same old barns that had been standing on their properties for over a hundred years.

"So anyway, Rafe wants a new barn," I told my foreman.

"I figured that's why you brought up the subject," he said. "Does he want the barn before or after we renovate his house?"

"Pretty sure it's after, but we'll double-check when we meet tomorrow morning."

We stopped at the front steps and stared across the wide field to the funky old barn where Rafe housed his small herd of milking cows and the odd assortment of hybrid farm equipment he was working with. The red paint was faded and peeling off. A few of the vertical slats were missing, and some of the remaining wood had started to disintegrate. The roof was uneven and missing some shingles.

"It looks ready to fall down."

That was an understatement. I stared at the old structure and felt a glint of excitement. I had never been one to shy away from a challenge, and replacing this clearly unstable outbuilding with a shiny new one would be fun. I turned to Wade. "We can do this. How tough can it be? It's just like any other job, only bigger, right?"

"*Way* bigger," he said. "But if anyone can get it done, Shannon, you can."

"It's nice of you to say so."

"You're my boss," he said with tongue in cheek. "I have to say nice things to you."

I smacked his arm and we both chuckled. But as we walked back to my truck, I sobered. "Rafe hinted that he's got a deadline for both of these projects, but he wasn't willing to mention what it was. Said we'd talk about it when we meet tomorrow."

"Does he know that the house alone will take at least six months, maybe longer?"

"I warned him."

"Okay," Wade said easily. "Guess we'll find out the rest of the details tomorrow."

"Yeah." The meeting with Rafe and my two foremen was scheduled for six o'clock in the morning. I just hoped we would all be awake enough to go over the final details of the job.

Wade pulled himself up into the truck and settled in the passenger seat. "Rumor has it the guy is made of money."

"Despite the condition of his house and barn, those rumors are true," I said mildly, starting the engine and putting it in reverse.

"Well, then, if he wants a barn . . ."

"We'll give him a barn," I said with a soft laugh.

With a firm nod, Wade pulled out his tablet and started a tentative list of supplies, equipment, and manpower. After a minute, he glanced up at me and grinned. "Guess we'll have to schedule some time to watch one of those barn-raising movies."

Early the next morning Wade and Carla showed up at my place driving Wade's wife's classy BMW sedan. I had offered to drive my truck — with Carla squeezed into the skinny backseat — but then I figured that since we were meeting with a genuine bazillionaire, the image of us driving up to his house in a luxury sedan would send a better message. Namely, that our company was successful. And that we had great taste in cars, too.

Not that my truck wasn't impressive. It was big, shiny, and powerful. And besides, Rafe was a farmer now. Wouldn't he appreciate that his new contractors were driving up in a big hunky truck?

I had to shake my head as I jumped into the front passenger seat. The fact that during our phone call last night the three of us had actually discussed which car we should drive was a testament to our nerves and the

11

importance of this job. A contractor was never so happy as when she had jobs lined up. And this job was a big one that could keep my crew and me busy for months.

"So tell us more about this new client," Carla said as Wade drove off toward the outskirts of town where Rafe's extensive property sat.

I turned in my seat so I could see both her and Wade. "I've only met him a few times and I think he's a pretty great guy. Business-wise, most of my information is from Marigold. Plus I looked him up online when we first talked about doing the job."

Raphael Nash, or Rafe, as he preferred, had made millions in the tech world by inventing, among other items, a unique solar battery that collected and stored energy in miniature solar panels, each the size of a deck of playing cards. From there, Rafe and his company were able to apply those panels to a dozen different uses, including small shingles that were attractive enough to use as siding on homes. They did twice the work of larger roof panels, storing up enough sun power to keep a home running for years.

Rafe was convinced that these small, attractive shingles would look perfect on the outside walls of the sorts of Victorian homes found along the Northern California coast, and while experimenting with the idea, he had discovered Lighthouse Cove. And Marigold.

After that first creative victory, Rafe and his company had gone on to invent a bunch of other products and gadgets that had revolutionized the alternative energy field.

Then, last year Rafe quit the business, leaving his tech company in his partner's good hands and moving to Lighthouse Cove, where he had bought the old Jenkins farm. He had hoped to live a quieter, more rural life, living off the land as much as possible. But instead of retiring to milk cows and fish, his mind wouldn't allow him to relax. He continued to dream up new and crazy ideas to improve life on the farm, mainly focusing on solar-and wind-powered farm equipment. He had even invented a self-reeling fishing pole that ran on solar batteries and he was currently experimenting with safe wind technology. He had installed three wind turbines on his property but had stopped using them after hearing that the big machines might endanger the birds. The guy was a marvel. And he was gorgeous, by the way.

No wonder my friend Marigold had fallen in love with him. And vice versa.

"Gorgeous? Really?" Carla said after hearing my rundown. "Tell me more."

"Well, let's see. He's tall, dark, and handsome. Classic good looks."

"Yummy," she said. "Where's he from?"

"According to Marigold, his mother is from Costa Rica and his father is from somewhere in the Midwest. Rafe was born and raised in San Diego. Also according to Marigold, the guy has already made enough money to last ten lifetimes. Now he wants to concentrate his talents on inventing ways to make life better for the poorest people on the planet."

"That's not a bad goal," Wade said as he made the left turn at Paradise Lane and continued east up and around the hill.

"I've heard he's one of the fifty richest men in the world," Carla said.

"He's definitely in the top twenty," I figured.

Carla bit her lip nervously. "I hope he'll be able to relate to us little people."

"If Marigold loves him," I said, "he's got to be a nice guy."

After a few seconds of contemplation, she nodded. "Okay. I'm holding on to that."

"We'll sit at the dining room table," Rafe said after I'd introduced him to my two

14

foremen at the front door.

"Wherever you'd like," I said.

He led the way into the cramped foyer, past an old wooden newel post that seemed to be the only thing holding the ancient staircase upright, and past the arched entry leading into the sparsely decorated living room.

"I'm not really living here," he explained, "so please excuse the lack of décor."

"No problem," I murmured as we followed him through another archway into the dining room.

"Whoa," Wade said, halting as we all stared at the spread Rafe had arranged for the meeting. The dining table was covered with platters stacked with donuts, pastries, and bagels. Another plate held cream cheese and all the other goodies that we might want to smear onto the bagels. There was a coffee urn, mugs, and a row of soft drinks lined on top of a sideboard.

"Wow," Carla said. "You expecting company?"

Rafe grinned. "You're it."

"This is so nice," I said with a big smile. "You didn't have to do it on our account, but I'm not about to complain."

"Good. Then grab some coffee and have a seat."

We happily followed his instructions and then sat down at the table.

"When I schedule a meeting this early," Rafe explained as he grabbed two fat donuts and put them on his plate, "I figure breakfast should be included in the deal. And since I'm basically a twelve-year-old kid when it comes to nutrition, this is my kind of breakfast."

"Mine, too," I admitted, chuckling. "Thank you for doing this. It wasn't necessary, but it's greatly appreciated."

"Don't thank me yet. I'm about to put you to work for the next few months."

"We're looking forward to it."

"Good. Then let's get started."

But instead of pulling out blueprints for the house or listing all the features he wanted in his new barn, he began talking about Marigold. "You know I've asked her to marry me."

I bit back a smile. "I might've heard a rumor about that."

His own smile was brilliant. "Then you know she said yes."

"I'm so happy for you both," I said, and laid my hand warmly on his forearm.

"She's like no one else I've ever known," he said in an awestruck whisper. "She inspires me to be the very best person I can

16

be. That's why I've started the Marigold Foundation."

"A foundation. That's . . . interesting." I blinked and somehow thought of my father's old saying that the rich were different than you and me. "Does Marigold know you did this?"

"I just told her last night."

"Did she run off screaming?"

Rafe barked out a laugh. "You do know her pretty well."

"Yeah, I do." I kept smiling. "And I know she's not generally impressed with grand gestures."

"No, she isn't," he said, meeting my gaze directly. "And while the gesture may be grand, it isn't an empty promise. The foundation is fully funded, and except for salaries for a small staff, all the foundation money will go toward grants to help eradicate poverty and hunger while saving the environment."

I stared into his eyes for a long moment, then nodded. I already knew that his goals were altruistic and humane, so why not accept him at his word?

He held up a hand. "Okay, let me rephrase that. I'm not looking for any pie-in-the-sky ideas." He smiled. "I don't want any *Kumbaya* moments from people applying for

17

grant money. I want to hear down-to-earth nuts-and-bolts stuff. I want to hear ways to use cutting-edge technologies that will actually help people."

I'd had a positive impression of Raphael Nash from the first minute I'd met him last month, but my loyalty was with my friend Marigold. I trusted my instincts, though, as well as Marigold's, and everything I'd just seen in Rafe's eyes and heard in his voice told me that he could be trusted.

I took a small bite of a bear claw and chewed it for a few seconds. I wondered why he had mentioned the Marigold Foundation and thought I'd better ask the question. "How is the foundation connected to the work we're going to do on your home and the new barn?"

"I'm glad you asked," he said, gulping down some coffee. "Let me explain what I have in mind."

The three of us pulled out our tablets and prepared to take notes.

Rafe folded his hands together and smiled. "I'm going to put on a conference."

I glanced at my two foremen. As announcements went, Rafe's wasn't exactly earth-shattering. But the more he talked it through, the more I could see that this conference of his could be a major event.

He already had a name for it.

"Future Global Survival Con," he said with a wide grin. "Impressive, right?"

He looked so guileless yet so proud of himself, I almost laughed. His twelve-year-old-boy sensibilities were showing again.

"Very," I said.

"I recently sent out two thousand glossy color brochures to companies and individuals who are active in all the fields I plan to target. So far, over three hundred people have registered to attend." He looked so delighted with himself, it was contagious. I smiled back as he added, "We'll be sold out at five hundred."

"Wow," Carla said again.

Wade nodded. "Double wow."

"Ditto." I chuckled a little. "I guess you can tell we're pretty fascinated by all of your plans."

"I'm glad, because the feeling's mutual."

"It is?"

"Oh, yeah," he said. "I can't wait to start working with you guys. Marigold insisted on driving me around town to show off some of the houses you've renovated. You do good work."

"We like to think so," Wade said with a grin.

I nodded. "Thank you."

He smiled sheepishly. "Also, I confess I did a little background research on your company."

"That's reasonable."

"Yeah, and I talked to a bunch of people around town."

"Oh boy," Wade muttered.

I immediately worried that he might've talked to Whitney Reid Gallagher, my worst enemy since high school. She would've given him an earful of reasons to avoid hiring me. None of her reasons were based in reality, but that wouldn't matter to Whitney.

Rafe chuckled. "It's all good. I was really impressed with what I found out. I admire your work ethic. And Marigold loves you, of course. So I'd say I'm pretty lucky to have you."

"I think you'll be happy with our work," I said, relieved that he didn't mention Whitney.

"I know I will," he said. "I just need you to assure me that my house will be finished before the conference starts."

"And when does the conference start?"

"Eight months from today."

"Oh." I blinked. I kept getting taken by surprise. "Well, that's completely doable, depending on the circumstances, of course."

"What circumstances?" he demanded.

"Supplies and equipment delivered on time," I said. "Available manpower. Co-operative weather. Things like that."

"I'm willing to pay whatever it takes to overcome all of those obstacles."

That was something you dreamt of hearing from a client — but rarely did.

"Then we will overcome all the obstacles," I said cheerfully.

Wade jumped in. "I know you and Shannon have discussed your plans for the house, but maybe you could go over it again with all of us. I assume you'll want to add square footage, open up some of the rooms. Modernize the kitchen. Maybe add on a bathroom or two."

"Yes, all of that."

I glanced at Wade and Carla. "I've already explained the city charter to Rafe, so he knows that the exterior style of the house will remain Victorian."

"It was never an issue," Rafe said with a shrug. "I've always liked the style. And Marigold loves it."

Lighthouse Cove had been added to the National Trust for Historic Preservation years ago, and the town council had decreed that all new buildings must conform to the Victorian style.

"But the materials and the construction

21

will be contemporary," I assured him.

"Of course," Rafe said with confidence.

"And then there's the barn," Carla added.

"Oh, yeah." Rafe's eyes lit up again. "About the barn."

"What about the barn?" Wade asked, immediately suspicious.

"It doesn't have to be finished before the conference," he explained. "Well, except for the foundation and a three-foot concrete block wall around the perimeter."

I hesitated, then asked, "What exactly do you mean when you say it doesn't have to be finished?"

"I'll explain later," he said breezily. "I'm getting ahead of myself." He reached for the stack of threefold leaflets and passed them around the table. "Here, have some conference brochures. Anyone want more coffee?"

Maybe it was just as well that we were taking a short breather because my head was starting to spin.

Once we all had more coffee — because we needed it — Rafe spelled out his plans, and I had to agree that with all of his connections throughout the world, this conference could be pretty amazing. Or a complete disaster. Time would tell.

I did know that Lighthouse Cove would

love having a big conference held so close by. The local hotels would be in heaven, and the shops and restaurants would get plenty of business.

"I've already booked a few dozen speakers," he said. "We'll have demonstrations and lectures and workshops on all sorts of future-forward ideas from every area of business, education, arts and sciences, space, communication, food and farming."

"You've already lined up all these people?" Wade asked.

"Yeah. Well, most of them are friends, so it wasn't too hard to twist their arms." He sat forward in his chair, getting into the subject. "We've got an eco-fisheries expert whose passion is tide pools. And another, my friend Julian Reedy, is a world-renowned plant expert who is determined to prove that plants can communicate with humans." He grinned. "Oh, and wait 'til you see the Stephanie vine. She's this huge, fast-growing plant that moves and grows in reaction to human pheromones. She's extraordinary."

"Wait," Carla said. "Stephanie is . . . a plant?"

"Yeah. You'll see. It's very cool. And another buddy, Arnold Larsson, is a pioneer in the field of smart mice studies."

Mice? I shivered. One of my deepest, dark-

23

est secrets was that I was deathly afraid of mice. But I wasn't about to mention it here and now.

"And, Shannon, I would love to display some of the tiny houses you've been building. They're perfect for people who're looking to step away from the grid and leave a smaller carbon footprint."

"Sure. I'll get in touch with some of the owners and see if they'd like to take part." I was so proud of the tiny houses my crew and I had started building last year. The four-hundred-square-foot homes had become so popular that I finally had to hire six full-time crew to work on them exclusively. We had sold sixteen homes so far and were still receiving offers daily.

"We've also got some fantastic chefs lined up to talk about the slow food movement," Rafe continued, and his eyes twinkled. "Which means, naturally, there will be a lot of food and wine tastings."

"Count me in," Carla said, and we all laughed.

"And we'll have a couple of thriller writers give a workshop on worst-case scenarios. You know, doomsday stuff. It'll be fun and scary at the same time." He glanced at me. "I'm hoping your boyfriend will agree to moderate that panel."

"Mac?" The gorgeous man who took up most of my thoughts and all of my dreams. I smiled at the thought of him heading that workshop. His bestselling thrillers were filled with doomsday plots and his hero, Jake Slater, always managed to avert disaster in the end. "He'll be great."

"Everyone who comes to the conference will be invited to submit a grant proposal and give a short presentation on how they would change the world. I'll be awarding a number of grants to help them finance their projects and ideas, put their words into action."

"Sounds like a wonderful opportunity," I said, caught up in his enthusiasm.

"I think so," he said. "I hope we'll get a lot of great ideas out of this."

"Logistical question," Wade said. "Since you're anxious to have the house finished by the time of the conference, are you planning to hold the conference on your property?"

"Yes, we'll do it here." He spread his arms out. "I've got five hundred acres so finding space won't be a problem. I've ordered two giant inflatable domes, one to be divided into separate rooms for workshops and small demonstration spaces, and the other to be used as a larger theater for the more

25

popular speakers and events. I might order another dome, but we'll wait and see. I'd like to have part of the land graded to accommodate the conference space and give people a good surface to walk on. And I'd like to set aside an acre or two for a gravel parking lot. And then there's the barn."

"The old barn?" Wade asked, his eyes narrowed. I knew what he was thinking: how could that wobbly old pile of rotting boards support five hundred people?

Rafe gave a light shrug. "I don't want to tear it down because right now it's where we milk the cows."

"Cows?" Wade repeated. "For real?"

"Yeah. You should check out my setup. I've got some happy cows in there."

"Cool," Carla said with a grin.

"I figure we can tidy up the old barn and use it as a space for vendors and some of the exhibits. And then there's the new barn."

Finally, I thought. "What is your plan for that?"

Excited now, he rubbed his hands together. "My plan is to have you finish the new barn *during* the conference. If you finish in time, we might be able to use it for some of the final events at the end of the week."

"I'm not sure I understand."

He took a breath. "Okay. Let me go over a few more of my ideas and we'll come back to the barn."

I tried not to frown. "Um, okay."

"Great. So I'll also want your crew to build a tower that we'll use as a vertical garden."

"Tower," I murmured, writing down the word three times. Maybe I'd consumed too much sugar because I was lost.

Carla piped up, "I've seen vertical gardens, but exactly what do you have in mind for this one?"

He pursed his lips in thought. "For the structure itself, I picture something similar to a fire department tower, if you've ever seen one of those."

"Sure," I said.

"Good. So basically it's a bunker built of concrete block, about three stories tall." He shifted in his chair and gazed at Carla. "It won't look like much on the outside, but inside we'll have a lush maze of plants and flowers growing up the walls and vines cascading down the walls. It's going to be amazing to walk inside and feel your entire body relax. There will be open windows with louvers that move with the sun to allow the maximum ratio of heat, light, and humidity for the plants to thrive."

"Wow," Carla whispered, clearly impressed.

"The louvers are automated?" I asked, regaining some of my brain power.

"Yes."

"And they're solar tracking?"

"Yes." Rafe beamed at me. "You've seen examples of them?"

"I have and they're awesome. I would love to get my hands on them."

He laughed. "Well, here's your chance." He set down his coffee mug. "The tower will be the tallest building on the property so obviously there's no possibility of shade. The louvers will go a long way toward moderating the temperatures inside. Structurally, I envision multiple mini-terraces, winding paths, ramps, and stairways leading up to an open-air rooftop."

"The tower will have to be built soon," I said, "if you expect to have lush plant life cascading down the interior walls by the time the conference begins."

"Yes. I'd like construction to begin as soon as possible."

"At the risk of repeating what we've said a dozen times, wow," Wade said. "You really seem to know a lot about this stuff."

"It's what I've worked toward my whole life," he said simply. "Green spaces in cities can lower temperatures and clean the air. It's important to me."

"It's important to us that we give you what you want." I had met dedicated people like Raphael Nash before, but I'd never met anyone who had the cash to make it all happen.

"I know you will," he said encouragingly. "And don't worry. We'll go over all of this again. Right now I'm just laying the groundwork, giving you an idea of what I have in mind."

"Okay. Good," I said, nodding as I made more notes. With all the work he had planned for us, this job could go a lot longer than eight months. *Nothing wrong with that,* I thought.

"Great," he said with satisfaction.

"Back to the parking lot for a second — I wouldn't use crushed gravel," I said. "But a small grade of gravel, say a pebble-sized rock, would be fine, if layered thinly."

"Sounds good. We can look at samples later. Also, I'll need my own driveway separate from the conference parking lot."

"Of course." I hesitated, then asked, "You didn't want gravel for that, did you?"

"No." He shook his head. "I'm not sure what I want."

"We could lay down stone," I suggested.

"Or brick, or a basic cement slab. Or blacktop, although I wouldn't really recommend that. It's practical, but not very attractive. I can get some samples and photos for you to look at."

"Great." He made a note on his legal pad. "Now let's talk about a timeline." He was still smiling easily, but now I could see a ray of steely resolve in his eyes. I almost sighed, knowing that with his fortune he could get whatever he wanted, including new contractors. I wouldn't let that happen. I intended to do the job he wanted us to do, but that didn't mean we wouldn't be asking a lot of questions.

"So let me get this straight," Carla said, reading through her notes. "You said that you don't need the barn to be finished by the time the conference starts."

"Well, yeah." He hesitated. "I wasn't very clear about that, but basically, I want you to start building the barn *during* the conference. My plan is to put on an old-fashioned barn raising."

I glanced at Wade and he grinned back at me. "A barn raising. Interesting."

"Yeah," Rafe said. "It'll be the first big event at the start of the conference."

I frowned. "But what does a barn raising have to do with future global survival?"

He leaned in closer and said, "It's going to be a *green* barn."

A green barn? They were usually red, but I suppose it didn't matter. It took a few seconds for the meaning of his words to sink in and then I felt like a numbskull. "By *green,* you mean environmentally friendly."

"Exactly." He smiled brightly. "I'm sure you know more about the actual materials than I do, but for instance, I'd like to see us use composite wood sidings, solar panels, a water reclamation system. We can talk about the particulars later, but you get the idea."

"Yes, of course." I was back in my element. "We're starting to do a lot more of that in our construction jobs."

"I've noticed," he said. "You built the solar panel canopies over the high school parking lot, so I figure you'll know how to get it done."

"We do and we will," Wade said firmly.

"And just a quick aside," Rafe said. "I'm going to want the new house to be as close to green as we can get it. What do you think?"

I lifted my chin and gazed right at him. "We can do it."

Now he grinned broadly. "That's why I hired you."

It was almost noon when we finished the meeting and headed back to town. I was glad Wade was driving because my brain was buzzing from information overload. We had spent another hour discussing Rafe's conference and then we had finally moved on to talk about the house renovation.

Currently, his fourteen-hundred-square-foot Victorian farmhouse was a two-story, three-bedroom, one-bath home. The rooms were small, the halls were narrow, and the closets were minuscule.

Rafe wanted the walls built out until we had over three thousand square feet with four large bedrooms, four updated bathrooms, an open, modern kitchen, a wide wraparound porch, and four fireplaces.

Piece of cake.

He also wanted an outdoor kitchen built on the large patio, complete with a fireplace and a pizza oven. Because, why not? I'd written it all down. The man knew what he wanted and I was determined to make it happen for him. And for Marigold.

"Can the patio and fireplace also be done by the time the conference starts?" Rafe had asked. "I'm going to want to show it off."

"Absolutely," I'd assured him. "My newest crew member is a very gifted stonemason from Scotland. He'll build you the fireplace of your dreams. And if you'd like to see some of his work beforehand, I can arrange to show you the amazing fireplace and hearth he built for his sister using reclaimed stone, brick, and glass."

His eyes lit up. "I was just about to ask if it could be done with reclaimed materials."

I grinned and nodded. "Absolutely."

"Who's the stonemason?" Rafe asked, curious now. "Maybe I've met him around town."

"His name is Niall Rose and he's a true artist. His sister Emily Rose is a friend of ours."

"Marigold's friend Emily?"

I smiled. "Yes."

Rafe frowned. "Is he the one who wears a kilt?"

"He sure is," Carla said with a happy grin. "You can't miss him."

"He doesn't wear the kilt when he's working," I added quickly, having asked Niall that very question when I'd interviewed him for the job. "Just when he's off to the pub or strolling around town."

Rafe and Wade had exchanged a purely male look, and I knew what they were thinking. How could any guy compete with a big burly Scotsman in a kilt?

The answer was obvious. They couldn't.

Two nights later, I invited Marigold and Rafe over for spaghetti and meatballs. While I stirred the pasta sauce, Mac poured the wine.

"Thanks," Rafe said after his glass was filled. "I'm glad you invited us over tonight because I wanted to talk to you both about the foundation."

"It's a great idea," Mac said.

"I'm glad you think so, because I want you both to be on my board of directors."

I turned away from the stove and stared at him. "Are you serious? I don't have any experience with that sort of thing. I wouldn't know the first thing to do."

"I can help with that," Rafe said with a grin.

"You're a vital member of this community, Shannon," Marigold said. "And you have lots of great ideas for improving people's lives."

I stared at her, then nodded reluctantly. "I do get a kick out of coming up with helpful innovations. But really, I'm just a small-town building contractor."

Rafe leaned against the counter. "You have

expertise in alternative energy sources and you know all the different types of environmentally sound products and materials that are on the market. And you use them for your home renovations. You know more than you think you do, and I know you would add a lot of good input to the board's decision-making process."

"What kinds of decisions are you trying to make?"

He took a sip of wine. "We'll be funding small companies and individuals who are leading the way, inventing new products and bringing their own brand of new technologies to the marketplace."

I gave the sauce one more stir and set down the spoon. "Your foundation sounds a lot like the company you used to run. What's the difference?"

Rafe nodded. "The company was involved in research and development of new products, then patenting them and finally producing them. The foundation doesn't do that work itself, but instead gives money to small companies and individuals who are focused on finding solutions to the world's biggest challenges." He chuckled ruefully. "My partners at the company didn't have such lofty aims. Which is one reason why I finally retired."

Marigold squeezed his arm. "But while you were there, you came up with wonderful ideas that are already helping to change the world."

He smiled at her and gave her a kiss. "Thank you." Finally he glanced back at me. "As a building contractor, you're on the front line. You're constantly learning about the latest innovations and choosing the most energy-efficient products and materials. And you're devising the newest and best methods for putting it all together."

I frowned. "You're making me sound like some kind of brilliant strategist, and I'm so *not* that."

"Yes you are," Marigold insisted with a smile.

I looked at her fondly. "You're sweet, but we both know I'm not."

She just grinned and swirled her wine, so I switched my gaze over to Rafe, who, lest I forgot, was my newest client. "I guess you're right in one aspect. I do keep up on the latest innovations in the building industry. But seriously, I'm no genius. I just want the best for my client."

Rafe flashed a big grin. "I appreciate that."

I let out a breath. "Well, then I'd be honored to help the foundation in any way I can."

"Good. Thank you." He immediately turned his focus to Mac. "Will you join us on the board of directors?"

"Sure. Sounds like a kick in the pants."

"I hope so." Rafe shook his head, laughing. "You also may have heard about the conference I'm holding next October."

"I've heard some rumors," Mac said. "Mainly from you."

Rafe laughed again. "Yeah, I'm pretty psyched about it. And I'm hoping you'll moderate a panel on worst-case scenarios."

I set down the sauce spoon and gazed at Mac. "You would be great at that. Your books are filled with so many of them."

"That's true enough." Mac stood at the chopping block, cutting up a cucumber for the salad. "Sure. I'll be happy to do it. Would you like me to come up with solutions or just present some problems?"

"You could do both if you want," Rafe said. "It's up to you."

"You want MacGyver stuff or Jake Slater stuff?"

Rafe looked puzzled. "What's the difference?"

Mac didn't even have to think about it. "Okay. Say there's the threat of a nuclear bomb going off in the lighthouse. Naturally, both Jake Slater and MacGyver will save the day, but Jake will do it by kidnapping the drug warlord who planted the bomb in the first place, dragging him into the lighthouse, and forcing him at knifepoint to call off the threat. But meanwhile, his entire army of cutthroats are already advancing and Jake will have to fight them off with his bare hands. And the knife, of course."

"Wow," Marigold whispered.

"MacGyver, on the other hand," Mac continued, "will devise a gadget made of toothpicks and a hairnet that he'll use to jam the timer and prevent the bomb from exploding."

Rafe's deep laugh was filled with delight. "I knew you'd be the perfect choice."

CHAPTER TWO

Two months later

"How's it going, boss?"

I looked up from the bucket of drywall mud and beamed with delight at the familiar face at the doorway. "Dad! How are you?"

"Couldn't be better," he said, looking relaxed and happy. I hadn't seen him in a while and I had to fight back the wave of emotion that grabbed hold of me. It wouldn't be cool to burst into tears on a construction site.

I glanced over at my head carpenter, Sean Brogan. "Can you take it from here?"

"Sure. I'll get Todd to help out. You go visit with your dad."

"Thanks." I wiped the beads of perspiration from my forehead, walked across Rafe's new master bedroom, and gave Dad a light hug. "I don't want to get any drywall powder on you."

"Wouldn't be the first time," he said with

a grin, then turned back. "Thanks, Sean."

"You bet. Good to see you, Jack."

Dad and I strolled down the wide hall toward the front part of the house. "Man, this place is going to be fantastic. Love the open concept."

"I do, too. It's slow going, though. The demo took a few extra weeks because instead of simply pounding down the walls with sledgehammers, Rafe wanted to save everything. You know, like the original woodwork and the plaster ceiling molds. All those special Victorian touches."

"I guess I don't blame him."

"I don't, either. He's into repurposing, so we've already got plans to panel his new office with the old wood planks from the porch. It's going to be awesome."

Dad nodded. "Sounds neat."

"Niall's going to use the bricks from the old chimney in the new patio, and Marigold snagged the staircase balusters to use in the garden. She thinks they'll be perfect for growing squash and beans."

"Everything old is new again," Dad murmured.

"Yeah. The master bedroom is the first room to be dry-walled. I want to finish one room completely so Marigold will be able to see how beautiful it's going to be. She visits for a while every day and watches us frame walls and install new pipes. We're still working on the wiring and yesterday we started on the ventilation system. It can get a little boring, you know?"

"How can you say that?" he demanded.

I laughed. "Hey, I'm never bored. But you know — civilians."

He chuckled along with me. "She's going to love everything."

"I think so, too." In the newly framed dining room I pointed up. "Coffered ceiling's going to be gorgeous."

He smiled warmly. "You do good work, kiddo."

"I had a pretty good teacher."

He slung his arm around my shoulder. "Come on, I'll buy you a cup of coffee."

We walked out the front door and down the newly built staircase, then crossed the wide plot of dirt that would become the front yard in a few months. Along the side of what would be Rafe's driveway was a utility table that held a large coffee urn, an electric teapot, plenty of mugs, cream and sugar, and a completely empty box of donuts.

We made small talk while we each poured a cup of coffee and strolled out to the bench that sat by the old barn. The sun was moving toward the highest spot in the sky but the air was breezy enough to cool me off.

I gazed at him fondly. "How are you, Dad?"

"I'm good. I've missed you."

"I've missed you, too. You don't park your RV in my driveway anymore."

He shrugged. "The marina has free parking for boat owners."

I knew that, but still. I sighed. "It probably wouldn't matter anyway. I've been so tied up with this job, I don't even know what day it is. What's going on with you?"

"I've been keeping busy," he said. "Helping out at the winery. Taking my boat out on the weekends."

"Fishing?"

"You bet. Brought home some beautiful salmon last week."

"Really?" I gave him a look. "I don't recall seeing any salmon in my freezer."

He grinned. Usually when my father and uncle went fishing, they brought back enough fish to feed the whole town. My freezer was always packed with their bounty.

"We just caught enough for one meal this time. Pete and I grilled it for some friends."

"That's what I get for being out of touch." I stared at him over the rim of my coffee cup. "Which friends are those?"

42

His smile had turned dreamy, causing alarm bells to ring in my head. "They're new in town. I don't think you've met them."

"You may be right. I don't get out as much as I usually do."

And the "friends" Dad was talking about would be gone in another week anyway, I thought. He and my uncle Pete loved the ladies, had always enjoyed dating women who were on vacation in the area. But there had never been a hint of a long-term commitment from either of them. They were perfectly happy to wine and dine a pair of visiting tourists for a week or two and then say good-bye.

"Do you have enough help on this job?" he asked. "I could get a couple of the guys together and we could give you a hand."

"Aw, thanks, Dad," I said, a little choked up by his offer. He and his cronies had been building houses in the area for as long as I had been alive. Last Christmas, they had helped me out on a project and it was wonderful to have them around. "But I've got a full crew and we're making good time. It's just that we've got several other structures to build in time for Rafe's conference in October, along with a full conference site and parking area to be graded and landscaped."

"Yeah, I've heard about that conference. Pete's doing a wine tasting one of those nights."

"That's right. Maybe you'll come with him."

"Maybe," he said.

"And we're doing a barn raising."

He did a double take at that. "A barn raising. Sounds serious."

I laughed. "It is."

He glanced around, then homed in on me. "Do you know what you're doing there?"

Still laughing, I shook my head. "To tell you the truth, no. I've never actually built a barn. But I've built everything else under the sun and the guys and I watched a bunch of videos and studied up on the techniques. And Sean just found out from a friend that there's an Amish family in Pennsylvania who's getting ready to build a new barn. I'm going to send him back to learn all about it."

"For real?"

"Yeah." I gave a quick shrug. "I'm hoping he'll bring back a consultant or two for the event."

Dad nodded, but still didn't look convinced. "Might be a good idea."

"Oh. And we've got a firm of structural

engineers working on the plans with us."

Now he grinned. "You could've mentioned that earlier."

It was my turn to laugh. "Have a little confidence, Dad. You taught me everything I know. Remember?"

"Yeah, and I did a pretty darn good job." He nudged his shoulder against mine. "And I have more than a little confidence in you, sweetheart."

I soaked up the closeness, breathed in his familiar scent of Old Spice mixed with fresh sawdust. Maybe the sawdust aroma was coming from me this time, but it didn't matter. It took me back to a time when we worked side by side every day.

"I miss you, Dad." I had to laugh. "I guess I might've mentioned that."

"Yeah. But you know I'm only a few blocks away." He chuckled. "But I miss you, too. We get busy and go along, forgetting that life could change in a heartbeat. I don't want so much time to pass before we get together again."

The breeze ruffled my hair and I pulled my baseball cap down more firmly. I could hear the sounds of a table saw whirring, the breathy rhythm of a nail gun, and the intermittent beat-beat-beat of a hammer in the distance. It was like familiar music, these sounds I'd heard my whole life.

After a few more seconds I straightened and gazed at my father. He was hedging. "What's really going on with you, Dad?"

He frowned. "Never could put anything over on you."

His expression was so serious, my eyes widened in real concern. "What's wrong? Are you sick?"

"No, no. Nothing like that. Shoot." He scowled, then rubbed his hands over his face. "I'm blowing this."

I jumped up from the bench. "Blowing what? I'm really worried now. Just tell me, Dad, before I completely freak out."

"It's nothing." He laughed ruefully. "Except that I'm a knucklehead."

"But why? Come on. Spill it now."

"Okay, okay." He shook his head, then started to smile, and finally his entire face split into a joyous grin. "It's just that, I've met a woman."

I stared at him, trying to figure out exactly what he was telling me. He met women all the time, but this sounded serious. And he looked so darn happy. But before I could ask him anything, I heard my name shouted from the house.

"Shannon! We've got a problem."

I turned and saw Sean waving from the

front porch. "Oh, shoot. Can you wait a few minutes, Dad?"

"No, you go ahead, honey. I've got to get going anyway."

"But we have to talk," I said.

"We will," he said, and gave me a big hug. "We'll talk soon."

A month later, the tower went up. Thanks to Niall and his small team of bricklayers and stonemasons, it took less than a week to finish. Record time, I thought. And it was just as Rafe had described it, a cement bunker, forty feet high and twenty-by-twenty-feet square. Inside there were three floors and a rooftop. There were stairs between the floors as well as ramps that led up to the next level. The second and third floors were open, like lofts, with railings where you could look over and see the floor below. It was a pretty clever design, if I said so myself. I had worked it out with Niall, Rafe, and Julian, the plant guy who would be filling the place with greenery.

We had left plenty of seemingly random open spaces in all four walls to act as windows where we would be installing the solar-tracking louvers Rafe and I had discussed.

Rafe had gone through a dozen names for

his concrete vertical garden tower before settling on the name "Ecosphere." He wrestled with the fact that the tower wasn't technically spherical, but calling it the "Eco-Tower" didn't work for him. Neither did Eco-Cube, Eco-Spire, Eco-Square, Eco-Quad, or Eco-whatever else we tried. "Eco-sphere" worked, and that's what he settled on.

Before Niall started working on the tower, I had asked Rafe whether or not he planned to have the tower demolished after the conference. He had decided to keep it intact and maybe use it for other purposes later. Because of this, I decided to add some flourishes to the basic design. Nothing fancy, just smooth wood framing around the ground-floor entryway and around each of the windows, plus a foot-wide ledge of thick, sturdy wood on top of the concrete block walls of the rooftop.

It looked good, and I had a fleeting thought that I would love to show it to my Dad. It had been a month since I'd talked to him. We had left messages back and forth, but I was so busy on this job that I just hadn't been able to find time to get together. I wanted to hear more about the woman he had mentioned. I would have to try and carve out some time to visit him, but knowing what my schedule looked like for the next few months, I wasn't sure when that would happen.

A week after the tower was finished, a large flatbed truck rolled onto the property and headed straight for the tower. The back of the truck was packed with every sort of tree, bush, and plant I could possibly name. Rafe and another man hopped out and walked toward me.

"Shannon," Rafe said. "You remember Julian Reedy, the plant guy?"

"Sure," I said, shielding my eyes from the sun. "Hi, Julian."

"Howdy," Julian said, his tone friendly as he reached to shake my hand. He had a full head of wavy brown hair and was good-looking in a tall, thin, and sinewy way. His arms and hands were strong, and I imagined he'd developed those muscles after hauling hundreds of large pots of trees and bushes and then shoveling dirt to plant them.

"Can my crew and I help you carry your plants into the tower?"

"No," he said curtly. "Nobody touches my plants but me."

I held up both hands. "Okay then."

Rafe grinned at me. "I'm not sure I mentioned that Julian isn't merely a plant

49

guy, but is actually an ethnobotanist."

"Huh," I said with a shaky smile. "I'm not even sure what that means, but I'm impressed."

I was relieved when Julian managed to lose the scowl. "Sorry to be so touchy. I'm usually pretty upbeat and easygoing, but when I see people hurting plants, I get defensive."

"We don't want to hurt any plants here," I said quickly.

"Good." And he smiled happily, as though he hadn't been ready to strike out a minute ago. "Among the many aspects of my job, I study the influences of human beings on plants. As you might suspect, the effects are mostly negative, so I have taken it upon myself to fight for the rights of the plant world. It can be frustrating, but every small victory is its own reward."

He seemed to lose himself in his words and now wore a dreamy smile.

He was one of Rafe's true believers, I thought. His plants were his cause, his raison d'être, the main thrust of his life. There would be plenty more like him at the conference in a few months.

I knew the Ecosphere was one of Rafe's most important exhibits so I wanted to make sure everything was perfect.

"I'll try not to get in your way," I said to Julian, "but I hope you'll allow me to assist you in the Ecosphere." I spoke carefully, not wanting another rebuff. "My guys and I can move stuff around or dig holes or get mulch or whatever."

He studied me for a moment. "You'll do as I say?"

"Of course. That's your world."

He twisted his lips, probably looking for a way to say no. But finally he nodded. "I will need help. So, yes. I appreciate your offer."

"Great. Just tell me what you need and I'll make sure you get it."

Four months later

As the sun began its slow slide down behind the hills along the western border of Rafe's property, I stood and stretched my aching muscles. I watched Niall Rose pack up his chisels and tools in his worn leather satchel and then pick up a broom and begin sweeping the patio area clean. He was a meticulous worker and took responsibility for leaving his work space in the same condition he found it every morning. Hiring him was one of the smarter moves I'd made this year.

"The fireplace and hearth look awesome, Niall," I said. "And the patio is just fantastic." I wasn't exaggerating. The fireplace and

51

chimney was the centerpiece, bordered on each side by an eight-foot wall of stone — mostly variegated slate, with bits of colorful glass and chunks of granite. On one side of the fireplace was a wide hearth perfect for sitting near the warmth of the fire. On the other side was an outdoor kitchen that included a massive barbecue grill, a wide counter, warming drawers, and a fully operational sink. As soon as Niall's stonework was finished, my guys would build a pergola over the spacious patio and Marigold would add lots of comfortable outdoor furniture.

"Aye, it's coming along," Niall said modestly, his thick Scottish brogue making even the simplest words tricky to comprehend.

But even if I couldn't understand every word, it was no hardship to talk with him. The man was, to put it bluntly, drop-dead gorgeous. He was well over six feet tall with the broad chest and shoulders of a WWE fighter. He had warm chocolate brown eyes and he wore his light brown hair in a close-cropped buzz cut. His usual work uniform consisted of faded blue jeans, work boots, and a black T-shirt that showed off his amazing chest and arm muscles. At the end of each day, he pulled on a thick plaid Pendleton jacket and drove off in a dirt-encrusted four-wheel-drive Land Rover.

The guy was just so . . . masculine. But he was a true artist as well and as gentle as a lamb, unless he was forced into a tangle — as he put it — with someone looking for a fight. My friend Emily, Niall's sister, had revealed that back home in Edinburgh, there were always one or two idiots in the pub looking to take on a guy like Niall.

Having grown up with only one sister, I just couldn't fathom the odd male characteristic that delighted in fighting. According to Emily, something similar had occurred in our very own pub right here in Lighthouse Cove. More than once. Maybe it was the kilt. I couldn't say for sure, but Niall still ran into the occasional drunken tourist who would take one look at him and decide he needed to be brought down a peg.

Emily's simple explanation was that men were crazy.

I wondered if maybe there were some guys who thought they could become an Internet sensation, courtesy of one of their friends' camera phones. Which again, equaled *crazy* when you thought about it.

Niall, not being as crazy as some, had made a strategic decision early on to get to know our police chief, Eric Jensen. The two big men had become fast friends and their small circle had grown to include Rafe, my boyfriend Mac, Emily's beau Gus, Lizzie's husband Hal, and some of the other good guys in town.

These days, if he ran into any tourists tanked up and crazy enough to want to start a fight, Niall simply signaled the bartender to give the chief a call. Naturally, the bar phone had Eric on speed dial.

"I don't know if I've mentioned it lately, Niall," I said as I walked him out to his car, "but I'm really happy to have you on my crew. You do beautiful work."

"Aye, you might've mentioned it a time or two," he said, grinning. "But 'tis I who's happier still to have a sister with such good taste in friends."

I gave him an appreciative smile. "We're all very lucky."

"Aye, we are," he said with a wink as he opened his car door. "See ya tomorrow, Shannon."

"Enjoy your evening, Niall."

I walked back to the front garden in time to see Marigold slapping her gloved hands together and swiping at the smudges of dirt on her sweatshirt. She had just finished planting a wide row of flowering succulents mixed with rosemary, lavender, and a few different grassy plants.

"That looks really pretty, Marigold," Jane Hennessey said, hands on her hips as she surveyed the results of our long day in the garden. She turned when she saw me. "Did Niall leave?"

"Yes. He's almost finished with the patio. Doesn't it look beautiful?"

Jane shrugged. "It's nice."

"Nice?" I tried not to gape at her. "You think it's just nice? Jane, the man is an artist. Everywhere he goes, he collects all sorts of beautiful glass and shells and rocks and then turns it into artwork. *Nice* isn't the word for it."

"Okay, it's very . . . it's very attractive," she said.

I chalked up her understatement to exhaustion and gazed around, taking in all the beautiful colors and clever designs. "This is coming together."

Marigold nodded. "We do good work."

"We sure do." I bent down to pick up my trowel and the three-pronged cultivator I'd been using to blend potting soil in with the dirt. "I don't know what we would've done without your help, Jane."

"It's my pleasure," she said, and gave a little curtsy.

She was joking around, but I knew she loved this stuff. The girl had a green thumb and a real gift for landscaping. The Hennessey Inn, owned and operated by Jane, had become renowned for its lovely gardens, so Marigold and I were both thrilled when Jane agreed to help us out.

Jane was my oldest — and still tallest — girlfriend. Ever since kindergarten when we were both taller than all the boys in the class, the height thing had been a running joke between the two of us. Jane had grown up to be a few inches taller than me, but I liked to think I held my own at a mere five foot eight.

Lizzie Logan leaned against me. "I'm so glad I came out here today. Got to hang with my buddies."

I wrapped my arm around her shoulders and squeezed. Speaking of height, Lizzie barely scaled five foot one. But as she always insisted, she made up for it with her great big heart. "Thanks for being here."

"I wouldn't have missed it." Lizzie was a few years younger than Jane and me, but she had grown up in Lighthouse Cove so we had known her forever. She and her husband Hal owned Paper Moon, the book and paper store on the town square. Hal had taken over the duties at the store while Lizzie pitched in to help us finish up the outside of Marigold's new home.

Lizzie, Jane, Emily, and Marigold were my best friends. The five of us tried to get together at least once a month for dinner, where we shared our deepest secrets, triumphs, and fears. And wine. And pasta. There was always pasta.

I was happy that Rafe had found jobs for all of us. Jane had been put in charge of hotel accommodations, naturally. Lizzie and Hal's books and paper shop had designed the conference programs and notepads for the attendees. They would also be setting up a number of book signings and had ordered books for those participants who had written them. Emily was the official caterer, of course. Marigold would be giving one workshop on quilting and another on her Amish background and ways that her Amish community had lived off the grid. The whole gang was involved, much to our delight.

"It looks fantastic, Shannon."

I turned and saw Rafe standing on the other side of the front gate, just staring at the beautiful results of our long day of landscaping.

"You like?" I asked, giving him a cheeky smile.

"I'm blown away," he said.

I smiled. "That was the goal."

"You guys really kick butt when you get together."

"We sure do." I gazed at my friends, who were finishing up in different areas of the spacious, colorful garden. "Jane is the real powerhouse. We just do whatever she tells us and it always works out."

Last month, Rafe and I had discussed xeriscape landscaping and he had confessed that despite wanting to stick with an environmentally responsible garden, he wasn't thrilled with the idea of seeing a bunch of cactus plants everywhere. His tone made me chuckle and I had quickly explained that there were a surprising amount of leafy green and flowering plants and grasses that were drought resistant, too. Of course, I had every intention of slipping in a few of my favorite cactus plants here and there because I knew they would add some striking pops of color and texture to the space.

But Rafe shouldn't have worried too much anyway, since our little corner of the world had an average rainfall way above the rest of the state. It had to do with the amount of fog that rolled in off the ocean and settled in the pocket between the coast and the nearby mountains.

Rafe had finally suggested that I work with Marigold to come up with something special for the landscape that would "blow him away."

From Rafe's reaction just now, it appeared that we had succeeded.

The landscapers had taken care of planting small and medium-sized trees all around the house and along the road. Once they grew in, they would provide even more privacy as well as a natural sound barrier.

Niall and his crew had built a smooth stone driveway from the road to the house, with two-foot-high stone barriers along the sides. The reclaimed stone was craggy and uneven and looked as if it had been standing there for a hundred years. Rafe loved the rustic look of it.

Marigold walked over, kissed Rafe quickly, and then turned to admire the whole picture. "Isn't it great?"

"Made even greater with you here," Rafe said with a grin and wrapped his arms around her.

"Okay, you two . . ." I laughed and some of the tension in my neck melted away. Rafe was a great guy, but he could be a little zealous. Seeing him relax and simply enjoy being with Marigold made me feel better about a lot of things, including their relationship. After all, they had gone through almost a year of home renovation craziness and were now plunging themselves into a very important business conference that promised to take up every minute of their time to the very end.

"You guys did an amazing job, Shannon," Rafe said.

"You know what? I agree." I laughed. "We really did."

The entire yard around the house was now bordered by a three-foot hedge with a front gate that opened to a charming brick and stone walkway that Niall had designed. The walkway led to the stairs up to the new porch and the very impressive thick oak double doors with classically Victorian leaded glass windows.

The interior of the house was sensational, if I did say so myself. It was now three stories and everything inside and out had been updated. New windows everywhere brought massive amounts of sunlight into all the rooms. The small top floor was one big room with windows on all sides, designed like a lookout post, ideal for watching the sunset — preferably while drinking a glass of wine.

The outside of the house was covered in thin horizontal wood siding that we had painted classic white with dark sage green trim on the shutters and eaves. The brand-new porch wrapped around the entire house and was wide enough to provide an outdoor seating area with a teakwood couch, two chairs, and several tables. At Marigold's request, we had also hung a pretty porch swing near the front door.

Rafe and Marigold were both very happy, to say the least.

I was happy, too, and relieved, because we had made our deadline with two weeks to spare. The house, the patio, and the landscaping were finished. The fireplace and hearth would take a few more days to complete since Niall had spent so much time constructing the vertical tower for the conference, along with the driveway and various decorative stone borders across the property.

The new barn foundation had been poured and the plumbing and electrical were mapped out. The framing for all the walls had been completed but nothing had been nailed into place. The massive side frames were currently stacked along the edge of the foundation and they would be raised and fitted into place on the second day of the conference.

The barn raising would be an immense undertaking. I had scheduled the manpower: fifty reliable construction workers, all vetted by Wade; Carla; my head carpenter, Sean; and me.

Rafe planned to give a short speech about green technology before we began the barn raising. He was pretty excited about it.

I was completely exhausted.

"Are we still meeting at the pub later for a celebratory burger and beer?" Lizzie asked. "I think I can talk Hal into joining us."

I winced. "I would love to see Hal, but right now I'm honestly ready to drop. Would you mind if we moved the celebration to later in the week?"

Jane drooped next to me. "Thank goodness you said that. I'm totally beat. And filthy." She grimaced as she held up her dirty hands.

"Yeah, we're all a mess," I said with a tired laugh.

But it had been a good day. Jane, Marigold, Lizzie, and I had met the landscapers at six o'clock that morning. Their big truck was loaded with dozens of trees, bushes, plants, flowers, succulents, rocks of all sizes, wood chippings, planting soil, and fertilizer. And we all got to work.

Niall had arrived shortly after that and went out to finish the patio.

At noon, our friend Emily had shown up with sandwiches, salads, and sodas from her tea shop on the town square. With Emily, our little circle of best friends had been complete.

Now it was after five o'clock and while the others cleaned up and prepared to leave, I took a stroll down the walkway and out the front gate to get some different perspectives of the house and surrounding yard and trees.

Wandering around to the finished back patio, I took a closer look at Niall's stonework. The fireplace itself was large and imposing, a beautiful work of art. The stones of the hearth had been fashioned into intricate wave patterns, while the floor of the patio was a winding, circular design that wove its way across the wide space.

I thought again how lucky I was to have him on my crew. And I would have to commend him for juggling all of the other jobs he'd done for Rafe, especially the three-story tower. We had started building it almost five months ago. It was a simplistic design, basically a bunker-style structure, and it only took the ten of us a few weeks to complete.

I gazed across Rafe's field to the tower that Julian Reedy had used to create the incredible vertical gardens, inside and out. The interior was now the lush green tropical haven Rafe had described in our very first conversation. A combination of magical fairyland and verdant jungle, with moss and ferns hanging everywhere and vines streaming down the walls. Every type of flowering plant and greenery was tucked along the pathways and ramps and terraces, and they had all grown so thick so quickly that you could no longer see the concrete structure beneath. Julian had even managed to plant a colorful circle of tulips in one of the corners.

The louvers that covered the windows were another amazing feature. When I first had them installed, I watched as they slowly moved with the sun as it passed over the tower. It was a real thrill to actually feel the temperature rise or drop inside the tower, depending on which way the louvers moved. I couldn't wait to install them inside some willing client's house. Or my own. Someday.

For some reason, the thought reminded me of my father. I wanted him to see the Ecosphere. He needed to come out here and see the progress we'd made. I was so proud of everything we had done here, and I knew I would see that same pride reflected on his face when I showed him around.

It was a miracle that we had been able to keep to our precise timeline for the rehab and all the added jobs we'd taken on for Rafe's conference. Those included building the tower; grading two acres of property to level the conference center area and make it comfortably walkable for the attendees; grading another acre, then trucking in enough pea gravel to make a suitable parking lot; and various other jobs. There could've been so many more problems if we hadn't worked out the logistics from the beginning. For instance, if Niall hadn't finished the tower on time, then Julian couldn't have started planting the vertical garden on time, and the Ecosphere would've been a bust. Instead, it was guaranteed to be one of the major highlights of the conference.

Now if only Julian would lighten up about people traipsing all over his ground cover. After all, that was the whole point of the Ecosphere, wasn't it? The conference goers were supposed to experience the green space, breathe the clean air, and make the connection that plants could be grown anyplace, no matter the climate or how small the space. And frankly, it worked. It felt like a miracle to walk those first few steps into the Ecosphere and actually feel every muscle begin to untwist. Maybe it was because the plants themselves were, according to Julian, resilient and renewable.

Julian, on the other hand, was anything but resilient. He had grudgingly allowed me to help him work with the plants to create the atmosphere within the tower, but he had made it more than perfectly clear that others were not allowed inside. He obviously loved his plants a lot more than he loved people, and he took everything personally, especially when anyone accidentally stepped on an errant leaf that had grown along one of the pathways. How would he react when hundreds of people began to descend on his beloved Ecosphere?

It was a mystery. Especially because, despite his curmudgeonly attitude, Julian had built dozens of these green-space environments all over the world. He knew how to behave. I wanted to believe that he would be professional at all times, but I would be watching him. I didn't want him to start haranguing the conference goers with dire warnings of severe penalties to anyone who brushed against one of his precious, fast-growing ficus trees.

I stopped and took a good long breath. In and out. In and out. Rolled my shoulders. Relaxed my neck. And sighed. It would all work out, I promised myself.

With fingers crossed, I packed up my

toolbox, said good-bye to my crew and my girlfriends, and trudged at last to my truck.

I parked in the driveway and miraculously managed to keep upright as I slid out of the truck, grabbed my backpack, and plodded through the back gate and into the kitchen.

"Honeys, I'm home," I called after locking the door, and was instantly greeted by Robbie and Tiger. Robbie, a gorgeous little Westie with a huge personality, barked for joy, while Tiger, my beautiful orange and white tabby, wound her way in and out of my legs and head-bumped my ankles, possibly in hopes of tripping me so I would tumble down to her level.

"Nice try," I murmured, and picked her up to rub my cheek against her soft fur. Naturally, this caused Robbie to bark even more loudly. In dog talk, I figured he was saying, *What am I, chopped liver?*

"Okay, okay. Equal time." I set Tiger down on the floor and switched over to Robbie, lightly rubbing his back and scratching between his ears. After a few seconds, he rolled over so I could rub his belly.

"You're so accommodating," I said with a laugh, then picked him up and snuggled for a minute.

Setting him down, I stood up and

stretched my back. "Oh. Oh. Ouch. I worked too hard. I need to take a hot bath."

Robbie and Tiger sat on the floor and stared up at me.

"Right," I said, instantly contrite. "Hot bath can wait. It's time for dinner."

I prepped their meals, and while they wolfed down their food and slurped from their clean water bowls, I sat down at the kitchen table and checked off the last few items on my spreadsheet for Rafe's house.

"Now it's bath time," I murmured, and headed upstairs.

A while later, I was halfway down the staircase when the doorbell rang. Robbie let out a happy bark and ran to the door. *Who could that be?* I wondered, and followed him through the living room.

"Mac," I said softly when I opened the door. "You're home."

"Hey, Irish," Mac said, then walked into the house and wrapped me in his arms.

MacKintyre Sullivan, world-famous author, former Navy SEAL, all-around hero, and love of my life, had been in New York for the past ten days. I had spoken to him every night and had enjoyed hearing about his meetings with agents, dinners with editors, and parties celebrating the opening of the film based on another one of his Jake

68

Slater books. And then there was the New York premiere of that film. He had invited me to join him, but I'd had to stay in town to finish Rafe's house.

"I missed you," he murmured in my ear.

Part of me still couldn't quite believe that when the fancy lunches and dinners and parties were all over, he continued to come home to me. But since we'd been together now for almost two years, I guess it was about time I started to believe it.

"I missed you, too."

He kissed me then and I could've stayed there in his arms all night.

He cupped my cheek with his hand. "You look a little tired, but you smell great."

I chuckled, happy that I'd had time to take a bath. "I'm exhausted. But more than anything else, I would love to have a glass of wine. Will you join me?"

"Absolutely." Wrapping his arm around my waist, we walked into the kitchen, where Mac received more frenzied greetings from Robbie and lots of head butts and slinky ankle strokes from Tiger.

I smiled at him. "Guess they missed you, too."

"The feeling's mutual. Hi, guys." He hunkered down to play with them for a few minutes while I poured two glasses of wine.

When he stood up, I handed him a glass. "I didn't think you'd be back until next week."

He shrugged. "I canceled a few lunches. A meeting or two. They weren't important. I wanted to get back home."

"I'm glad." We sat at the kitchen table and quietly sipped our wine, enjoying the moment. Finally I said, "You're home just in time for the survival conference."

He said nothing, but scowled, surprising me.

"What's wrong?"

"I'm not sure I'm going to do the workshop Rafe wanted me to moderate. Just found out who else is on the panel with me."

"Who?"

His lips tightened. "Have you heard of Sketch Horn?"

"Sure. He's a writer."

"If you want to call him that," he grumbled.

"What do you mean?"

He breathed heavily through his nose, clearly annoyed. "He's a blowhard and a liar. He claims to have been an Army Ranger. Did a bunch of black ops missions, he says. But I don't believe a word of it."

"Seriously? You think he's lying about something like that?"

"No doubt in my mind."

"So I take it you've met him."

"Oh, yeah," Mac said. "I've met him plenty of times at writers' conferences and book events." He stood and began to pace the room "You know, I don't even think *Sketch Horn* is his real name."

"Oh?" I smiled weakly. "Well, but a lot of writers use pseudonyms, right?"

He brushed aside my logic and muttered, "Pretentious jerk."

I almost laughed. "You really don't like this guy."

He glared at me. "You think?"

"Just a feeling I'm getting."

He gave me a reluctant half smile and sat back down to finish his wine. "Sorry. Can you tell that I just can't stand him?"

"But why? I mean, besides the fact that he's apparently a liar and a blowhard and a pretentious jerk?"

"He cheats on his wife. Blatantly. And he's just not very smart. He says stupid things, interrupts conversations, talks out of school."

"What does that mean?"

"He once revealed to a room full of readers that his agent got a nose job."

"Ew. That's not good."

"Right? And another time, he was drinking with some other writers and he started whining about his wife. Said some horrible things about her that I won't repeat here."

"That's just stupid. And awful." I reached out and touched his hand. "Okay, you're right. I'm sorry you're stuck with him."

"Ah, but I'm not." His eyes narrowed as he seemed to map out a plan. "I have a few alternatives. I'll propose them to Rafe tomorrow."

"Good." I stared at my wineglass and wondered. "I've never read a Sketch Horn book, but I guess he's pretty popular. Is he a good writer?"

He hesitated. "I wouldn't say he's a *bad* writer, but that's only because I'm certain that his wife writes his books for him."

"You've got to be kidding."

"It's been a rumor for years, but I know it's true." He frowned. "His wife knows a lot more about the books than he does."

I frowned. "It must be weird to do all the work and have someone else take all the credit."

"I'm surprised she hasn't strangled him in his sleep," he grumbled.

I would've laughed if he didn't sound so miserable. "I'm sorry you have to deal with this."

"I'm the one who's sorry." Frustrated, he

raked his fingers through his thick, dark hair. "I really hate to hear myself whining."

I grabbed the wine bottle and poured us both another half glass. "As soon as you talk to Rafe, you'll feel better. I'm sure he can switch things around for you."

But I had to wonder why Rafe had invited the other man to speak at his conference in the first place. If all those rumors were out there, Rafe had to know about them. He made a point of researching anything that touched his life, plus he was aboveboard and earnest about everything else. Why would he have invited someone like Sketch Horn to his conference?

"I don't want to make trouble for Rafe," Mac said, "but you know, I spend a lot of time writing out questions and working on notes before I show up for a panel or a workshop. I don't want to expend all that energy and then wind up dealing with someone I don't respect." He took a slow sip of wine, then set the glass down and shook his head in disgust. "And now I sound like a sanctimonious toad."

"No, you don't. I think you're being perfectly reasonable. Your panel will be discussing a really serious subject. How can you expect the audience to trust your words if you can't even trust the other people on the panel?"

"Good point," he murmured. He leaned over and kissed my cheek. "Thank you."

Mac's presentation was centered on worst-case scenarios and ways to overcome them. The subject fit perfectly with Rafe's overall conference theme of survival, but it would also be entertaining — because it was Mac, who always made things more interesting and fun. Or maybe I was just biased.

A while back, Mac had told me that because we lived so close to the ocean, he wanted the panel to explore topics like flooding and tidal waves and boating accidents. Serious stuff. And who knew more about overcoming disasters than someone famous for writing those very scenarios for their characters? But again, knowing Mac, he would have fun with it because that was how he lived his life. He was a really wonderful speaker so I had a feeling his workshop would be one of the highlights of the conference.

But having to work with Sketch Horn would take all the fun out of it for everyone. I couldn't blame Mac for wanting to get rid of the guy.

Sketch Horn was turning out to be the actual living embodiment of a worst-case scenario. How weirdly ironic was that?

CHAPTER THREE

"I didn't think this day would ever arrive," Marigold said, grabbing my hands and squeezing them excitedly.

"It feels like it took forever," I admitted.

"Rafe is just thrilled. I'm so happy for him."

"I am, too." But mostly I was nervous. Tonight my work would be on display for hundreds of people to admire — or pick apart. I was so pleased with the way Rafe's house had turned out and I was pretty certain everyone else would be impressed, too. But still, I was feeling my nerves as I dressed for the party in black pants, a fancy white tuxedo-style shirt, and a trim black velvet jacket.

I was dressing up because Rafe had asked me to give a short presentation about the green aspects of the barn and the house tonight as part of the opening introductions. I had agreed to do it, of course. It was hard to say no to Rafe.

Under ordinary circumstances I would have no problem talking to anyone about, well, almost anything. I liked people and I really enjoyed talking about my work. But the majority of conference attendees were scientists, biologists, and serious educators and experts, and I had to admit that I felt a little intimidated.

"You look pale, Shannon," Marigold said.

"She just needs some extra blusher," Jane said, giving me a conspiratorial wink. She knew me too well, could recognize the signs of apprehension setting in.

The three of us were in Marigold and Rafe's lovely new bedroom suite, getting ready for the cocktail party. I was pleased with the size of the room, which was basically massive. The king-sized bed sat on a platform beneath a domed ceiling that opened to the sky when the weather was good. Opposite the bed was a sitting area with a comfortable loveseat, a matching chair, and a table, the perfect space to enjoy a morning coffee and read the paper. Wide windows on either side of the room looked out onto the woods and surrounding green hillside.

Marigold had popped open a bottle of champagne to enjoy while we dressed.

"I think she's nervous," Marigold murmured as she fastened dangly gold earrings to her ears.

"I think you're right," Jane agreed.

Yes, they were both right, but I wasn't going to say so. Instead, I waved away their concern. "I'm fine. Just going over tomorrow's program in my head. I've still got a lot of work to do. I probably shouldn't drink tonight."

"Too late for that," Jane said with a smile, and raised her champagne glass in a toast.

"You deserve to celebrate, Shannon," Marigold insisted as she sipped her drink. "You accomplished a miracle here. Rafe is thrilled with the work you did on the house. So am I, just so you know. And because you were so awesome and totally in charge with getting the house done, Rafe was able to concentrate on the conference."

"That's nice to hear," I said as I slipped my feet into short black boots. "But I'm not exactly finished with the job."

"What do you mean?" Marigold wondered. "The house is completely finished."

"Besides, you deserve one night off," Jane said.

"The barn," I repeated for emphasis. "My work is not completed until the barn is raised."

"But you told me that Wade and Sean were the point men on the barn raising." Jane spoke while staring in the mirror and fussing with her necklace. "And they know exactly what they're doing, right?"

"But I'm the boss," I muttered.

"She's so stubborn," Jane said to Marigold.

"I know," Marigold said, shaking her head. "I guess it's part of her charm."

"Hmm." Jane smirked. "I suppose charm is one way to put it."

"I'm standing right here," I reminded them.

They both grinned, and after a moment, I joined them. Two of my best friends in the world were here with me. Mac and other friends would arrive in just a short while. I would have all the support in the world with me tonight. I mentally shook myself, knowing there was no reason to feel intimidated. Instead I should've been jumping for joy.

And why not? The house was finished. Niall's beautiful stone fireplace and hearth were finished. Firewood was already stacked inside the firebox, ready to be lit and enjoyed by Rafe and Marigold on some cool fall evening very soon.

My crew had spent all morning putting last-minute touches on the yard, patching up a few interior spots where the furniture movers had made marks, and adding the final bits of décor to the porch. And now we were essentially done — except for that pesky barn.

Other than a few small private tours given by Rafe or Marigold, none of the guests would be allowed inside the house during the opening cocktail party. But Rafe still wanted the outside to look beautiful, especially for tonight's party. And it did look fantastic, thanks to all the friends and helpers we'd called in to lend a hand. There were twinkling lights in all the trees and colorful lanterns placed strategically around the property.

And the house itself was amazing. Honestly, it was one of the best rehab jobs my company had ever done and that was saying a lot. And, I had to wonder, how many more jobs might come from people attending this conference? Attendees would be milling around, strolling Rafe's acres of property, and enjoying the venues and the events. But the centerpiece was Rafe's new home. If even one or two of those attending were to hire my company to work on their homes, I would be thrilled.

Rafe had realized there might be prospective clients here tonight and had given me permission to show the house to anyone who was serious about hiring my company. And his confidence thrilled me almost as much as his generous paycheck had done.

Emily's catering staff had set up four separate cocktail bars at opposite corners of the outdoor conference area. In the middle of the big space were a few dozen bar-height tables and chairs where people could sit and chat while enjoying the food and drinks. Each of the tables had a cluster of candles in the center to add sparkle to the scene.

Along with all of the conference attendees and speakers, many of our town's luminaries would be in attendance tonight. And everyone from Rafe's old company would be here, too.

I gulped down another glass of champagne and forced myself to lighten up. After all, tonight promised to be a party for the ages.

Rafe took to the stage to welcome everyone to the conference and then said a few words about the Marigold Foundation. "The focus of our foundation is basic: food, shelter, clothing, and survival. How do we sustain our own quality of life and how do we help others who are suffering? I hope that the speakers and events will begin to address this massive question.

"Also, this week we'll be interviewing grant applicants who have submitted the best ideas and projects and products. And at the end of the week we will award a number of cash grants to the best of the best. There may be some job opportunities offered as well.

"For everyone who's applied to receive a grant, please check your conference envelope for your appointment time.

"Now," Rafe continued, "I want to quickly introduce the Marigold Foundation board members. When you hear your name, please come up to the stage, give us a one-sentence introduction to your field of study, and take a bow."

He introduced Julian Reedy, the plant guy — that is, the *ethnobotanist* — who was in charge of the Ecosphere. Julian took the microphone from the intern and said, "Love plants, don't hurt them. They will keep you alive."

Pithy, I thought with a smile.

Next, Rafe introduced Arnold Larsson, a renowned pioneer in the field of smart mice studies. "Come visit the mice," Arnold said. "They're happy, social creatures who want to coexist with you."

It felt like a sliver of ice was dripping down

my spine at his mention of mice. It was embarrassing to admit it, but I really hated those creepy crawly critters.

"Now, please welcome Midge Andersen, our eco-fisheries expert, whose passion is tide pools."

Midge ran and jumped onto the stage. She was petite, barely five feet tall, and quite pretty, about forty years old and very lean. She had what I could only call a pixie face and prematurely white hair worn very short. I had met her briefly last night when Rafe had his private meeting with the board members and conference speakers. I was amazed by her energy and enthusiasm for her subject matter.

Now she waved to the crowd and grabbed the microphone. "Yo! Tide pools, people! They hold the key to survival of the planet. And if you see me during the conference, ask me about sandcastle worms!" She waved again, handed the mic back to the intern, and jumped off the stage.

Oo-kay, I thought. Everyone was truly in their own little bubble world here. And now, darn it, I really wanted to know about sandcastle worms.

With a fond smile for Midge, Rafe took the microphone. "And of course you all know Mac Sullivan." Mac didn't bother walking up to the stage, but simply turned to the crowd and waved to warm cheers.

"Mac will be moderating the 'Worst-Case Scenarios' workshop later this week," Rafe said, "and it promises to be a fabulous event."

Hearing Rafe's words reminded me that I had been too busy to ask Mac if he had been able to get rid of Sketch Horn yet.

The other board members included Marigold, of course, not only because she was Rafe's fiancée and the namesake of his foundation, but also because she had grown up in the Amish world and was familiar with that strain of off-the-grid living, a favorite topic of the conference goers.

There was also an astronaut and a renowned chef who traveled the world with his entourage, providing thousands of meals for people affected by natural disasters. I was on the board, too, but since Rafe had asked me to speak about green construction, he was saving my introduction for later.

Rafe held up his hand. "Just a couple more announcements and I'll let you all go enjoy the cocktail party."

There were more cheers, obviously in favor of the cocktail party. Rafe added, "Speaking of cocktails, you won't want to miss the wine tasting tomorrow night.

Lighthouse Cove's own Pete Hammer will bring his world-class organic wines for all of us to taste and he'll talk about the French water-saving techniques he's now using in his vineyards. Don't miss that."

I smiled at the thought of seeing my uncle Pete tomorrow night.

"Okay, last announcement. Promise." And with that, Rafe gave a speedy overview of what else to expect during the week, including expert speakers in space communication; solar and wind power; sustainable foods; alternative food sources; algae snacks; smart plants; biofuel ponds; alternatives to cotton and wool clothing; and hemp products.

"In the old barn," he added, "you can learn all you ever wanted to know about bamboo, jet packs, and shoes made from recycled plastic bottles."

I had helped spruce up the old barn with a coat of paint and some replacement boards. Inside, the lighting had been reworked so that vendors could show their products and Rafe could give tours of his latest inventions.

So far, Rafe's ten dairy cows didn't seem to mind the crowds, just continued to chew grass and amble back to the barn for milking. Rafe's farm manager had been advised to keep an unobtrusive but careful eye out for anyone who might be inclined to disrupt the cows from their twice daily milking regimen.

After another round of excited applause — for plastic shoes? — Rafe finally introduced me.

I climbed up to the stage and stared down at the faces of hundreds of people. I took a quick scan, trying to find my friends. Instead, I found Whitney Reid Gallagher staring up at me with complete contempt. I gulped, quickly glanced away, and found Niall beaming up at me. Calmer now, I spied Jane standing near Niall and I gazed at both of them for moral support as I began my short speech on green construction. Four minutes later — or was it four hours? It felt like it — I walked away from the podium, surprised to hear loud, enthusiastic cheers.

"You were brilliant," Mac said as I stepped down from the stage.

"Right," I said, laughing. "This is definitely a green crowd. But talking about it was kind of fun."

"You sound surprised."

"I am, sort of. It's a real treat when most of the crowd actually gets what I'm talking about."

Sadly, *most of the crowd* did not include Whitney Reid Gallagher. She had managed to look bored and angry at the same time, but maybe it was just me.

And now I recalled that Marigold had mentioned months ago that Whitney had approached her, hoping to get the job as decorator for the new house. Naturally, Marigold had turned her down because she knew how awful Whitney could be. I had forgotten all about that. No wonder Whitney had been giving me the stink eye more than usual lately. I'd just thought it was her natural look.

"This is an enthusiastic group." He glanced around. "Guess everyone here is pretty much into saving the planet."

"I guess. They definitely got emotional over the idea of composite shingles."

He grinned. "There wasn't a dry eye in the place."

I laughed again, feeling better that Mac was close by.

"Hey, Shannon," Rafe said, and Mac and I both turned to see Rafe walk up to us. He had two other people with him, a short, pale man in his mid-thirties and a blond-haired woman who looked a few years younger. "Wonderful speech."

"Thanks, Rafe."

"Hey, Mac." Rafe gave him a manly smack on his back. "I wanted to introduce you both to my business partner, Dillon Charles. And this is Hallie Wilkes, our associate."

He turned to face them. "Guys, this is Shannon Hammer and Mac Sullivan. Shannon did a fantastic job of completely rebuilding my house, and tomorrow she'll be in charge of the big barn raising."

"Oh, great," Dillon said. "We're raising a barn."

Well, that was snide, I thought, but just smiled and extended my arm to shake his hand.

"Yeah, hi," he said. "Good to meet you. You're the decorator?"

"No, I'm the building contractor. My team did the rehab on Rafe's house. And tomorrow I'm raising a barn."

I'd imitated his snarky tone, but he didn't seem to catch the sarcasm.

"Right." He nodded rapidly. "The old farmhouse looks a hell of a lot better than the last time I saw it."

I smiled tightly. "It was an extensive renovation."

Meanwhile, Hallie only had eyes for Mac. I couldn't blame her for that. Clearly awestruck, she murmured, "I've read all your books, Mr. MacKintyre. I can't wait to

87

attend your workshop."

"Thanks, Hallie," Mac said with an easy smile. "I hope you'll find it interesting. And please call me Mac."

"Oh," she said breathlessly. "Thank you."

"Stop fawning, Hallie," Dillon snapped. "You look ridiculous."

"But I —"

"You're embarrassing yourself and the rest of us." Dillon turned to me and Mac. "Excuse us. We have some business to attend to." Then he grabbed Rafe's arm and pulled him a few yards away to speak privately.

Rafe shot us both an apologetic look, then walked off to carry on a quietly heated discussion with his old partner.

Mac and I exchanged a quick glance as Hallie's cheeks reddened. As far as I was concerned, the only thing she had to be embarrassed about was the fact that her boss was an obnoxious bore.

"Don't worry, Hallie," Mac said gently. "As an insecure writer, I have a deep appreciation for anyone who's willing to fawn in my presence."

She gave him a grateful smile. "Thanks. Please don't mind Dillon. He's under a lot of pressure."

Or he was just a jerk, I thought, but didn't

say so. Hallie was young and pretty and maybe a bit naïve. Her long blond hair was twisted into an elaborate braid and she wore a bright purple sweater over a short pleated purple skirt with black boots. The bright candy colors made her look even younger than she probably was.

I moved on to a new subject. "It's nice that you could be here for Rafe's conference. Are you staying all week?"

"Yes," she said, then lifted her shoulders self-consciously. "Well, to be honest, I'll be working most of the time, but I plan to check out a few of the events and workshops."

"So what do you do as an associate for the company?" I asked.

She leaned in closer. "Rafe was being nice by calling me his associate. I'm actually just a secretary. I'm Dillon's and Rafe's secretary."

"There's nothing wrong with being a secretary," I whispered. "I'm pretty sure secretaries run everything."

She chuckled. "That's kind of accurate."

I took a moment to study her two bosses. Dillon Charles was doing most of the talking in hushed, urgent tones. Seeing them next to each other made me wonder how the two men had ever gone into business together. Rafe was so friendly, clever, and dynamic, while Dillon seemed guarded, snarky, and downright rude. But maybe he was just having a bad day.

They were complete opposites in looks, too. Where Rafe was tall and darkly handsome, Dillon was short and thin, except for a small paunch around his middle. While Rafe wore a white linen shirt with the sleeves rolled up to reveal his tanned, muscular arms, Dillon wore a black turtleneck sweater that did nothing to disguise the paunch and made his skin look even paler. And I doubted if his wispy, dark blond hair would hold up in a strong wind.

After another minute, Hallie gave up waiting for her bosses to finish their private conversation. Giving Mac and me a weak smile, she said, "It was nice meeting you both. I think I'll go get something to drink."

"Nice meeting you, too," I said, and watched her walk away.

"Let's take a walk," Mac murmured.

"Sounds good. I can show you the tower where we planted the vertical garden. Otherwise known as the Ecosphere."

"Cool." He snagged two champagne flutes from a passing waiter and handed one to me.

"Oh, perfect. Thanks," I said, and we

90

turned away from the cocktail party area and headed for the tower.

Glancing back, Mac said, "I didn't realize there would be so many people here."

"Rafe said there's at least eight hundred people here for the cocktail party, can you believe it? Five hundred are attending the conference, but Rafe also invited a bunch of local people for the opening party. The mayor is here, and Chief Jensen and Tommy."

"Yeah, I saw them earlier."

Tommy Gallagher was the assistant police chief and my ex-boyfriend from high school. He was here with his horrible wife Whitney, my aforementioned worst enemy from high school. It wasn't like I didn't hope they were happy, because Tommy was as sweet as he'd ever been. But Whitney could be such a twerp sometimes. She was the original "mean girl" and she hadn't improved with age.

"And Marigold said that Rafe invited his entire company," I added. "So that's another forty people or so."

He glanced up. "Good thing the weather cooperated."

"It's such a nice evening." I gazed up at the sky. "And there's a full moon."

I'd heard the old wives' tales about bad

91

things happening under a full moon, but I didn't believe it. Mostly. In any case, I wasn't going to let silly superstition ruin this beautiful night.

Mac slipped his arm through mine and we continued walking toward the tower, just beyond the old barn.

"So what's with Rafe's partner?" I said.

"He's clearly a jerk and a bully," Mac said easily.

"I feel bad that Hallie has to work with him every day."

"Yeah. Poor kid."

We walked a ways in silence, and as we passed the old barn, I couldn't help but take a quick look inside. Rafe had mentioned that a number of vendors would be using the space to exhibit their products, so I thought I'd try to get a sneak peek. It took me two seconds before I was able to focus on what I was seeing. Then I gasped and moved away from the door.

"Well, that's cozy," I muttered.

"What is it? What's wrong?"

"You need to see for yourself," I said quickly. "I couldn't possibly describe it." Actually, I could've described it, but a picture was worth a thousand words, as they said.

Inside the barn, a man and a woman were

kissing passionately. Not that I cared, but seriously, couldn't they get a room? Anyone could've walked by and seen them. Like us, for instance.

I suddenly realized who the woman was. That white hair was instantly recognizable. What was she doing in there?

Meanwhile, Mac was staring at me intently. "Your cheeks are so pink. I can't wait to see what you were looking at." He was laughing as he pulled the barn door open an inch and stared inside. "Oh, crap."

He slammed the door shut, pulled me by the arm, and kept walking.

"Why are you angry?"

He grumbled under his breath, then admitted, "I'm just annoyed."

"Why?" I asked, thinking I would have to look up the difference between *angry* and *annoyed.*

"That couple in there," he said, scowling. "It just figures."

"You recognized Midge Andersen?"

"Yeah, yeah," he said, disgusted. "But the guy with her is Sketch Horn. And by the way, Midge is not his wife."

"Oh no." I winced. "That's sleazy."

"Especially in a funky old barn that anyone could walk into at any moment." He rubbed his forehead wearily. "I just saw his wife earlier."

"She's here?" I asked.

"Oh, yeah. She comes to all the conferences with him. This could get ugly very quickly."

"In that case, he can't be too bright."

"He's an idiot."

"They were moaning," I said. "In the barn. I thought it was the cows."

He began to laugh and within seconds we were both giggling like children over horny Sketch Horn and bad girl Midge.

"He's just such a hound dog," Mac muttered. "It's embarrassing."

I was still shaking my head. "Let's stop and take a few deep cleansing breaths. And try to forget what we just saw."

"Not much chance of that." He managed another chuckle. "The image has been burned onto my brain."

A minute later we started walking again and several minutes after that we found ourselves standing in front of the concrete tower. "Welcome to the Ecosphere."

He stared up at the three-story structure. "Glamorous name for something that looks like a concrete block bunker."

I had to agree. The outside of the building was still as gray and boxy as it had been from the beginning, but now there were dozens of drought-resistant plants tucked into small pockets randomly carved out of the concrete blocks. These outdoor plants had grown more slowly than the ones we had planted indoors, but they still managed to bring some color and dimension to the austere outer shell.

"Wait 'til you see it from the inside."

We stepped through the doorway and entered the tropical wonderland.

"Wow." Mac gazed around. "This is fantastic."

"Isn't it?"

I hadn't been inside since Julian and his team had installed small spotlights in various parts of the garden. It gave the space a wonderfully ethereal quality that I really loved.

"The air is cool," he marveled. "I thought it would be warm."

"No, the plants help clean the air and cool it down. And the louvers help." I pointed to the nearest window and the wide horizontal blinds covering them. "They move with the sun in order to keep the interior from getting too hot at any time during the day."

"That's just amazing."

"It's beautiful, isn't it?"

"Yeah." He continued to look around, taking in the verdant carpet of ferns that edged the pathway and the thick vines that draped the walls. Aloe vera plants thrived in every corner. Dozens of pothos plants, with the most abnormally large leaves I'd ever seen, cascaded down from the second-floor balcony. Succulent snake plants cast eerie, tongue-like shadows on the walls.

"I could set up a table and write in here." Mac moved in a circle, studying the greenery all around us. "In fact . . ." He took out his phone and began taking photos. "I can see Jake Slater getting trapped in here."

I had to smile. "That's a great idea. And wait until you meet Stephanie."

He began to walk up the ramp, but stopped and turned. "Who's Stephanie?"

"Let's keep going up to the next level. I'll show you."

As we reached the second floor of the Ecosphere, the tendrils of the Stephanie vine brushed against Mac's legs.

"What was that?" he demanded, jumping back.

"That's Stephanie," I said, laughing. "She's a fast-growing vine and seems to move toward anything human."

"That's freaking weird."

"Yeah, it's weird. But it makes sense when Julian explains it. Something about its DNA causes the plant to react to human phero-

96

mones. Apparently it's attracted to our breath, too. There's a bunch of other details Julian talked about that I couldn't begin to explain to you, but he'll be giving Ecosphere tours starting tomorrow."

"I'll sign up for that. I want to hear all about Stephanie. And the rest of this place, too."

I gazed at him fondly. "You're already plotting your next book, aren't you?"

"You bet I am," he said, still snapping pictures as he explored the second floor. "This place is wild. It's inspiring all kinds of murderous thoughts in me."

"I'm so happy for you." I laughed and grabbed his hand. "Let's go check out the roof."

The top of the tower was open to the sky and provided a 360-degree view as far as our eyes could see. With the full moon and star-studded sky, we could easily see the acres of rolling hills and woods that bordered Rafe's property to the west. Turning toward the eastern rise, I could see the three giant wind turbines Rafe had erected over a year ago. The blades weren't moving now and I knew that the engines had been deactivated while Rafe experimented with a safer, bird-proof technology.

To the north, I could just make out the

tip of the lighthouse three miles up the coast. "Isn't this great?" I said. "You can see the whole world from here."

"It's beautiful," Mac said. "You're beautiful." He pulled me into his arms and kissed me, and for a long time we just stood and enjoyed the view and the cool night air.

"I'm surprised there aren't more people inside this tower tonight."

"Most of the people here tonight have come for the food and drink."

"Ah. You're probably right." He laughed, then suddenly jolted.

I jumped back out of his way. "What happened?"

"That," he said, pointing toward his foot.

Glancing down, I saw him holding off the precocious Stephanie vine with his boot.

"This is getting weird," he said, then grinned. "But I love it."

I had to agree. After another few minutes, I said, "We should get back."

We tramped down the ramps to the ground level and, holding hands, walked back toward the party. I pointed to the giant air domes, set up last week and now fully inflated for the conference.

"Let's go check those out," Mac said.

I marveled at the massive structures. "Rafe described them to me a few months ago, but nothing could have prepared me for the reality."

"They're huge," Mac remarked. "They must be the size of a football field."

"I think they look like giant snowballs."

"Yeah, they kind of do," he said, chuckling.

I had peeked inside a few days ago, and just as Rafe had explained, the first dome was subdivided into smaller conference rooms suitable for the many different workshops and presentations.

The second dome was set up like a theater, with rows of chairs for the major speakers and events.

"These structures are so smart," Mac said. "Pretty brilliant of Rafe to think of using them for the conference."

"They look futuristic, don't they?"

He nodded. "Sure do."

"We got a little mini-tour the other day," I said, "and it was amazing. The air inside the domes is pressurized, so to get inside you go through two parallel doorways with an inner chamber that minimizes any loss of air pressure."

I glanced at him. "And with all the research you do, you probably know all that already."

He smiled and squeezed my hand affectionately. "I've been inside some of these domes so I'm familiar with them, but I still find the concept intriguing."

We approached the first dome. When I heard voices, I moved more quickly. "Hey, that sounds like Rafe. Maybe he's giving a tour. You want to check it out?"

"No," he whispered, and drew me into the shadow of a live oak tree near the old barn. "It's Rafe, but he's arguing with his partner, Dillon."

"Are you kidding?" I squinted to see if I could make out the two figures. "They're still arguing?"

"Yeah," Mac said quietly.

Settled in the shadows, I could finally hear their words.

"I've told you a thousand times, I'm not coming back," Rafe insisted. "Stop bugging me."

"You lied to me," Dillon said with hissing intensity.

"I did not. I told you I wanted out. I trained my team to carry on without me. I signed everything over to you. Now handle it."

"I'm the money man," his partner said angrily. "I handle the money. I don't do the creative crap."

"Creative crap?" Rafe said quietly. "You mean, the *crap* that turned you into a billionaire?"

Dillon waved his hand angrily, sweeping his words away. "Since you left, we've got over a hundred new patents to deal with. They're all connected to ideas you came up with. I need your expertise to get those ideas into production."

"My team can —"

"Screw your team!" Dillon cried. "They're all a bunch of drones. They don't have an ounce of innovative spirit. As much as it pains me to say this, we need you."

"It won't work, man," Rafe said, and he sounded exhausted.

If he had been arguing with Dillon all this time, I couldn't blame him for sounding dog tired.

"And now you've got this ridiculous conference," Dillon said sarcastically. "And this stupid foundation of yours. Are you kidding me? You're actually giving money away to people whose ideas we could've monetized. What's wrong with you?"

"What's wrong with *me*?" Rafe sounded incredulous, and then he started to laugh. "We don't need the money, Dillon."

"Speak for yourself."

"We've both made enough money to last a few hundred years. How much more do you need?"

"As much as I can get," Dillon groused.

"Damn it, Dillon. You promised you would stop the gambling."

"I just do it to blow off steam," he fumed. "It's got nothing to do with anything. What I'm talking about is the big stuff. What if the company stock goes down? What if you get sick? You can't be giving all this money away."

"It's going to good causes."

Dillon ran his hands through his hair, clearly frustrated. "You always were a do-gooder." It was definitely not a compliment. "It's not like you can single-handedly save humanity. Just give it up and come back to work."

"You've never even tried to see it my way."

"Your way sucks." Dillon started to walk away, then turned and stormed back. Poking his finger at Rafe's chest, he said, "You're an idiot. And that little country bumpkin you call your fiancée is a total joke. She's as dumb as you are."

"Don't you ever —" Rafe grabbed Dillon's shirt and hauled him up off the ground. For a long moment the two just stared at each other. Then Rafe dropped him and Dillon stumbled backward.

"What is wrong with you?" Dillon said, tucking his shirt back into place. "You used to be a class act. You dated the most beautiful, sophisticated women in Silicon Valley. Now you're living on a farm with freaking cows and a milkmaid for a girlfriend. You're an embarrassment."

Rafe's voice dropped to a threatening whisper. "If you ever talk about Marigold like that again, I will kill you."

"Marigold." Dillon shook his head in disgust. "Even her name is dumb."

Rafe took a deep breath and blew it out slowly. "Do us both a favor and walk away, Dillon. Leave now. Go home. And don't come back here."

"I don't have to come back here," he said scornfully. "But one of these days you'll come crawling back to the company and I'll slam the door in your face."

"Where's my sledgehammer when I need it?" I muttered, and started to rush forward. "I'm going to kill him."

"No." Mac managed to grab my jacket and dragged me back into the shadows. "Leave it alone, Shannon."

My hands were bunched into fists and I was so furious, there had to be smoke coming out of my ears. I watched silently as Dillon stormed away. After a long moment, Rafe walked slowly back to the cocktail party.

"Did you hear what he said about Marigold?"

"Yeah. I heard him," Mac said. "And I heard the lethal fury in Rafe's voice. He'll make sure the guy doesn't come back here again."

"What a horrible person." I paced back and forth in the small shadowy space under the live oak tree, wishing I could do something to avenge my friend. "If Rafe lets him back into the conference, I will personally kick his butt."

"Rafe's butt or Dillon's?" he asked.

"Both." I bared my teeth and growled like an irate mama bear.

"Whoa," Mac said, holding up both hands. "Easy, girl."

I shook my fists in the air. "I can't help it, I'm so angry. He's a complete jackass."

"That's not being very fair to jackasses," Mac said, and I recognized that he was trying to diffuse my rage.

It was working, sort of.

"Sorry," I said, blowing out a breath. "But wow. How did Rafe ever get partnered up with that guy?"

"It's a mystery," Mac said.

"I'll say," I muttered. "I wonder if he always upsets everyone he comes into contact with."

"He's lucky Rafe is such a good guy," Mac said, still watching Dillon's retreat. Finally he said, "Let's get back." He held my hand a little more tightly as we walked back to the party.

Despite all the turmoil we had seen and heard, I managed to get a good night's sleep and woke up early the next morning, anxious to get started on the barn raising. I arrived at Rafe's at seven a.m.

Since it had been touted as one of the first big events of the conference — after the introductory remarks and cocktail party of the night before — there were bleachers set up in the field next to the wide concrete slab that was the site of the new barn, and several hundred people were already sitting and waiting for things to happen.

Sean was in charge of wrangling the fifty workers we had hired for today. I found him on the far side of the concrete slab with Carla and Wade. As I walked up, Sean handed me a cup of coffee.

"Thanks, Sean," I said gratefully. "I owe you big time."

Carla snickered. "Emily's got a whole catering table laid out near the air dome. He had to walk about forty yards there and back to get that for you."

"Hey, I had to hold two cups all the way over here. I could've spilled coffee, but I didn't."

"You're a real hero," Wade said.

"Don't mind them," I said with a laugh. "I appreciate the thought, no matter what."

Sean nodded at me. "You're welcome."

It felt good to shoot the breeze for a few minutes with the three people who had been with me from the very beginning. I had gone through grammar school and high school with all of them, and when I took over my father's company, they all came to work for me. Each of us had been through plenty of highs and lows since then and had managed to survive and thrive. I truly trusted them with my life.

For the last few months we had been studying barn-raising videos together. And a few weeks ago, Sean had returned from the real live barn raising in rural Pennsylvania. He had taken his own videos and given us a detailed tutorial in the art of raising barns.

So today would be the real test.

Our carpenters and workers had parked their trucks on the opposite side of the new barn site, away from the conference area and the bleachers. I recognized many of the workers — both male and female — and felt an air of excitement coming from them. I had a feeling that this was going to be a day that people would remember for a long time.

Rafe walked over to get things started. "Welcome," he began. "The barn raising is an important event for the conference because, well, first of all, I'm getting a new barn."

There were gales of laughter and Rafe was chuckling as he signaled for everyone to quiet down. "The other reason I'm excited to present this barn raising is that it's a perfect way to demonstrate the uses of green technology and the supplies that are available to anyone who wants to make a small difference in the world."

The applause interrupted him, but not for long. He spoke for another minute and I was grateful for the kind words he said about our crew. When he'd finished and stepped away from the microphone, Sean and the rest of us moved quickly to the far side of the concrete slab, where all the side frames were stacked.

Rafe managed to grab my attention for a minute. "Just wanted you to know, I'm going to get Marigold and watch the barn raising from the top of the Ecosphere."

"What a good idea," I said, staring at the

tower in the distance. "That's the perfect observation spot."

"I think so, too." He patted my back. "Good luck."

"Thanks, Rafe."

I jogged over to rejoin my guys. Over the last week, my crew had constructed the wood base for the side walls of the barn. They had taken ten-foot-long two-by-fours and screwed them horizontally into the foundation wall to create the base for the side frame. Once that base was secured to the concrete, we could hoist the large side frames and secure them onto the wood base.

And earlier this morning, Sean had handed out assignments to all our workers, so all I had to do now was give the orders.

I climbed a few rungs up my own ladder and Wade handed me the megaphone we used on big jobs like this. "Okay, let's get started," I said. "Thanks to everyone for being here today. First thing we're going to do is lift this first frame up, hoist it over the concrete wall, and screw it to the wood base. Team number one, you know who you are, right?"

"Yo," a bunch of them shouted, and waved their power drills.

The audience went wild with laughs and applause and we were off and running. It took that first team of twenty guys about fifteen minutes to complete the task. I was impressed, especially now that I could see that huge wood frame standing upright along the side of the barn.

"Good work, you guys," I shouted.

Every one of my workers cheered loudly. It was a rowdy group, but I loved them all.

"Ready for the second wall?" I cried.

"Yo!" another team of twenty shouted from the other side of the barn, and I laughed.

They repeated the same task on that side, and I marveled at their ease and speed. The momentum was amazing, and at this rate, we would be finished well ahead of schedule. Of course, I was especially pleased that we had built all the pieces beforehand and now we just had to put everything in its proper place.

Suddenly the sound of a woman's shocked screams filled the air, followed by several guys shouting and running to the other side of the barn.

What in the world? I thought. I looked around, trying to locate my team to find out what was going on. I picked up the megaphone and yelled, "What's happening over there?"

Carla dashed over. "Tell everyone to stop

working and quiet down. And then you have to come see this."

"So much for momentum," I muttered. But after making the announcement, I scurried down the ladder and took off running around the massive foundation.

"What's wrong?" I demanded, out of breath from the run. I recognized the woman who had screamed. She'd gone to our high school but she was a few years older than me. She wore her hair in a ponytail pulled through the back of a navy blue baseball cap. "You're Rochelle, right?"

"Yeah," she said, breathing heavily. "Yeah."

"So what's the problem?"

"Tha-that's the problem," Rochelle said, pointing a shaky finger toward the stacked wood frames where they touched the cement foundation.

I stared, then took an awkward step backward. It was a problem, all right. There was no way this could be happening. No way.

But it was most definitely happening.

The first thing I noticed was the short, dark blond hair, then the black turtleneck sweater.

Bile collected in my throat, but I managed to control my reactions. I had seen dead bodies before, maybe too many times, and it never got easier.

And here was another one. He had been shoved facedown next to the remaining frames. A pile of loose lumber had been tossed on top of him for good measure, so not only did someone want him dead, but they wanted him buried, too, if only symbolically.

It was Dillon Charles, Rafe's mean bully of an ex-partner. He was dead.

CHAPTER FOUR

I wanted to kill him and now he's dead, was all I could think as I watched Police Chief Eric Jensen hike soberly across the field to view the scene of the crime. If this was karma, I had to wonder whose it was. Mine or the dead guy's?

I was instantly remorseful for that self-centered reaction. This wasn't the time to worry about my karma. This moment was all about Dillon.

But speaking of karma, I glanced around, looking at faces. Was anyone else feeling guilty right now? After all, I wasn't the only one who abhorred the guy. The man had made at least one other enemy last night besides me. Hallie had been mortified by him. And Rafe had been even more furious with Dillon than I was, as hard as that was to believe. Still, even unpleasant ex-partners or bosses didn't deserve to be murdered.

I walked over and joined Eric as he directed his officers to handle crowd control. I recognized Mindy and Dan, both uniformed officers and friends of mine, jumping into action.

When Eric broke free for a moment, I got his attention. "I can have my guys move these frames, unless you'd rather have your people do it."

He gazed down at me and shook his head. "Shannon Hammer, what a surprise to see you at a crime scene."

"Not my fault."

"Never is," he mused.

Despite the serious look on his face, I knew this was his way of teasing me. The joke fell a little flat, though, I thought, given the number of dead bodies I'd stumbled upon over the past few years. Sure, I happened to show up at crime scenes more often than most people, but trust me, it wasn't something I enjoyed. It just seemed to be my lot in life. Or my karma. Go figure.

"Do you know who he is?" Eric asked quietly.

"Yeah," I said. "I met him last night. He's Dillon Charles, Rafe's ex-business partner. He was at the party, and frankly, I don't think he made any new friends."

"Apparently he managed to make at least one enemy."

"I was just thinking that same thing."

Eric continued to stare at the body. "I didn't meet him."

"You're one of the lucky ones," I muttered.

"You'll explain that comment to me in a moment." He was frowning, but I was onto him now. That frown wasn't meant for me, but for the situation.

"Sure will. But anyway, what about the frames? Do you want us to move them out of the way?"

"Wait on that. I don't want to disturb anything until we can get a closer look."

"Okay." I was a little relieved. I just wasn't ready to get any closer to the dead body yet. "Just let me know and I'll have my guys help with anything you need."

"Thanks." He turned and shouted for Tommy, who came running.

"Hey there, Shannon," Tommy said jovially, and gave me a friendly peck on the cheek. The man had the uncanny ability to remain pleasant and happy in the worst situations. I imagined his cheery attitude was how he managed to get through life, given that his wife was the supreme queen of the mean girls' brigade.

"Hi, Tommy," I said.

"Man, this must be such a bummer for

114

you," Tommy said. "I was watching the barn raising from the air dome. Looked like you and your guys were having a blast."

"We were." We'd done so much prep work for that job, it was hard to admit that finding the dead guy had ruined a good time. "Not sure we'll be able to continue working today."

Hearing my words, Eric turned and flashed me a sympathetic smile. "Not likely."

"I didn't think so."

Life was funny, I thought. The police chief had recently fallen in love with my sister Chloe, so our normally friendly relationship had grown into a more familial bond. This meant that Chloe was visiting us more often, which made me happy. She lived in Los Angeles, where she hosted a top-rated home renovation show on the Home Builders Network.

For a long time, she had avoided coming home, but now she was becoming a familiar face around town. It was good to have her back, and I wasn't the only one in town who thought so.

Too bad she couldn't be here for the conference, I thought. If nothing else, she might've been able to help with the barn raising. Unfortunately, not even her presence would help cajole the police chief into letting my team finish the barn today. The site was going to be a crime scene for the foreseeable future.

I looked up as Rafe and Marigold hurried across the field.

"Good God," Rafe said. "I just heard. What in the world happened? Was it an accident? How . . . ?" He rubbed his face with both hands, showing his stress and grief. "I was just talking to him last night. How can he be dead this morning?"

After seeing the way Rafe had yelled at Dillon last night, I was surprised to see him so upset. But that wasn't fair. Rafe and Dillon had known each other for years and they had once been friends.

"I don't know what happened yet. Eric probably knows. I can try to find out if you want me to." But after seeing how many people Dillon had run afoul of last night, I seriously doubted that his death was an accident.

Rafe wrapped his arms around Marigold and she pressed her head against his shoulder.

"Oh, Rafe," Marigold said. "I'm so sorry."

At that moment, Hallie the secretary walked up to Rafe. "What happened?"

When Rafe didn't respond, she glanced around at the crowd with a puzzled expression. She finally followed Rafe's gaze and noticed the body, then had to do a double take. And she began to scream like a wild banshee. "No! No! Dillon! No!"

Rafe immediately turned away from Marigold and pulled Hallie close, stroking her hair and crooning, "Shh. It's okay, honey. Shh."

"Dillon," she screamed, inconsolable. "Why?"

It seemed like a way over-the-top reaction from someone who'd been berated and humiliated by the man less than twelve hours ago. And I had to admit that Rafe's instant coddling was a little confusing as well. I glanced at Marigold, whose eyes were dry. She met my gaze and walked over to stand next to me.

I squeezed her hand. "Are you okay?"

"Yes," she said, leaning closer. "I feel so badly for Rafe, but I'm not sorry Dillon's dead. I didn't like him."

I blinked in surprise. Not that I blamed her, but I was pretty sure that this was the first time I'd ever heard Marigold say something so negative about anyone. She was usually such a kind, friendly, cheerful person. Ordinarily, she liked everyone.

"What a coincidence," I whispered. "I hated his guts."

"Apparently we weren't the only ones." Marigold began to wring her hands together. "I probably shouldn't have said that. Isn't the old saying, *Don't speak ill of the dead*?"

"Yes," I said, "but if you didn't like him alive, I don't think you'll get punished for saying it after he's dead."

Marigold smiled. "Still, that was unkind of me. I'm sure there were plenty of people who liked him very much."

I doubted it. But that was Marigold for you. My lips twisted in a frown at her repentant tone. "Look at it this way. It could've been an accident."

Her eyebrows shot up. "Oh, I hope so, for Rafe's sake. I would hate to think there's a murderer loose at the conference. He worked so hard to pull this together, and he really wanted it to go well. What if everyone leaves?"

I let that thought sink in for a long moment. You could never predict how people would react to something like murder. There were times when everyone in town would hide in their houses. But more often than not, you couldn't keep them away from the scene.

"I don't think Eric's going to let anyone leave, even if they wanted to. At least, not

118

until he's talked to them all."

"Good point," Marigold said, and shot another quick look at Rafe, still soothing Hallie.

"So what's with the drama queen?" I whispered.

She sighed. "Hallie is very attached to Dillon and Rafe."

I watched the way the woman was still clinging to Rafe, and said, "Well she certainly is at the moment."

"I understand why she would like Rafe," Marigold said, "but I don't get that she's wailing and weeping over Dillon. He was not a nice man."

"He certainly wasn't nice to Hallie," I murmured, and gave Marigold a shortened version of last night's scene.

And he hadn't been nice about Marigold, either. Remembering what he'd said about her last night made me want to kick him, dead or not.

We talked quietly for another minute and then stopped to watch Eric and Tommy carefully make their way, stepping over each two-by-four of the framing, to get to the body. Once there, they knelt down to examine Dillon and the crime scene close up.

Marigold turned to me. "Let's get together with the girls later on. I might need to vent."

119

"I'll set something up," I said, then watched her walk back to comfort Rafe, whose secretary still had her arms wrapped around him and continued to wail against his chest.

Attached was right. Marigold might need a crowbar to pry the woman off Rafe.

Marigold took hold of Rafe's free arm and leaned against him. He gazed down at her, giving her an awkward smile. Yeah, it was awkward, for sure. But it seemed he was used to Hallie's theatrics.

And maybe I was a horrible person for criticizing the girl. But come on. Dillon had been unforgivably rude to Hallie last night. So what was with the melodrama now?

As Marigold's friend, I didn't like what I was seeing. But then, Hallie had known Rafe and Dillon a lot longer than any of us had. And Rafe was simply a great guy. Maybe Hallie had learned how to take advantage of his kindness. Of course, maybe she was looking for more than kindness. I was going to keep my eye on her.

Whatever was going on, I would be texting my girlfriends as soon as possible to set up a late night chitchat session for Marigold.

Tommy passed by and I grabbed him. "Do we know how he died? Was it an accident?"

His eyes narrowed. "You know I can't

discuss that with you, Shannon."

I gave him one of my patented ex-girlfriend looks. Very intense, very focused. It worked every time.

He rolled his eyes, then muttered, "Okay, fine. But don't say anything to anyone."

"You know I won't."

He moved close enough to whisper in my ear. "Knife in the stomach. Multiple times."

It took me a few long seconds to absorb that information. "Wow. Harsh."

"I've got to go," Tommy said. "Keep it to yourself."

"Of course I will." I patted his arm. "Thanks, Tommy."

I walked away, rubbing my stomach. Wow. Someone had stabbed Dillon Charles in the stomach. Multiple times. So, not an accident, obviously. It was a deliberate, violent, up-close-and-personal act. Dillon's killer had wanted him to suffer. It wasn't like a knife in the heart or a bullet to the head, which would've killed him instantly. No, with multiple stab wounds in his stomach, Dillon would have been left bleeding and writhing in pain for a long time out there in the cold night air.

His killer must've had a lot of pent-up anger to do something so vicious. Of course, I had seen firsthand the kind of intensely negative emotions Dillon Charles could stoke in people.

People like Rafe, for instance. And me, I had to admit. Still, I wouldn't have stabbed him in the stomach. Ouch.

Without another thought, I pulled out my cell phone and called Mac. He answered on the first ring.

"Hey, Red. I'm working on the new book. How're you doing? How's the barn raising coming along?"

"Not so well," I said. "Dillon Charles was murdered. His body was found by the new barn this morning. He was stabbed in the stomach multiple times."

"What?" he shouted.

So much for keeping it to myself. I gave Tommy a silent apology and took a deep breath. "Dillon. Murdered. Stabbed."

"Got it. Oh, man. Are you all right?"

"Yeah, I'm fine. It was a shock, of course. And Eric has canceled the barn raising for the next day or two."

"Sorry about that."

"It's fine. I just wanted you to know."

"It touches my heart that when murders occur, you think of me."

I laughed a little. "Who else would I call?"

"Are you all right, babe?" Mac asked, serious now. "Do you want me to come down there and hang out with you?"

I wanted to say yes, but I knew he wanted to work on the book. "I'll be fine, but thanks."

"Okay. Love you, Red. I'll see you later tonight."

"Good luck with the book."

We ended the call and I turned to find out what the police chief was doing. Eric stood staring at the lumber pile where the body was still lying. Then he began to wave and I gazed across the field to see Leo Stringer stride toward us, carrying his stainless steel briefcase of crime scene tools. As Lighthouse Cove's one and only CSI guy, Leo was a vital member of the team. He also happened to be a nice, talkative guy who was always willing to give me a little inside information. I was almost as happy to see him as Eric was.

An hour later, I finished an impromptu meeting with Sean, Wade, and Carla. We had a new schedule for the continuation of the barn raising and Sean had the names of forty-six workers who had agreed to return anytime this week to complete the job. *Not a bad number,* I thought.

Once Eric and Tommy had gone over the crime scene and checked out Dillon's body, and Leo had performed his CSI magic, Eric gave me the heads-up to move the frames.

I grabbed my megaphone and called my workers to action. "May I have your attention, please?"

I waited until my people settled down to listen, then said, "Police Chief Jensen has given the okay to move these frames now. Can I get thirty strong workers to help lift the frames and move them twenty feet to the west?"

I counted forty-two workers who hustled over to help out. With Chief Jensen's direction, they lifted the frames and moved them away from the body.

"Thanks, everybody," I said when the job was done. "Really appreciate your help and cooperation. Please see Sean Brogan for an updated schedule of when we'll be able to finish the barn raising. Thanks again."

I was pleasantly surprised to hear the cheering that occurred when I finished my little speech. Even with a dead body, people seemed happy to be here. *It made a strange kind of sense,* I thought, *that being faced with someone else's sudden death would give some people a new lease on life.*

Once Dillon's body was bagged and carried off the property, I finally had a chance to talk to Rafe. "I'm so sorry about Dillon.

I know his death must be a huge loss for you."

"Thanks, Shannon." He rubbed the back of his neck, clearly distressed. "We had our differences. Everyone does. But we had been friends and partners for almost twenty years. It's a real loss for me and my company."

"I'm so sorry," I said again. I hesitated, then added, "I hate to bring this up, but are you thinking of canceling the conference?"

"Are you kidding?" He chuckled ruefully. "I've had over five hundred new requests for registrations just today. We've been adding names to the waiting list and we'll send them all a brochure for next year. But the attendees who are here today are ecstatic. It's weird, isn't it?"

I'd seen this kind of reaction before, so I wasn't really surprised. "Yeah, it's weird."

Rafe blew out a breath. "But it's also heartening that they're willing to stay and take part in what we've got planned this week."

I gave his arm an encouraging squeeze. "It's important to them. I'm glad."

And it was just as I'd always thought. Murder brought out the crowds.

At sunset, the wine tasting was in full gear.

The police had given permission for the conference to continue but had closed off the area around the new barn. I was grateful to Rafe for keeping to the conference schedule, too, because it was so nice to see my uncle Pete holding court, lifting a glass of rich, red wine as he spoke of his Anderson Valley vineyard and winery and his gradual acceptance of the French method of watering grapevines.

Thirty-five years ago, Pete had fulfilled a dream when he bought an acre of land near the town of Navarro twenty-five miles inland from Lighthouse Cove. He and my dad and a bunch of their buddies planted the first grapevines back then. And, as they say, the rest is history. Now Uncle Pete had three hundred acres of healthy grapevines, a thriving winery and tasting room in Anderson Valley, and a popular wine bar and restaurant on Lighthouse Cove's town square.

After Pete's presentation, twenty of his winery employees strolled through the crowd, pouring wine and chatting with the enthusiastic conference attendees. I snagged a glass of pinot and sidled up to the main table, where Pete had a line of people waiting to ask him questions.

"Shannon!" Pete bellowed, and grabbed

me in a bear hug.

"Uncle Pete," I mumbled into his barrel chest. "It's so good to see you."

He held me at arm's length and grinned. "You get prettier every day."

I laughed. "You've been saying that since I was three years old."

"And it's still true."

"I've missed you. It's been a few months since you've been around."

"Things are hopping at the vineyard, kiddo."

"That's what Dad says. I've hardly seen him around lately, either."

"He's keeping busy," Uncle Pete said, his gaze darting around the crowd to see who needed help. He turned back to me. "Heard about the trouble out here today."

"Yeah. Rafe's business partner was found dead."

His eyes narrowed. "Did you find him?"

"No, thank goodness." My father and Uncle Pete didn't like my proclivity for finding dead bodies, either. "But I saw him. It was pretty bad." I shook my head, not wanting to think about Dillon Charles. "Now what about Dad? What's he keeping busy with?"

"Oh, this and that." His smile was vague as he grabbed the wine bottle and poured a

127

small serving for the next person in line. "Hey, how about if we all get together for dinner next week at Bella Rosso? My treat."

"I would love that. Call me."

"I will, sweetie."

I was getting ready to ask him about Dad's new girlfriend when I glanced over my shoulder. "Oops. You've got a crowd of people waiting, so I'll let you go. We can talk later."

"Wait," he said. "I want you to meet someone."

"Okay."

He grabbed my hand and pulled me over to the end of the bar, where a woman was pouring wine and answering questions.

"This is Belinda McCoy," Uncle Pete said with a happy grin. "Belinda, this is my niece Shannon."

"Is this the talented woman who builds houses?"

"Yup, the very same."

Belinda beamed at me and shook my hand heartily. "It's great to meet you. I've heard all about you."

"Good to meet you, too." *Although I haven't heard a word about you,* I thought, but just smiled.

"You're doing the barn raising," Belinda said.

"Yeah. We were supposed to start this morning, but now it'll be a few days before we get things rolling."

"I wish I could be here for that, but I've got my own work to do."

"We'll take pictures," I said.

She chuckled. "Perfect."

She didn't seem inclined to turn away and my uncle was still standing there, so I asked, "How do you like working for my uncle Pete?"

She smacked his arm and gave him a wink. "Best boss ever."

Pete elbowed her. "Best winemaker ever."

Winemaker. I felt my eyebrows rising. This was unexpected. "You're the new winemaker?"

"Sure am. Been there almost four months now."

"Wow." Where had I been? Then I remembered. "I've been tied up on this job for the better part of a year so I'm out of the loop. But congratulations. I hope you're enjoying it."

"I love it. The Anderson Valley is gorgeous."

"I think so, too. Where were you working before this?"

"I had my own vineyard in Napa. Sold Cabernet Franc grapes to just about everyone in the valley. Then I sold the land to a German firm for way too much money and was looking forward to some time off. Thought maybe I'd go for a slow cruise around the world."

"That sounds nice."

"Yeah, for someone else. For me, I was antsy after a week. Couldn't wait to get back to working the soil, working with the grapes, experimenting with new blends." She picked up a wineglass and swirled the liquid expertly. "But I didn't want Napa anymore. Talk about a rat race."

"That's what I hear." I sipped the pinot, enjoying Belinda's no-nonsense style. She was somewhere in her mid-forties, I thought, with dark red hair cut bluntly so that it swung just above her shoulders. She was tall. At least an inch or two taller than me, which put her around five-ten. My first impression of her was a good one. She seemed solid, funny, a hard worker.

"So I flipped a coin," Belinda continued, "started driving north, landed in Anderson Valley, and spent a week hitting every single one of their wineries. I met this big buffalo" — she jabbed her thumb into Uncle Pete's muscular arm — "and never looked back."

Pete looked especially pleased to be called a big buffalo.

I studied her for another long moment. "Are you the one who suggested the move to the French watering method?"

"Yeah, that was me. I worked at Château Margaux for three years and picked up some pointers."

"Some pointers?" I laughed. "From Château Margaux?"

She grinned. "Maybe one or two."

"Uh, right." It figured that the most famous wine producer in the world might have a few pointers to share.

Then I noticed there was still a line of people wanting to talk to the wine experts.

"I'd better let you get back to work," I said.

"Guess so. But hey, let's get together sometime soon, have a glass of wine, and swap lies."

"I would love to," I said easily. "Pete has my number so just give me a call when you're in town."

"Great. See you soon." She picked up the bottle of Pinot Noir. "Shannon, wait. You might need this." She poured a generous helping of wine into my glass.

"Thanks, Belinda."

With another wink, she turned to the next person at the table.

I stood near the end of the bar for a few

minutes, sipping my wine and watching Belinda and Uncle Pete chatting up the crowd. They worked side by side, casually moving around each other to open bottles and pour more wine. They helped each other answer questions and would interject a comment or a joke or two with ease. It looked as if they'd been working together for years.

And watching them, I couldn't help but wonder if Belinda and Uncle Pete had a thing going on.

I also had to wonder about my dad. Why wasn't he here tonight? He had mentioned that he might come by for the wine tasting. Of course, once again I had let a few weeks go by without talking to him. And with that, I felt an instant punch of guilt. I had been so wrapped up in Rafe's conference that I'd lost track of time and neglected checking in on my father. Again.

I wandered away from the wine bar and stopped to gaze around at the crowd. *Where was Mac?* I wondered. I really needed to talk to him.

"And who are you?"

I turned and saw a very tall, very skinny man standing next to me. He wore a severe black suit that gave him the look of a funeral director. His hair was combed flat against the pale skin of his forehead, signaling that he was a serious nerd. His question was more demandingly inquisitive than just friendly banter, which told me that his social skills might be in need of some tweaking.

"I'm Shannon Hammer."

He lifted his chin, which meant that he was now looking down his nose as me. "You are the one raising the barn."

"That's right." I took a sip of wine. "Who are you?"

"I'm Wesley Mycroft."

He announced it as though I should've known who he was. *Mycroft,* I thought. The name suited him since he looked like a caricature of a Victorian gentleman fallen on hard times.

Wesley swept his arm out to indicate the party crowd in general. "What do you think of all these people?"

I glanced around. "I hardly know any of them, but if they're here because they admire Rafe, I assume they're mostly decent folk and very smart."

He sniffed and it sounded like a retort. "Oh yes, I'm sure they're 'decent folk.' "

I forced myself to keep smiling. Wesley was definitely a nerd, and oddly fascinating. "But not smart?"

He shrugged, but said nothing.

"Why are you attending the conference?" I asked.

Another sniff. "I'm only here to win the grant."

"Ah." I supposed there were plenty of people here for that reason, too. "Do you have a particular field you're interested in? Or some kind of invention you're presenting to the judges?"

"I have made several important scientific breakthroughs and my inventions reflect that." He straightened up to his full height and lifted his chin. "One is a machine that will clean up a square mile's worth of greenhouse gases in five minutes."

In spite of his personality, I was impressed and told him so. "That sounds amazing."

"It is." He lifted his chin so high that if it started raining, he'd drown. "Unfortunately, the government stole it."

Hmm. "Oh, dear. I'm sorry."

He sniffed again. "I've also created an unbreakable encryption repeater to communicate with aliens — but it was stolen, too."

"Good heavens," I murmured. "What are the chances?"

"My encryption device is also useful in thwarting credit card theft. But as I said, it's been stolen."

"That's unfortunate."

"And I plan to present a new idea to the foundation's judges at the earliest opportunity."

"Do you have an appointment with Rafe?"

"Of course," he said, his tone chastising.

"Can you share your new idea with me?"

Again he stared down his nose, considering me. Then he shrugged. "I've already patented it, so I don't see why I shouldn't share it with the world."

"Please do."

"I've created an attachment that fits onto the hull of a specially outfitted ship. It is capable of collecting six metric tons of ocean garbage in one gigantic scoop and depositing it into a trash compactor built into the stern of the ship. It will take two months to completely clean all the garbage currently floating on the surface of the ocean."

"That is fantastic." *Fantastic,* as in weird and eccentric and completely unbelievable, I thought. "Is there some company that's underwriting all of this?"

"I won't go into my connections, but suffice to say, we will be ready to roll it out next year."

"I hope it happens for you." I meant it. The world could use a contraption that cleaned up the ocean's garbage.

"It's for all of us."

"Of course." I smiled. "Does it have a name?"

"Yes." He cleared his throat. "I call it the Scoop-Monster."

"Oh." I prayed I wouldn't lose control and burst out laughing. "Oh, that's . . . perfect." I scanned the crowd, searching for Mac. Or anyone. Wesley had left oddly fascinating behind and had veered right into weirdo territory.

"There you are."

I whipped around and almost whimpered when I saw that it wasn't Mac. Worse, the person wasn't even speaking to me.

"I have your special cocktail, Wesley," the newcomer said, and handed Wesley a half-filled martini glass.

"It's about time," Wesley groused, clutching the glass.

"It spilled a little," his friend muttered.

Wesley took a sip. "Damn it, Sherman! It's not dry enough."

"I'll get you another," Sherman said immediately.

If I were Sherman, I'd show him how dry it was by pouring it onto his head. But then, Sherman's behavior was so obsequious, I wondered if he might be Wesley's manservant. His voice had a simpering quality that reminded me of Dr. Frankenstein's knuckleheaded servant, Igor. Any minute now I fully expected him to bow and say, *"Yes, master."*

"Never mind," Wesley grumbled, shooting a furtive glance my way. "I'll drink it anyway."

It made me wonder if he still would've given Sherman a pass if I weren't standing there listening to every word.

Wesley glanced at me and gestured toward Sherman. "Sherman is my colleague."

"How do you do?" Sherman said, extending a sweaty hand to shake mine.

"Just fine, thanks. I'm Shannon Hammer."

He nodded. "How did you meet Wesley?"

I was asking myself that same question. "I was just standing here and he started chatting me up."

"Oh my," Sherman said, his eyes wide. "I can't believe your luck."

I wasn't sure I'd heard him correctly. Unless he meant *bad* luck. "*My* luck?"

"Oh, yes," he said breathlessly. "Wesley barely deigns to speak to anyone. You must recognize what a gift you've been given."

"Yeah, he's a gift all right." I glanced up at Wesley, who preened. He clearly agreed with everything Sherman was saying.

"Wesley is a genius," Sherman whispered loudly.

"Stop!" Wesley cried.

"Thank you," I said with relief. The sycophantic sucking up was starting to make my eyes bleed.

"Stop!" he yelled again.

"Oh no," Sherman cried, and began wringing his hands. "Oh dear."

"What is it?" I asked. "What's wrong?"

"The clicking," Wesley hissed, pressing two fingers against his temple. "It's going to drive me mad."

"What's he talking about?" I asked.

"Can't you hear it?" Sherman asked me.

"Hear what?"

"The clicking," Sherman repeated, then lowered his voice. "It's the government. They follow Wesley everywhere. He hears them constantly. Click. Click. Click."

Hoo-boy.

"Really?" My eyes narrowed in on Sherman and I chose my words carefully. "And do you . . . hear the clicking, too?"

Sherman whispered, "I've personally never heard the click, but I'm not as sensitive as Wesley."

"Ah. I'm going to bet that no one is as sensitive as Wesley." I coughed to clear my suddenly tight throat. "So. It was lovely meeting you both, but I must go."

"I'll see you again. I sense it." Wesley nodded, and shut his eyes tightly against the clicking.

"Can't wait for the moment." I turned and walked as quickly as I could until I'd made it to the outer edge of the throng. I heard a sound and wondered if the clicking was following me. I took a few cleansing breaths and centered myself. Okay, no clicks. Must've been my imagination. Good grief.

Was this conference filled with odd people like Wesley and Sherman or had I just had a short run of bad luck? I glanced around at the faces of people nearby. Everyone looked normal. I decided to relax and sip my wine and soon I was feeling normal again, too. Whew.

From the snippets of conversation around me, I could tell that a lot of people were caught up in the fact that a dead body had been found that morning.

I hadn't heard the word *murder* mentioned yet, thank goodness. The assumption was that Dillon's death had been a tragic accident.

"And there she is."

I turned and saw Niall walking toward me, holding a glass of wine. He wore his kilt and I saw women gazing at him as he

139

strolled through the crowd. Couldn't really blame them. He was looking fine this evening, like he'd walked right off the cover of a romance novel.

"Hi, Niall," I said. "Hope you're enjoying yourself."

"I am, indeed. And you?"

"I'm not sure." I glanced over my shoulder to make sure Wesley, Sherman, and the clicking were nowhere near me. I had a feeling, though, they might be visiting my nightmares. "I just had a conversation with two of the strangest people I've ever met."

"Are ye sure they're the strangest?" He glanced around. "There's some mighty stiff competition here tonight. I just spoke to a woman who was a swordfish in a past life."

I laughed. It was good to have a friend to share this odd experience with. "Are you enjoying the wine?"

"Aye, I am. I'm here with Emily, helping carry some of her catering tables, so I thought I'd take advantage of the wine bar." He clicked my glass in a casual toast and took a deep sip. "This is the Pinot Noir. It's a lovely wine, isn't it?"

I smiled. "Uncle Pete makes great wines."

"Emily mentioned that the winery owner is your uncle. That's a wondrous thing to have in a family."

"It really is."

We sipped in silence for a moment, then he leaned in. "My sister also mentioned that you've a knack for finding dead bodies."

"Did she?" I attempted to keep my cool as I gulped down the wine.

He chuckled. "I see it's true, then."

"I suppose so," I said with a sigh. "I don't know why, but yes, I appear to be a dead body magnet. And God, that sounds terrible."

"Have they determined yet how this morning's victim was killed?"

I couldn't meet his gaze. "Not yet."

He frowned so deeply that the lines in his forehead became canyons.

Since he didn't know I'd been sworn to secrecy, that frown couldn't have been meant for me.

"What's wrong?" I asked.

He breathed heavily. "Emily says I must tell you what I saw."

"Oh." I nodded. "Then you absolutely must."

"Aye, then I will." He glanced around at the people standing nearby. "But not here."

"Let's take a walk." Not only did I want to hear what he had to say, but it was a good excuse to get away from the crowd for a few minutes.

■ ■ ■ ■

We strolled out toward the three wind turbines on the hill. The area was deserted. Niall didn't say anything so I waited, sipping my wine as I gazed at the colorful party going on across the field.

"Quiet out here," he commented.

"Yes."

"Well, then. No point in lingering over the telling of it, is there?"

"Nope."

"Right, then. I went to check on the patio last night," he began. "You understand, I feel a kinship there because it's my work."

"I totally understand that," I said with a soft smile. I felt an attachment to every house I'd ever worked on.

"That man, Rafe's partner, the one who died soon after, was sitting on the hearth. I didn't know who he was at the time, just thought it was bold of this fellow to trespass. I was tempted to toss him out, but didn't, of course. Though it was a near thing."

"His name is Dillon," I said. "I'm sure Rafe gave him permission to go and look at the work we've done."

"Aye, perhaps." He shrugged massive shoulders. "I moved closer, but then stopped when a woman approached him from around the other side of the house."

"Who was she?"

He scowled. "I don't know names. She was there last night at the opening ceremony. She was up on stage when Rafe introduced his people."

"His people?" I thought for a second. "You mean the foundation's board of directors?"

"Yes," he said, excited that I could follow along. "She's the fish lady. The one I told you about."

"The swordfish lady?"

"Aye. But she also works with the fishes now."

I was going to need a translator to get through this conversation. But I mentally went through everyone on the board and then realized: fish. "The eco-fisheries lady, you mean. Midge Andersen."

"That's the one!" He patted my shoulder with enthusiasm, then his expression darkened. "She was angry, there on the patio. I could barely hear her words because she was whispering at first, you see. But her vitriol was so venomous that it caused her voice to rise. Am I making sense to you?"

"Yes, I understand." *Not completely,* I thought, given his heavy brogue, but I was able to follow along as he spoke. And the woman had been talking to Dillon, after all, so that would make anyone's vitriol rise.

"Despite the hushed tone, I found I could hear her words," he said. "I shouldn't have stayed and listened in, should've left them alone to have their private chat. But I confess I stayed and heard every word."

It would be so wrong of me to squeal with pleasure at his decision, so I just said, "So . . . what did you hear?"

"A vicious argument." He winced. "She accused him of cheating. Of stealing and lying and ruining her life."

"Wow," I murmured. Midge Andersen had really been making the rounds last night. First fighting with Dillon, then off to an assignation with Sketch Horn in the barn.

That reminded me of what Mac and I had seen, peeking into the barn where Midge was getting hot and heavy with Sketch Horn. Dang, Midge had been busy. She must've gone directly from yelling and threatening Dillon to shagging with Sketch.

Troubled, Niall scratched his head, leaving a few strands of hair sticking out in all directions. "At first I thought the woman was speaking of a romance gone wrong. You know, cheating, lying, all the ways two people can treat each other badly."

144

"Yes," I murmured.

"But then Dillon began to defend himself, began speaking about the price of doing business, and how she should've known when she came to him with her idea that he would naturally put his own name on the patent, because after all, he would be doing all the work. I soon realized it was a business deal 'twas making her skin boil."

I knew my mouth was hanging open. But had Dillon actually put his own name on a patent that should've gone to Midge? Wow.

I stared at Niall. "What did she say to that?"

He gazed up at the early evening sky. It was still blue, I noticed, but darkening by the minute. Then he looked down at me and said absently, "She's such a little thing, you know."

"Midge? Yes she is." Midge Andersen was barely five feet tall, I thought, and figured that was where she got the nickname *Midge.*

Niall continued, "But after getting her steam up, she had the strength of an Amazon." He held up one clenched fist dramatically. "She moved in, got very close to him, and said, 'I will kill you for this.' "

Hearing those words almost made my eyes bug out, but I quickly recovered. "Did Dillon say anything to that?"

"Not exactly." Niall sneered in disgust. "He just laughed in her face."

"Ouch." Oh, that was so not a good thing to do to anyone. To a furious woman, it was even more foolhardy.

"Aye, it was cruel," Niall agreed. "The wee fish woman stared at him for a moment, then slapped his face hard and walked away." Niall took a quick sip. "It was quite inspiring."

I had to take a minute to think. I gazed at the hillside and reveled in the light evening breeze. It was another beautiful night, except for the fact that murder was in the air.

"So let me get this straight," I said. "Midge went to Rafe's partner Dillon and told him about an idea she had. He later stole her idea. And then last night you heard him admit it to her face and then you heard her threaten to kill him. Is that the gist of it?"

"Yes!" He beamed at me. "You're a smart one, Shannon Hammer."

I had to chuckle at his praise. But I sobered up immediately. "We have to go to Chief Jensen and tell him exactly what you heard last night."

He downed the rest of his wine and gave

an abrupt nod. "Aye, there's no escaping it. So let's go."

CHAPTER FIVE

Halfway to the car, Niall and I ran into Mac, who was just arriving.

"Hi," I said after Mac had planted a brief but solid kiss on my lips. I touched his cheek. "You made it."

"Sorry I'm late. I really got into the new book."

"That's wonderful." I grinned. "Will there be an Ecosphere in there?"

"Oh, yeah. I spoke to Julian the plant guy earlier." He grinned and rubbed his hands together. "It's going to be awesome. That's one of the reasons I had to start the book. Get it all down while it's fresh in my mind."

"I can't wait to read it." I glanced up at Niall, then back at Mac. "We're on our way to see Chief Jensen."

"Turning yourself in?" Mac asked lightly.

I smiled indulgently. "Funny, but no. Niall overheard someone threatening to kill Dillon. He wants to make a statement."

"Now that's interesting." Mac checked his wristwatch. "I came out here to find you because I'm supposed to meet the chief at the pub in an hour for a beer. I thought maybe you'd like to join us."

"I would. And Niall would, too, right?"

"Aye, a beer would be helpful." He looked like a drowning man who had just been tossed a life preserver.

"I'll bet." Mac grinned. "I'll give him a call." He gazed at me. "Why don't I ask him to meet us at your place?"

"I like that idea," I said. "I was going to have to stop at home anyway to feed the creatures."

"I'll order a pizza," Mac said. "I'm starving."

"My hero." I turned to Niall. "Does that work for you?"

"Och aye," he said. The phrase came out in one smooth, breathy syllable.

In spite of the serious situation, I had to sigh. I could listen to him talk in that Scottish brogue all day. And I felt the same way about his sister Emily. I wasn't always certain we were speaking the same language, but I loved the sound and rhythm of their voices, the appealingly musical quality of it. And I had to be honest, just looking at Niall while he talked was no hardship, either.

Mac looked at Niall. "I can give you a ride home later if you need one."

"No, no," Niall said. "But I thank ye. I'll call Emily, have her pick me up on her way home."

"Well, then," Mac said. "We're all set."

Fifteen minutes later, I pulled into my driveway and turned off the engine. Mac drove his car in behind me and we all walked through the backyard gate together. I could already hear Robbie barking like a maniac and I had to laugh. He was going to go bonkers over my guests. I couldn't blame him.

"You have a dog," Niall said, his eyes lighting up.

"How did you guess?" I said with a grin. "He's a Westie and very friendly. And loud."

He grinned broadly. "A perfect guard dog. I expect we'll get along just fine."

The three of us walked into the kitchen and watched Robbie go insane.

"His name is Robbie," I explained over the barking, "short for Rob Roy, and he loves people."

"Well, then, we have a few things in common, don't we, Robbie?" Niall hung his leather satchel on the back of a kitchen chair, then sat down and patted his legs.

150

"Up you go, lad."

I laughed as I watched Robbie wiggle his butt until I thought he might shake it off. Once in Niall's lap, he managed to sit still for a few seconds while he got his back stroked. Then he flipped over for stomach rubs, staring all the while at the big Scotsman with sheer adoration in his eyes.

"He's a darling thing, isn't he?" Niall said. "A true warrior."

I laughed. "Yes, he is."

Tiger the cat, meanwhile, managed to maintain some dignity. She gave her attention to Mac, who held her and scratched between her ears. Then, hearing the sound of cans being opened, she jumped down and slunk across the room to the counter where I was preparing dinner. Wending her way in between my legs, she meowed loudly and head-butted me mercilessly.

"I'm hurrying," I said, reaching down to ruffle the fur between her ears. "Chill out, why don't you?"

Barely a minute later, I carried both of their dinner bowls over to their assigned spots and the two starving animals raced to gobble up the food. The humans were forgotten. For now.

I got beers out for Mac and Niall, then jogged upstairs to change out of my jeans and boots into yoga pants, a sweatshirt, and socks. I sent a quick text to Emily, Marigold, Jane, and Lizzie, asking if we could all meet tomorrow morning around ten o'clock because Marigold needed to vent.

Marigold quickly responded by inviting everyone to her new home with Rafe. *He'll be busy at the conference so we'll have the house to ourselves,* she assured us.

Emily wrote that she would be on-site and would provide pastries and coffee.

Lizzie said, *Yay! I'll be there.*

Jane said, *Can't wait to see y'all.*

Marigold thanked us all for the support.

That's what we do, Jane typed, and wished us all sweet dreams.

Chief Jensen and the pizza delivery guy arrived at the same time, so the four of us sat down in the dining room and ate pizza and salad, drank wine or beer, and talked about murder.

Once Niall had dictated his statement to Eric, the chief asked him to sign it, and then slipped the handwritten sheets of paper into his notebook. Then he turned back to Niall. "I apologize again for the informality. I might need you to come down to the station if I have any other questions."

"I understand," Niall said. "I'll do what-

152

ever you need me to do."

"Thank you." Then Eric looked at me. "I apologize to you, too."

"Why?"

"Because I've got to take care of this right now. Otherwise, I'll have to drag you all down to the station."

"Then you won't get any pizza," I said lightly.

"That's why I'm staying right here." Eric had his briefcase opened on top of the low cabinet across from the dining table. He twisted around in his chair and removed a small manila envelope marked EVIDENCE from his briefcase. Then he turned to Mac. "I'd like to ask if you can identify this item."

"Looks like an envelope," Mac said.

"Very good," Eric said. "Smart-ass."

Mac bit back a smile. "Can't help myself."

Eric reached into the manila envelope and pulled out a clear plastic bag. Enclosed inside the bag was a dangerous-looking knife. He handed it to Mac. "We don't want any contamination, so don't remove it from the bag. Just examine it as well as you can through the plastic and let me know what you think."

We were obviously staring at the murder weapon. Blood from the blade was smeared against the side of the bag. I really tried hard not to look at it, but it was hard to look away. I felt my stomach wobble and folded my arms tightly across my chest.

"It's a knife," Mac said, but he wasn't being funny this time. He took the bag from Eric and stared at the knife for a long time. He turned it this way and that, then over to examine the backside.

"It's not a regulation weapon," he said finally. "But then, there's really no such thing these days."

"Explain," Eric said.

"When it comes to knives," Mac began, "the military will occasionally issue a particular type to everyone. Maybe it's because they got a package deal, or because some corporation wants the endorsement. But more often than not, we choose our own. Not everyone likes the same weight, texture, embellishments, whatever."

"Embellishments," Eric muttered, writing it down.

"You know, doodads, fancy stuff. Colors. That sort of thing." Mac carefully set the sealed bag down on the table and grabbed a piece of pizza. "Some of the SEALs teams were issued a specific knife when we graduated, but nobody was forced to use them. I never used mine. It didn't work for me. The manufacturer's label was raised and it was right where my thumb sat." He shrugged. "It was irritating. Now I carry a mini-reflex. It's small, easy to hold, and the blade is retractable."

"Retractable," I repeated. "You mean, like a switchblade?"

"Yeah. I'll show you sometime."

"I'd like that," Eric said.

"I'd like to see it as well," Niall added. "I use a number of different knives for work. Always in the market for something new."

Mac nodded, then held up the bloody bag again. "This blade is fixed. Not retractable. A buddy of mine has something similar to this. He was an Army Ranger, if that helps."

"Army Ranger?" I said, frowning. "Doesn't Sketch Horn profess to be a former Army Ranger?"

"That's what he says," Mac groused. "But if he ever served one day in his miserable life, I'll be a blue-nosed gopher."

I stared at him. "A blue-nosed . . . gopher?"

He shrugged. "It's an old saying my father always used."

" 'Tis a good one," Niall said cheerfully.

"Were you in the military, Niall?" I asked.

"Aye." He downed the rest of his beer. "British Army. Served in the Middle East for six years." He gazed at each of us. "I

155

built a lot of walls. The British military loves their walls."

I patted his arm. "If they put you in charge of walls, they clearly recognized one of your strengths."

"Aye." He nodded. "Our military forces are issued knives, but they're fancier than this one. Stainless steel, with gadgets attached. Very handy."

"Gadgets? Like a Swiss Army Knife?" I asked.

"Much the same, but sharper, stronger blades." He winked at me. "British steel, you know."

Eric rested his elbows on the table and looked at Mac. "So you don't think Sketch Horn was an Army Ranger."

"Not a chance. He's a fake," Mac insisted. "One soldier recognizes another."

Niall gave a brief nod. "Aye, it's true."

I pointed to the bag he was still holding. "Maybe he's faking it right down to his Army-issued knife."

"Maybe," Mac allowed. "Knowing Sketch, he probably read about some knife or other being 'army issued' and went out and bought it. But trust me, when it comes to knives, that whole 'military issue' hype doesn't hold a lot of water. Now if you want to talk about guns, that's another story."

"Good to know." Eric took the plastic bag from Mac, slipped it into the manila folder, and then set it inside his briefcase. "What do you know about this Sketch Horn character?"

"At the risk of repeating myself, I don't like him," Mac admitted. He took a sip of beer as if to wash the taste of the Sketch conversation out of his mouth. "I don't trust him. He's a liar and a cheat. But to be honest, I doubt that he killed Dillon, mainly because he's a coward. But also, I'd be surprised if he even knew how to handle a knife like this. And more importantly, I don't think he knows the guy."

Eric sat back in his chair. Took a deep breath and blew it out. "That all makes sense. But since he pisses you off, I won't remove him from the suspect list yet."

Mac laughed out loud. "Thank you."

I leaned forward in my chair. "I'll bet there are a bunch of other people who hated Dillon Charles just as much as Midge Andersen did." I winced, remembering something important. I quickly averted my eyes and stared at the pizza. "Mmm, I might have another slice."

"Shannon," Eric said sharply. "What aren't you saying?"

"What do you mean? I didn't do anything."

He laughed, but it wasn't the carefree ha-ha-ha laugh of a happy person. "You are by far the worst liar I have ever met."

"What're you talking about? I'm a good liar."

Mac reached over and squeezed my arm. "You're digging a hole, babe."

I glared at him. "You were there, too. You heard them fighting. Why didn't you tell Eric?"

Mac grinned. "God, I love you, Red."

Despite wanting to bask in his words, I frowned. "That's a non sequitur."

"He wants to hear it from you," Mac prompted.

I rolled my eyes. "Fine, but I'm having this last slice." I reached for the pizza, then added, "And I love you, too."

Eric took a slow sip of his beer. "You're stalling. You should know that I'm not leaving until you talk."

I pointed to my mouth, which was now full of pizza.

"I can wait," he said. "You can't chew forever."

Briefly I considered trying. But then I swallowed the bite, drank some of my beer, and sighed. "All right. I'm sure it doesn't mean anything in terms of adding to your suspect list, but Rafe had a horrible argument with Dillon last night."

That caught him by surprise and he stared at me for a long moment. "Rafe."

"He wouldn't have killed his own partner," I insisted.

"*Ex*-partner," Eric murmured.

"I think maybe they were still partners," I said. "I guess you could find out. My point is, Rafe wouldn't have killed him because Dillon was running the company for him. Rafe didn't want to do it, so why would he kill the guy who was taking care of business?"

"Unfortunately," Mac added, "that's exactly what they were fighting about."

"Right," I said. "Dillon wanted Rafe to come back to work, but Rafe wouldn't do it. Dillon said some really awful stuff about . . ."

"About what?" Eric demanded.

I scowled. "About Marigold."

"You're kidding me," Eric muttered as his hands turned to fists. "What an ass."

"I know, right?" I felt better seeing Eric get so angry about Dillon insulting Marigold. "And that's when Rafe told him to get off of his property and don't come back."

"Good," Eric said.

Mac and I continued talking, going back and forth, adding little details, but that was the gist of the argument.

Eric's eyes were narrowed to sharp points. "He really said that about Marigold?"

"Yeah," Mac said. "I'm not saying the guy deserved to die. But I sure didn't blame Rafe for kicking him out of the conference."

"Me neither," I insisted. I wasn't about to mention that I'd clearly heard Rafe say that he would kill Dillon, mainly because there had to be a dozen other people who had those same feelings for the guy. Including me.

Eric continued writing for another minute, then looked at me. "Do you think Marigold knows what Dillon said to Rafe?"

"I hope not," I said. "But I was just thinking that Mac and I probably aren't the only ones who overheard their conversation. I mean, they were right out in the open."

Eric nodded. "There were a lot of people out there last night. Someone else easily could've heard them and then told Marigold what was said."

Mac winced. "It's possible that the killer heard them arguing and knows that Rafe had a motive. Whoever it is could use that against him if it comes down to it."

"That's a horrible thought," I said. But

then my mind flashed on Hallie. "I wonder if their secretary heard them yelling."

"Is she the clingy one?" Eric asked.

"So you saw that," I said flatly.

"Couldn't miss her," he admitted. "Her wailing caught my attention at first, but when I noticed twenty minutes later that she was still stuck like glue to Rafe, I had to wonder."

"Did you talk to her?"

"Briefly. She didn't have a lot to say except to insist that everyone in the company was like one big happy family. Definitely a case of protesting too much. Everyone loved working there, everybody loved Dillon, et cetera, et cetera."

Mac snorted. "And if you believe that, I've got a bridge I'd like to sell you."

"Don't bother," Eric said, shaking his head. "Nobody's happy all the time, especially at work. And I've rarely seen a high-powered business where there weren't undercurrents of some really ugly stuff."

I gazed at Eric. "I guess Hallie didn't mention that Dillon was horribly rude to her when we met her last night."

Eric shook his head. "No, she didn't. Tell me about it."

Mac took over here, explained what Dillon had said about Hallie fawning over Mac.

161

"It was a real crappy thing to say. Hallie was humiliated, and it embarrassed all of us, not just her."

Eric continued to write in his notepad.

Finally I asked, "Did you talk to Rafe?"

"Yes," he said.

He didn't add anything else, and it gave me a sinking feeling. Maybe it was because I'd eaten too much pizza, but I didn't think so. "So did Rafe mention the fight he had with Dillon?"

For a long moment, Eric locked his gaze on me in that Zen-like way of his that usually had me crying for mercy within a nanosecond or two. Eventually he looked away, checked his notes, checked his watch, and then glanced around the table at each of us. "I'm afraid this investigation is hitting a little too close to home for all of us. I'm going to take off now, but if any of you remember anything else, or you talk to anyone who has information, you call me. Is that clear?"

"Absolutely," I said, and Niall and Mac murmured their agreement.

Eric stood. "I hope I don't have to remind all of you that everything you've heard tonight is confidential. If you need to talk about it, you talk to me."

"Sure will," I said.

162

Mac saluted. "Got it."

"Yes, sir," Niall said smartly.

Eric nodded. "Good. That's good." He nodded at Mac. "I like the salute."

Mac chuckled. "Thought you would."

Eric's phone buzzed and he pulled it from his pocket. Staring at the screen, he smiled so softly that I almost didn't recognize him.

"It must be Chloe," I said.

He grinned. "It is. Let me just say hi and I'll call her back."

"I want to say hi, too." My sister Chloe had confided in me that she and Eric spoke on the phone every night. He didn't seem to be getting tired of the arrangement. In fact, I'd never seen our big tough police chief happier.

It was nice for me to see that Chloe's love was reciprocated, if Eric's dreamy expression was any indicator.

I took the phone. "Hey, sis. When you coming up?"

"We'll be on hiatus starting in two weeks," Chloe said. "And then I'll be able to stay for a month."

"Fantastic. Can't wait to see you."

"Me, too. Send my love to Dad and Uncle Pete."

"You bet. Love you, bye." I handed the phone back to Eric, who said a few more quiet words, then hung up.

He snapped his briefcase closed, then pulled it off the counter. I could tell he had shifted back into Police Chief mode.

He glanced at all of us again. "I know you'll call me if you think of anything else."

"We all will," Mac assured him.

"And hey, thanks for the pizza and the beer," he said cheerfully, as if we had spent the evening watching a football game.

"Glad you could join us." I stood and gave him a hug, then watched as Mac walked with him out to his SUV.

After taking another slug of beer, I turned and smiled at Niall. "That went well, I think."

The next morning, the smart mice escaped.

The news sent Antarctic-sized chunks of icy chills sailing up and down and around my spine. The sight of that bloody knife the night before was nothing compared to the horrific possibility of having mice scampering all over the place.

Smart ones. Ugh.

Plus, if this were a science-fiction movie, those smart mice would start breeding, and within a couple of months, we'd have whole herds of them running around. And that thought creeped me out so much, I knew

I'd be dreaming about it.

The thing was, I couldn't talk about it with my closest pals, and I didn't dare tell anyone how I felt. I was a kick-ass contractor, after all. I wore a tool belt with panache and could swing a hammer better than anyone on my crew.

How could I confess that I was afraid of a silly little mouse? It was a phobia that, like many phobias, had no basis in reality. Mice were not terrifying to most people. They were cute, furry little creatures. They were fun pets for children.

And that thought was just gross.

In my mind, there was nothing *fun* about them. And *these* mice were smart. *How smart?* I wondered. Could they devise plans to take out the human race?

Double ugh.

I drank my coffee and thought about it. Why were the smart mice being featured at this conference? I suppose they might be useful for gobbling up the piles of food scraps left behind by humans. I had to wonder just how smart these smart mice were.

The escaped mice situation was scrambling my brain.

Maybe it was a good thing that these were supposed to be *smart* mice. Maybe they would be smart enough to stay away from me. But I doubted it. Just as a cat could recognize the one person in a room with allergies, a mouse would sniff out my fear and come a-running.

Maybe they were so smart, they would know enough to gang up on me. As a mouse squadron, they could drive me crazy, terrorize me to such a point that I would become comatose, unable to speak or react. Then they would start to nibble at my feet, then move up to my ankles. My shins. Knees. Oh God. Pretty soon I would have mouse bites all over my body. Could I bleed to death?

My imagination was clearly working overtime. I was sick of feeling so helpless. If I could figure out where the mice had gone, maybe I could simply avoid that area and be perfectly fine. That was sort of proactive, right? In a really passive way.

I was determined to find out just how smart these mice were. I grabbed my bag, pulled out my conference program, and looked up Professor Arnold Larsson. I wanted to find out exactly what his smart mice were capable of.

I considered myself extraordinarily brave when I found his cubicle in the old barn and walked inside to meet him.

"Dr. Larsson?"

"Ya?" He whipped around, his white lab coat flapping. "Hello."

"Hi. I'm Shannon Hammer. I wanted to find out about the mice that escaped."

"Oh, ya. No worries. We are in control of the situation." He had a charming Swedish accent. "The mice will be back in their cages within a few hours."

"Really?" I asked. "Because this property is huge. They could be halfway across the state by now. And there's the woods. Mice love to hang out in the woods, don't they? Lots of places to hide in the woods."

"No, no, not my mice." But he said it through tightly clenched teeth. "They love their cages. They love me. This is where they feel safest."

"Seriously?"

"Oh, ya. I take good care of them. They remember. Smart mice have long memories. They are also very docile and easily captured."

"How will you capture them?"

He smiled. "With food, of course."

Of course, I thought. The same way you would capture anyone. Me, for instance. Spaghetti or cheeseburgers would do the trick. And just like that, I wanted to have a cheeseburger. But since I'd had one just the other day, I would try to restrain myself.

"How did they escape?" I asked.

"It's a mystery," he said, frowning. He made several sweeping gestures with his arms. "Look around you. These conditions are luxurious. Their cages are pristine. I feed them only the finest quality fruit and grains."

I did as he said and took a look around. It was pretty cramped in here, but it wasn't like mice need a lot of room. What did I know?

"What makes them so smart?" I asked.

He stared at me for a long moment, then shrugged. "Gene manipulation, of course."

Another icy chill slid down my spine. "Gene manipulation? So you actually perform surgery on them?" Could this get any worse?

"Ya, of course."

"So you could manipulate them to do anything?"

"No, not *anything*," he assured me with a quick smile. "But for instance, I have strengthened their memories and given them better recall. I have made them quicker to react to changes. And I have taught them to fear."

"Wait? What? Fear?" I took a deep breath to calm down. "But won't fear make them more aggressive?"

"Oh no, it will simply make them more careful. They will make better decisions."

"Like what? Don't walk on the freeway? Don't take a shortcut with anyone named Donner? What decisions can they make?"

He laughed. "You are a funny one. But no. Not those kinds of decisions. Those are not within their scope."

"And you control what is within their scope."

"Ya, of course. We want to keep them alive. And by making them more careful, more *fearful,* if you will, they will live longer."

"Oh, that's just great." Mice living forever. A dream of mine. "Well, I sure hope you find them."

"The traps will be set this afternoon."

"Traps?"

"Humane traps. They will enter for the food and won't be able to leave. We should have them all back by dinnertime."

"That's great news, Doctor. Thanks."

I walked out feeling even worse than I had earlier. Mainly because now I felt *sorry* for the mice. I didn't like that the scientists were conditioning them to be more fearful. How did they do that? And did I really want to know? It was just weird. But then, if they could actually make decisions, maybe they would decide to take revenge on the sickos experimenting on them.

Maybe I should wear a sign that says I LOVE MICE.

But no. I couldn't do that. They would see right through me.

My phobia was still intact, but I had to admit I was feeling some camaraderie with the mice. And maybe that was the first fledgling step toward friendship with the little creatures. Baby steps, right?

Right?

No freaking way! I screamed silently.

Good grief.

I checked my watch. It was time to meet Emily. I tiptoed all the way back to the catering area, scanning every inch of ground for roving gangs of mice. But I had a feeling, if they were really smart, they were long gone by now.

I met Emily and helped her carry a basket of pastries and croissants over to Rafe and Marigold's house.

"Marigold made a pot of coffee," Emily explained, "so I don't have to drag that over there."

"Good."

Emily glanced at me as we entered the front yard and walked to the porch. "Do

170

you know what this is about?"

"I don't, but I have a feeling it's connected with the murder."

"Oh dear." She frowned at me. "But I suppose you would know."

I shrugged, accepting my fate as chief murder magnet among my friends. "I guess I would."

"Here we go," she said. "I'll get the doorbell."

But before she could push the button, Marigold opened the door. "Thank you guys for coming."

"I'm glad we could get together," Emily said.

Marigold gave us each a hug and took the basket from me. She led us into the small sitting area off the kitchen, where Lizzie and Jane were already seated, drinking coffee and munching on apple slices.

There was a coffeepot on the table along with mugs, cream and sugar, and butter and jam for the croissants.

"Everything looks wonderful," I said.

"I love this room, Shannon," Marigold said softly, wrapping her arm around my shoulders. "Especially in the morning when the sunshine comes pouring through the windows."

I was thrilled to hear her say that because

I had designed the room with her in mind. Warm and friendly, with comfy furniture and wide glass walls that opened onto a view of the farm that stretched on forever. This morning the blue sky was studded with thick white clouds and sunlight played on the grass.

I didn't even want to think about how Whitney would've decorated this house. Chrome and glass everywhere, stiff black leather couches and shiny red chairs. The woman thought she had good taste, but she was wrong. At least where Marigold was concerned.

"Your house is beautiful, Marigold," Lizzie said.

"Thanks to Shannon," Marigold said, giving me a light squeeze. "I love this place. I can't tell you how happy I am. I'm just so . . . happy."

And she promptly burst into tears.

"Oh my God, Marigold!" Jane jumped up from her chair and grabbed her in a tight hug. "What is it? What's wrong?"

I rubbed her back. "Tell us how we can help."

"There's nothing you can do," she wailed.

"Sit down," I said firmly, and taking her hand, I led her over to the big comfy chair on the other side of the coffee table. "Sit down and tell us what happened."

"You can't tell anyone," she cried.

"Of course we won't tell," Lizzie said staunchly.

"Just talk, sweetie," Jane crooned. "We're here to listen."

Emily sat down on the rug by Marigold's chair and handed her a tissue.

"I love you guys," Marigold began through her tears.

"And we love you, too," I said, sitting down on the couch. "Now spill."

"I — I — I . . ." She hiccupped the word.

"Take a deep breath," I said. "Do you need some water?"

"I'll get it," Lizzie said, and jumped up to take care of it. A few seconds later, she handed a glass of water to Marigold, who gulped it down.

"Okay?" Lizzie asked. "Want some more?"

Marigold shook her head, still sniffling. "Thanks."

"Tell us why you're sad, love," Emily said softly.

She tapped her fingers on her knees nervously. "Okay. It's just that, something happened and . . . and I can't tell Rafe. I probably shouldn't tell you guys either because it'll get back to him, but I can't keep it inside."

"We can all keep a secret," Emily said. "You know that."

"This is a pretty big one," Marigold whispered.

Jane shook her head, as confused as the rest of us. "What is it, Marigold?"

"I'm just afraid that if he hears what happened, he'll be so upset. Maybe he'll just want to walk away from everything."

"He loves you," I said quietly. "Whatever happened, he'll understand. There's no way he'd leave you."

"My darling girl," Emily said, her soft melodic brogue cushioning her words. "Have you fallen out of love with him then?"

Marigold's eyes widened. Her mouth opened, but no words came out. And suddenly she was crying again. "No! Why would you think that? Rafe is wonderful."

Now I wanted to cry, too. Our darling Marigold was a sweetheart, but when she was upset, she could talk circles around the point until everyone was dizzy.

"We all agree, Rafe's a sweetie," I said. "So what's the problem? What the heck happened?"

She blinked a few times and stared at me. "You met his business partner, right?"

"Yes, we talked about that," I reminded her. "I met Dillon the first night of the conference. And now he's dead."

"Right," Marigold said, nodding slowly. "He's dead."

"Murdered," I added.

Lizzie flashed me a furious scowl and all I could do was smile weakly. "Well, it's true."

"That's right, he was murdered," Marigold said, her tone suddenly harsh. "And I couldn't be happier."

And I couldn't blame her. But Marigold was so rarely fierce, it threw the rest of our friends off.

"Whoa, sweetie," Jane said, alarmed. "You don't really mean that, do you?"

Marigold's eyes were dry now and focused on each of us. "Oh, yes, I mean every word." She pushed herself out of the chair and pounded her fist into her palm. "I only wish I had killed the bastard myself."

Chapter Six

The other girls began to speak at once, loudly and emphatically. Marigold sat quietly and watched them carry on, freaking out and pacing around the room for a good solid minute.

Jane frowned as she stared down at Marigold. "I don't believe you meant that. Not really."

"Of course she didn't mean it." Emily folded her arms across her chest. "She's just upset."

"That's right," Lizzie insisted. "You just moved out here with Rafe and you're going through a period of adjustment. It's natural to feel overly emotional."

Overly emotional? Just because she wanted to kill the guy? I found her reaction perfectly reasonable, but then, I had actually *met* Dillon Charles. Watching Marigold, I could see that our friends' best intentions were only making her feel worse. Well, I could take care of that just by telling everyone the truth about the dead man.

I hesitated, but then plowed ahead. "I don't think you're being emotional, Marigold. I think you're right on target. The guy was a horrible person and I'm okay with him being dead. But that doesn't mean I killed him. And neither did you."

They all stared at me in shock, for speaking ill of the dead, maybe? I just shrugged. "Did any of you meet this guy?"

"No, but . . ." Lizzie fiddled with her hair nervously, not making eye contact.

Jane frowned. "I saw him during the cocktail party, but I didn't get a chance to meet him."

"Well," I said, my tone overly cheery. "Let me tell you a little bit about him. He was one of the biggest jerks I've ever met. Mac and I overheard him saying awful things to Rafe about Marigold and about our nice little town." I glanced over at Marigold. "I'm sorry, but he was just horrible. Rafe kicked him out of the conference."

"He did?"

"Yeah," I continued. "Dillon even humiliated his own secretary in front of Mac and me. It was mortifying for her and for us. And apparently he stole ideas and patents from at least one person at the conference.

Probably more. Who knows what else he did. He was a major son-of-a-you-know-what. I'm not saying he deserved to be killed, but I'm also not mourning his loss. And neither should any of you."

We all stared at each other for a long, silent moment.

Lizzie aimed her gaze directly at me now, and nodded. "I didn't know that. If it's true, then Marigold's got every right to be pissed off about this guy."

"Yeah, she does."

"Okay, then," Emily began, "I understand why you didn't like this fellow Dillon. But why do you think you can't tell Rafe?"

"Because." Marigold took a deep breath, let it out slowly, and whispered, "Dillon Charles, his best friend and business partner, tried to . . . well, maybe I'd better just tell you what happened."

There was a long moment of silence.

I had a terrible feeling and had to force myself to breathe. "Yes, maybe you'd better."

"Don't say a word," Emily insisted. "I'm going to make another pot of tea."

Lizzie rolled her eyes. "You're killing us, Emily."

Emily lifted her chin. "Everything's better with tea."

I wouldn't have thought so, but Emily's words caused Marigold to giggle. So maybe a pot of tea was the answer to all the world's problems.

We waited patiently until Emily carried the newly filled teapot and set it down on the coffee table. She poured the tea into cups and handed them to each of us.

And finally Marigold told her story.

"It was the night before the conference started," she began. "Raphael had to drive into town for a meeting with some of the conference sponsors. I was home alone and I was so happy. So comfortable. I was drinking a glass of wine and unpacking the last few boxes. The doorbell rang and I jumped. I was startled. I'd never heard the sound before. I laughed at myself, but then I began to wonder, who would drive all the way out here at night? I decided it had to be one of you guys, or another one of our friends. I ran to the door, checked the peephole, and saw Dillon. I didn't know him very well, but I knew that he and Raphael were close, so I couldn't let him stand out there in the cold.

"I felt okay about inviting him in because I'd met him a few times in the past. He came out here for the first time when the old farmhouse was here. Way before you started the rehab, Shannon."

"That was just over eight months ago," I explained to the others. "So let's see, Rafe had been living in Lighthouse Cove for a few months and even back then, he was well into planning this conference."

"That's right," Marigold said. She took a sip of tea, then continued. "My first impression of Dillon back then wasn't too great. He was angry with Raphael for moving so far away from the Bay Area and he was letting Rafe know it. But Rafe just teased him and Dillon lightened up a little. Or so I thought.

"I had no idea that Dillon was still so angry with Rafe for leaving the company. I thought they were still close friends. When he showed up the other night, he was flirtatious and funny and sort of charming. I figured he had worked out his feelings about Raphael not going back to work with him. After all, Dillon had the company all to himself now. Wouldn't most people like being the one in charge?"

"You'd think so," Jane said.

"Right?" Marigold raised both hands up in confusion. "But whatever. I let him into the house and told him that Rafe wouldn't be home for a while. Dillon said that was okay, that this was a good chance for the

180

two of us to get to know each other better. He asked for a glass of wine and I poured one for him. Then he asked if I would show him around the house. He was very complimentary about everything. The house, I mean. And me. And Rafe's farm. And the town. Everything. He was very positive, very pleasant."

That did *not* sound like the Dillon I knew. And I was getting a really bad feeling about the whole scenario.

"He said that Rafe must really love it out here," Marigold went on, "if he was willing to give up the great life he'd had in the Bay Area. It was a nice thing to say, I thought. But then he began to list the names of all the beautiful women Rafe had dated in San Francisco. One was more gorgeous than the next, he said. Not much chance of meeting those kinds of women up here, is there?"

"He honestly said that to you?" I asked. I knew the guy was a jackass, but he kept raising the bar.

"Yeah." She pressed her lips together. "It got weird."

"You mean, *weirder,*" I muttered.

She nodded. "At some point, his words and his tone turned really bitter. He accused me of trapping Raphael, of lying to get him to marry me."

"That's hateful," Lizzie said.

"I don't have much experience with men," Marigold admitted. "But I've never heard that kind of talk from Raphael or any of the guys around here."

"Most men aren't like that," I assured her.

She shrugged. "I guess my negative reaction must've shown on my face because his expression instantly smoothed and he smiled. Warmly."

"What a psycho," Jane muttered.

This really was nuts. Dillon was an even bigger jerk than I had thought. If that was possible.

"Yes." Marigold nodded. "Definitely psycho. Now I wonder if he was happier because he'd gotten a rise out of me. Did it cheer him up to upset me? Is that what he wanted?"

"Of course that's what he wanted," I said. "He wanted to give Rafe a hard time, but he was too much the coward, so he figured by hurting you, he'd get back at Rafe the long way around."

"Probably," Marigold murmured.

Jane gave a brisk nod. "He wanted to hurt you."

"He succeeded," Marigold said flatly. "Anyway, I tried to switch gears, tried to keep it light. I smiled and told him how well

182

Raphael had taken to life here in Lighthouse Cove. How he had so many good friends in town and how we had such a wonderful life. I talked about the farm and the cows and how we were starting to make ice cream from all the milk. How he'd bought a little sailboat and we were having so much fun with it. I was rambling, just trying to keep things upbeat."

She rolled her eyes. "I sounded like some kind of Pollyanna. Or maybe I just sounded like myself."

I chuckled. "You do tend to see the glass half full."

"And that's a good thing, right?" Marigold said.

"Absolutely," Emily said, patting her knee.

Marigold sighed. "Unfortunately the more I gushed about Rafe's new lifestyle, the more Dillon's expression turned ugly and sour."

"I'll bet." Lizzie was pacing again, flexing her knuckles in frustration. "That's exactly what he *didn't* want to hear."

"True," Marigold said. "Finally he said, 'So now you've got yourself a sugar daddy. How'd you do it? You're nothing to brag about, you know. You're not sophisticated. You're not beautiful. You're nothing but a hick. A bumpkin. What does he see in you?' "

"He's wrong," Emily said. "You are beautiful."

"I'm so glad he's dead," Jane whispered, her jaw clenched so tightly that I reached over and rubbed her shoulder in sympathy.

Marigold had to take some more deep breaths. "It was so hurtful of him. And what did I do? Lifted my chin like a brave little soldier and said, 'All I know is that Rafe loves me.' "

"What did he say to that?" I asked.

"He just about fell on the floor laughing."

I scowled. It sounded like the same reaction that Midge Andersen had received from Dillon, according to what Niall said he'd overheard the other night.

"And that's when he got really disgusting," Marigold said. "He grabbed hold of both my arms and yanked me up close to him."

"Oh, jeez, Marigold," Lizzie moaned. "What did you do?"

"I was so shocked, at first I couldn't think what to do." Shaking her head, she seemed to be looking back on the moment in complete disbelief. "I tried to pull my arms free and back away from him, but he squeezed my arms so tightly, I knew I would have

184

bruises."

"Bastard," Lizzie muttered, not for the first time.

"After a few seconds I managed to escape his grip, but then he yanked me back so hard, I thought my arm would break." She took a shaky breath. "You guys, I was petrified. He was taunting me the whole time and I won't even repeat the vile stuff he said, but I finally got so angry that I kicked him. I only hit his knee, but I guess I caught him off guard because his leg crumpled. He let go of me and I ran down the hall and out the front door." Marigold was breathless, as though she'd just run a marathon. "I hid in the old barn until I heard him drive away."

"Thank God for the old barn," I said.

"When Rafe got home," she continued, "I had already showered. I'd scrubbed and scrubbed until my skin was one big patch of red. I had to get the hideous feel of him off me. I had my pajamas on and I was sitting up in bed, pretending to read."

Emily asked, "Did you tell him?"

"No. I couldn't. Not right then. He was so happy to see me and I was pitifully happy to see him. He told me how much he loved me. He lay down next to me and just held me. I started crying and he sort of laughed and teased me, thinking I was crying because I missed him after only four hours. And I *had* missed him, but he had no idea why.

"And I still can't get the nerve up to tell him. I just can't."

"You'll tell him when you're ready, Marigold," I said. "But I'll bet he would *want* to know."

"Of course he would," Lizzie said. "But you'll tell him in your own time."

"The thing is," Marigold continued, "I think you're right. Dillon was just an awful person. He attacked me because he wanted to hurt Rafe. He wanted to ruin my relationship with him and humiliate me in the process."

"He was a coward," I said flatly. "Thank God you were able to push him away. He was a truly evil guy."

She huffed out a laugh. "That's for sure." She grabbed a croissant and absently munched on it. "I'll have to think about how I'll tell Rafe." She blinked away the tears and gazed at each of us. "I just need some time."

"You might want to talk to a counselor," Jane said. "You know, a therapist. Someone besides us who can actually give you some good guidance."

186

"Yeah," Lizzie said. "Because we just basically want to kill him all over again. So maybe that's not much help."

Marigold laughed out loud and it was such a lovely sound that we all joined her.

"The counselor idea is a good one," Lizzie said. "I would recommend Sally Collins."

I nodded. "I like her, too."

Jane turned to Lizzie. "How do you know Sally?"

Lizzie averted her eyes. "Um, we've met a few times."

"She's wonderful," Emily said, looking back and forth at the rest of us. "I was seeing her for several months last year."

Jane's mouth opened and closed. Finally she said, "You were?"

Lizzie blinked. "You, too, Jane?"

Jane swallowed. "After Uncle Jesse died, I needed to work some things out."

"I . . . I went to see her a few months ago when Taz was about to turn twelve," Lizzie said, referring to her adorable young son. "He was bent on fraying my last nerve and I just needed a little perspective, you know? I'm pretty sure she kept me sane."

I stared at Lizzie. "Wow. I never knew." Turning, I grinned at Marigold. "I guess you can count on Sally to be discreet."

Marigold pressed her lips together, then

187

tried to smile. "Maybe I'll call her."

"Do what feels right for you," Emily said, reaching out to clutch Marigold's hand. "You were attacked. Thankfully you weren't hurt. You saved yourself. But you need time to process all that."

"Emily's right," I said. "You'll tell Rafe when you're ready, but your mental health and wellness comes first."

Marigold closed her eyes and breathed slowly. Then her eyes opened and she met each of our gazes. "I don't know who killed Dillon Charles. But if I ever find out, I plan to bake them a cake, shake their hand, and say 'thank you.' "

I headed for the new barn, but wasn't sure I could face my guys just now. I had lost my appetite, but I was light-headed enough to know that I needed to eat something. Maybe it was all the adrenaline that had been coursing through my system during Marigold's harrowing tale, but now it had dissipated and I felt like I was crashing. I needed protein and I needed to get away from the conference center for a while. Without another thought, I jogged to my truck, jumped in, and took off for town.

Seventeen minutes later, I was ensconced in a booth at the Cozy Cove. The welcome aroma of burgers and fried food wafting from the kitchen made my appetite spring back to life. Glancing around, I took in the familiar walls covered in old black-and-white photographs of Lighthouse Cove from its earliest days. I had been coming here with my family since I was a little girl and we lived just a block away. I still lived a block away in the same house I'd grown up in, and I still loved coming to the Cozy Cove.

More recently, I would often meet my dad and Uncle Pete here on Saturday mornings, but it had been a while since the three of us had gotten together. I suddenly had to sniff back tears that were springing up unbidden. It had been an emotional morning. And I was smelling French fries.

"Hey, Shannon, it's been a while."

"Hi, Cindy." I closed the menu and smiled up at the waitress who had been working here for as long as I could remember. "I haven't been around much. Just finishing the rehab on Rafe Nash's farmhouse."

"I heard it looks fantastic."

"It's pretty awesome," I said with a grin.

"I'll drive out there sometime and take a look." She grabbed my menu. "What'll you have, sweetie?"

"Cheeseburger, medium rare, French

fries, lots of pickles. The usual."

"Cola?"

I thought for a minute. I had gone from having zero appetite to wanting to eat my feelings. Well, if I was going to do this right, I couldn't waste my time with soft drinks. "I'll have a chocolate milkshake."

"Going hard." She grinned. "I like it." She slid her notepad into her pocket. "That'll be up in just a minute."

"Thanks, Cindy."

She started to head for the counter, then stopped. "Hey, your daddy was in here the other day with his new girlfriend."

"Is that right?" So Cindy had seen my father's new girlfriend but I hadn't. I really was out of touch. But now that Rafe's house was finished and the conference was in full swing, I would be able to call Dad and set up a date to meet his new lady.

"Yeah. She seems like a sweetheart. Really down to earth. And your father is clearly smitten."

"Isn't that nice?" I said. But was it? I had no idea since I hadn't even met her yet. I was the worst daughter ever.

"And man, I just love her hair," Cindy continued. "That color reminds me of yours. A little darker. Can't tell if it's natural or not, but I just like the way she's got it cut real blunt and swingy, you know? It's as cute as can be and it suits her perfectly."

The cook yelled an order out and Cindy turned and yelled back, "Coming." She whipped back around. "I'll get your order out ASAP."

"Thanks, Cindy."

I leaned back in the booth. I couldn't catch my breath for all the thoughts speeding around my head at a thousand miles an hour. I closed my eyes to try and slow them down. Because according to Cindy's description of my father's new girlfriend, she sounded an awful lot like Belinda McCoy, my uncle Pete's new winemaker.

And the other night, watching Pete and Belinda together, I had been pretty darned sure that my uncle had his eye on Belinda to be *his* girlfriend.

So how was it that she and my father had looked cozy enough that Cindy thought they were a couple? Was Belinda playing the two men against each other? And if she was, how quickly could I hunt her down and smack her 'til her head spun? Nobody hurt my father or my uncle. Not on my watch.

I had really lost my appetite now. And that irritated the heck out of me. I took a few more breaths to calm down. There could be a perfectly reasonable explanation for all of this. I could've been reading Uncle Pete wrong, but I didn't think so. And I hadn't talked to my father in a couple of weeks, which was a rarity. Usually we talked several times a week. But because I hadn't talked to him, I had no idea what was going on in his life. And that made me sad.

Unfortunately, with everything I had to do for the conference, the barn, the small houses display, and everything else, I wouldn't have time to meet the new GF for another day or two. Maybe longer. But when I finally did get a chance to hear Belinda's explanation, what would I do? Maybe it would be better to talk to my father first. No, maybe I would call my sister first and then set up a conference call with Dad. We could double team him. *Yeah, I* thought. *That would work.*

With that happy thought, my appetite was starting to return and my stomach was growling from all the savory smells emanating from the kitchen. I wanted that cheeseburger. Almost as much as I wanted to get to the bottom of whatever game Belinda McCoy was playing.

That afternoon, Eric showed up at the conference site. He found me walking the perimeter of the new barn's foundation, examining the wood base for the frames to make sure they were still holding and ready to go. Maybe I was being paranoid, but I wanted to check every inch of it. Yes, it had only been two days since the barn raising had been interrupted by Dillon's death. But I figured with some of the odd occurrences happening at the conference, like the escape of the smart mice, I would rather be safe than sorry.

And frankly, I'd wanted some time to myself to think over everything Marigold had told us. I had been so furious on her behalf and so helpless with it, that it felt as though my whole body was vibrating.

And that was because I couldn't tell anyone. It was so frustrating! I could've hunted down Jane or Emily to talk about it, but what I really wanted to do was talk to Mac. I needed to share with him everything Marigold had told us this morning. He was so intuitive that I knew he would feel the pain and make things better. But I couldn't say a word. I could never betray Marigold's confidence.

I suppose it said something about my feelings for Mac that he was the first person I thought of when I needed to dump my fears and worries and terrors on someone else.

Wasn't that the whole point of being a couple?

The thought made me shake my head. Gee, must be true love if you trusted the guy enough to dump some horrible news on top of him. But it was true love, and the whole dumping thing worked both ways. So I was okay with it.

I was so wrapped up in my own thoughts that I didn't hear Eric walk up. I jumped when he spoke.

"I wanted to let you know you can continue the barn raising tomorrow."

"Great news," I said, recovering quickly.

"You okay?" he asked, clearly concerned with my reaction.

"Me? Yeah. Sure. Thanks for the news. That was fast."

"Yeah, we got all we could get from the crime scene," he said, "so now it's a matter of interviewing people and figuring out who had the most to gain from Dillon's death."

"Have you talked to Hallie?"

He gave me a look that I interpreted to mean, *Mind your own business.* But of course, that wasn't going to happen.

"Yes," he said finally. "I tracked her down this morning. She's still despondent, still a little teary-eyed." He thought for a moment, seemed to consider his words, but then came out with it. "She said something strange."

"Really?" My ears perked up. "What's that?"

"She said she's glad that Rafe is coming back to work now that Dillon's gone."

That made zero sense. Rafe was out of the business and devoted to Marigold and his new life in Lighthouse Cove.

"Did Rafe tell you that?"

"Nope. In fact, he told me he's going to try to find new jobs for his employees, then liquidate the company and work on his own up here."

"Then it looks like Hallie's doomed to disappointment. Oh well. She's young, she'll snap out of it."

He cocked his head, giving me a look. "That's a little harsh."

"Sorry," I said, although I wasn't. "I'm not in the best of moods this morning."

"Why? Something happen?"

"Um." I couldn't say anything, but he would know something was bugging me. "It's not my story to tell. And really, it's not that important." Not now that Dillon was dead, I added to myself.

His eyes narrowed. "Does it have anything to do with the investigation?"

I stared at him for a few long seconds. "No."

He stared back. "You sure about that?"

He was right. I was the world's worst liar. "I'm sorry. I'd rather not say anything else right now."

He must have seen the concern in my eyes, because he nodded and let it go. "Let me know if anything changes."

"I will. I promise."

He walked away and I felt the weight of the world settle on my shoulders. There was simply no way I could tell him about Dillon's attack on Marigold. Not only was it *not* my story to tell, but also it had just dawned on me that there was no one else who had a bigger motive to kill Dillon Charles than my friend Marigold.

Except maybe Rafe.

I set up a conference call with Carla, Wade, and Sean. "We got the high sign from Chief Jensen. Barn raising's on for tomorrow. Can you guys rally the troops?"

"I'll send a group e-mail right now," Sean said. I could hear him clicking on a keyboard. "Okay, I had forty six workers say they would be able to come back, but I'll send a message to all fifty. There's always a few who can't make it after all, but then there might be one or two who said no at first but will be able to do it now. I'll let you know the final count ASAP."

"Thanks, Sean."

On my way over to the air dome, Marigold found me. I gave her a big hug and asked her how she was feeling.

"Much better after talking to you guys this morning. I'm still working up the nerve to tell Raphael what really happened, but I definitely feel a little lighter for having gotten it off my chest."

"I'm so glad. Whatever you decide to do, it's going to be the right thing for you."

"What would you do, Shannon?"

"Well, you know me. I would probably tell him because I'm not very good at keeping secrets." *Not to mention, the world's worst liar,* I thought. "But that's me. You need to figure out what's right for you. You might want to call Sally Collins to talk. Or, I don't know. It sounds silly, but believe it or not, sometimes just taking a long bike ride helps settle my mind."

"I know what you mean, and it doesn't sound silly at all." She sighed. "I just don't want to add to Rafe's pain. Dillon was his friend and now he's dead. Rafe is already feeling guilty enough that he was killed on his property. During his big conference. You know? He's worried about everything else and now his oldest friend and partner is dead. It's really tearing him up."

"I can see how it would. But you remember I told you about the argument I overheard between Rafe and Dillon, right? Dillon said a lot of awful things, personal things that were really hurtful, and Rafe ordered him to get off his property. So I don't think there was any friendship left between them." I rubbed her arm. "That's just something to consider, but it's not the most important thing."

"What is it?"

"You, Marigold. I care about your feelings more than anything else. Whatever you decide to do, I'm right there with you."

She hugged me. "Thank you."

"Just take care of yourself, okay?"

She didn't speak for a long moment, then nodded slowly. "I will. You always make so much sense, Shannon."

"I'm a smart cookie," I said with a grin, then sobered. "And, Marigold, if you do decide to tell Rafe and you need some support, just say the word and we'll be there with you."

"Thanks, Shannon." She hugged me again

tightly. "I'm so lucky to have you as my friend."

"I'm the lucky one."

An hour later, Marigold called me to invite us over for an impromptu dinner at their place.

"Rafe wants to christen the new grill with a few of our closest friends," she said. "And he needs a break from the conference hubbub."

"Sounds like a great idea," I said. "We would love to come. What can we bring?"

"Just bring a bottle of wine," she said. "And just so you know, before you all arrive tonight, I plan to tell Rafe what Dillon did. I hope it won't ruin the party, but I need to get it off my chest before another day passes."

When she hung up, I said a silent prayer that everything would turn out right for her and Rafe. Then I walked into the air dome to watch Mac moderate his "Worst-Case Scenarios" workshop. There were only three writers on the panel so he had clearly been successful at getting rid of Sketch Horn.

I found a seat in the third row of the nearly packed auditorium, and shortly after I sat down, Rafe walked up to the stage to introduce the panelists. There was Mac, of course, along with a romantic suspense author named Cheryl Meyerson, and another thriller writer, Brett Barlow.

Once Rafe had introduced the three, he added, "In case you were here to see Sketch Horn, I'm happy to announce that he'll be moderating another panel tomorrow called 'The End of the World as We Know It.' It should be highly entertaining. But now, let's get started with 'Worst-Case Scenarios.' "

The applause was deafening inside the air dome, and I was proud and happy to know that Mac's panel had managed to fill the massive theater to its capacity.

Mac started out by saying that worst-case scenarios could occur in any situation, any hour of any day. "Think about it. Any of you in this room could come up with a worst-case scenario about something as simple as crossing the street. I'll give you a minute to consider the possibilities."

There were some chuckles, and then all three panelists started spit-balling their own ideas.

"Runaway bus," Mac began.

"The signals go out because terrorists have destroyed the grid," Brett Barlow suggested.

"A toddler gets loose and runs into traffic," Cheryl said, causing a number of people to moan with worry.

Brett grinned. "A bike messenger pops a tire."

"You spot your husband on the opposite corner," Mac said, "locked in a passionate embrace with another woman."

I laughed when that last one got the biggest gasps from the audience.

Mac was chuckling, too. "Now, unlike the other examples, that last idea doesn't put anyone in physical danger — except maybe your husband."

After that, the three writers scared us with harrowing situations. Cheryl presented the scenario of a diabolical serial killer obsessed with pipe bombs. Brett was a big fan of what he called "doomsday scenarios in everyday life."

Mac came up with a tsunami scenario featuring Lighthouse Cove and he asked audience members to come up with all sorts of solutions to save the town. The suggestions ran the gamut from storing lifeboats in every house, to building underground bunkers along the Alisal Cliffs, to constructing a forty-foot-high, three-mile-long breakwater across the cove. One person insisted that the town council needed to pass a law making swimming lessons mandatory.

The banter between the panelists was

hilarious, and at the end of the hour, the audience gave them a standing ovation.

I stepped into the aisle and watched dozens of people race up to the stage for a chance to meet the authors and ask questions. Mac was surrounded and I knew I wouldn't be able to get close to him for another half hour or more. I sent him a quick text to meet at my house in two hours so we could drive together to Rafe and Marigold's dinner party.

I turned to weave my way through the hordes and found myself face-to-face with weird Wesley's even weirder friend, Sherman. Well, not exactly face-to-face since he was a good six inches shorter than me. Today he wore a green polka-dot bow tie with a gray sweater vest tucked into trousers belted tightly above the waist. And brown suede Hush Puppies on his feet. It had been a while since I'd seen a pair of those, but I had to admit they suited him. It wasn't necessarily a compliment.

He pointed at me. "You."

A real social animal, I thought. "Me."

He frowned. "Er, hello."

"Hello, Sherman. Are you enjoying the conference?"

"How can I?" he demanded. "Did you hear about the mice?"

202

I shuddered at the mention of the M word. "I hear they escaped."

"They escaped?" His eyes narrowed. "Or were they liberated?"

Good question, I thought.

"Either way," he continued, "they have yet to be found." He shook his head peevishly. "This conference is descending into chaos. First an unexplained death, now mice. What next?"

For some reason, thoughts of a tsunami came to mind. I didn't even want to think about Wesley and the clicking.

I just shook my head. "Dunno what's next. But sure nice talking to you."

He ignored my attempt to escape, saying, "I'm trying to get to the front of the room to ask Mr. MacKintyre Sullivan a question."

I glanced over my shoulder at the throngs of people gathered around the stage and particularly around Mac. "Good luck."

"Never mind. I won't make it through that flock of mindless sheep." He turned around and changed direction, and inched along with me and the rest of the audience toward the back exit.

Lucky me, it seemed that Sherman was my new best friend.

"You know him," Sherman said, scowling up at me.

"Who?"

"Mr. MacKintyre Sullivan."

I smiled. "I do."

"Will you please get me an audience with him?"

"He's not the Pope, Sherman. He's just a guy. You can walk up and talk to him anytime during the conference."

"I would prefer to use my connections to guarantee a serious meeting with a like-minded scholar."

"And I'm one of your connections?"

"I've seen you with him, so yes."

"And Mac is a . . . scholar? Like you?"

"Like *Wesley,*" he corrected.

I considered Mac really smart, but I wasn't sure he qualified to be a scholar. Or at least, not a scholar — or a nut job — like Sherman. Er, Wesley. But Mac would probably love to hear it. I couldn't wait to tell him.

"I can't promise anything," I said, shuffling along at a snail's pace, trying not to run into the people in front of me. "But I'll see what I can do."

"Good."

"Where shall I tell him to find you?"

"Have you been in the Ecosphere?" he asked.

"Yes. It's wonderful."

He scowled. "Wesley has some issues with the space."

"What about you?"

"I'm not important. Wesley is the one who matters."

Hoo-boy. "So is this meeting with Mac for you or for Wesley?"

"Wesley, of course." He shook his head as if I were a complete dolt. "I'll leave you now. I must find Julian Reedy to arrange an audience regarding the Ecosphere."

"An audience for Wesley?"

"Of course for Wesley," he said irately. "I suppose you do catch on."

I didn't know why I was finding his insults amusing.

"Good-bye," he said.

"There's nowhere to go," I said, staring at the hairdo of the woman directly in front of me. It was a good thing I wasn't claustrophobic in this insane crowd of people.

But Sherman had managed to slip between the couple in front of us and disappear into the crowd.

"Bye-bye, then," I muttered, not the least little bit sorry to see him go.

After hearing Marigold's story that morning, I had been uncertain whether she would be able to enjoy herself at the first social get-together in her new home. But I shouldn't have worried. She and Rafe were having the time of their lives and my girlfriends and I couldn't be happier. It made me suspect that Marigold had already told Rafe everything.

The party was in full swing by the time the sun began to set. I was pleased to see that the nearby conference area was deserted. According to Rafe, the horde of conference-goers had disappeared an hour ago to attend a gourmet Slow Food event in the large banquet room of the Inn on Main Street. The two world-class chefs had designed a menu that sounded fantastic and there was nothing like the promise of free food to attract a conference crowd. I had no hope at all that there might be leftovers.

We all hung out in the kitchen for a little while until Rafe took the steaks out to the grill. Then, as with almost any party anywhere on earth, the women continued to chat in the kitchen while the men stood outside and kibitzed around the grill.

"I'm sorry Emily couldn't be here," Marigold said, "but we plan to have plenty of dinner parties in the future that she'll be able to attend."

Emily was catering a small private party tonight for Julian Reedy and his fellow ethnobotanists. And didn't that sound like a good time?

Marigold had finished chopping tomatoes and added them to the salad, then put the bowl into the refrigerator. Closing the door to the fridge, she whipped around and blurted, "I told him."

There was a long second of silence and then we all grabbed her in a big group hug.

"I'm so relieved that you were able to talk to him about it," I said.

"So am I," she said.

"So how did he react?" Jane asked.

"Just as Shannon predicted," she said, squeezing my hand. "He said he wished he could've killed Dillon himself."

"Good answer," Lizzie said with a curt nod. "I'm glad, since we all feel the same way."

"I know I do," Jane muttered, scowling at the reminder of Marigold's attack.

"So do you feel better?" Lizzie asked.

"So much better," Marigold said with a sigh. "And now I don't want to talk about it again tonight. I just want to relax and have fun with you guys for a few hours before we have to jump back into the conference scene tomorrow."

"Sounds good to me," Lizzie said. "I'll pour more wine."

I dutifully held out my glass for a refill, then led the way out to the patio. I was happy to see that Rafe had invited Niall to dinner as well. The two men had bonded over the virtues of reclaimed glass and stone during the months of construction of the patio and the other outlying stonework around Rafe's property. Now Niall was regaling Lizzie's husband Hal with exploits of his days as a teacher in an Edinburgh high school. It seemed that Niall had done a little bit of everything before finding his bliss as a stonemason.

Marigold went over to sit on the hearth near Rafe, who was keeping an eagle eye on the steaks being grilled.

It really was a relief to know that Marigold had told him about Dillon's duplicity. It had been so deeply painful for her that it might have haunted her throughout their marriage. But looking at them now, so animated and happy to be with each other, I could only hope that things would be wonderful for them from now on.

I could still remember the night last year when Marigold had admitted to all of us that she was dating the new guy in town. Raphael Nash and she had met at the historical society, where Marigold was exhibiting her quilts and Rafe was giving lectures and demonstrations on installing solar shingles on Victorian homes. It was pretty much love at first sight for Rafe, and after a few dates, he asked Marigold to marry him. But she had refused his proposal.

Undeterred, Rafe went on a campaign to win Marigold's heart, even going so far as to paint marigolds on the old wooden water towers around town. I had seen one of the brightly painted wooden towers while I was out driving one afternoon and had questioned Marigold about it. She was furious, but finally admitted that she was falling in love with Rafe. But since she had been raised Amish and had deliberately moved away from her community, the last thing she wanted to do was become a farmer's wife.

When Rafe realized why she was refusing to marry him, he quickly assured her that she would never have to milk another cow, ever again.

And he had kept his word. It helped that he was ridiculously wealthy and could hire a dozen people to milk cows and run tractors.

I smiled at the memory.

"What are you thinking about?" Mac asked as he joined me by the patio table and wrapped his arm around my shoulder.

I told him where my mind had gone and he agreed that it was nice to see Rafe and Marigold so happy.

"Especially in the middle of all this up-heaval," he added. "First the house renovation, now this conference. And the death of his partner, of course. No matter how big a jerk that guy was, it had to be traumatic for Rafe. The two of them are going to need a vacation after this."

"I think we're all going to need one," I said.

We strolled lazily around the new patio, checking out the fascinating patterns in the stones. When we reached the edge of the patio, where newly planted trees blocked off the view of the conference grounds, I frowned and squinted at the shadows along the side of the house. "Who's that?"

"It's Niall," Mac murmured.

"But that's . . . oh." I whipped around and, slipping my arm through Mac's, quickly headed in the opposite direction.

"Are you all right?" Mac whispered in my ear.

"Yeah. Wow. Just a little . . . surprised."

"I'd call it a shockwave, based on your reaction."

"Well, yeah. Because that was Jane with

Niall." I shook my head, still dumbfounded. "I had no idea. And you know, I'm pretty sharp when it comes to figuring out who's doing what with whom."

He grinned. "Guess Jane knows how to keep a secret."

"What kind of friend is that?" I said huffily. I was kidding of course, sort of. But I couldn't wait to corner Jane at the earliest opportunity.

"By the way," Mac said, changing topics, to my relief. "I didn't ask if you enjoyed the panel this afternoon."

"Oh, yes." I stood on tiptoe and gave him a quick kiss. "I loved it. I was so proud of you. The crowd loved you. And you were so funny. The subject matter was a little scary, too. But all three of you were really creative and entertaining."

"I can't believe we filled the air dome," he admitted. "And I'm glad you found it a little scary. It was supposed to be. But we wanted to play for some laughs, too."

"You succeeded. It was really fun." I took a deep breath and said, "Would you be upset if I went to Sketch Horn's panel tomorrow? I've never officially met him, but from everything you say about him, I'm dying to see how he handles things."

He gazed down at me, shaking his head.

"No, I won't be upset. In fact, I had the exact same thought just a few minutes ago. It's like you were reading my mind."

"If I can sneak away from the barn raising for an hour, we can go together."

He kissed the top of my head. "It's a date."

I watched Marigold grab the steak platter and take it into the house. Jane followed her inside as Rafe, Hal, and Niall argued about marinades while they continued watching the meat.

"Isn't it a beautiful night?" Lizzie said, coming over to join us.

Mac grinned. "Sure is."

"You can see a million stars out here," I said, marveling at how clear the sky was, once you got a few miles away from all of the ambient lights of town.

Without warning, the sound of rifle fire exploded in the night air.

"What the hell?" Rafe said. "Everybody get down!" Then he raced into the house and disappeared.

"Was that a gunshot?" Lizzie demanded.

Mac hurried over to me. "Stay down." Then he dashed away.

"I'm already there." Instinctively, I hunkered down and stared out at the surrounding hills. From where I was perched, I could see Mac running around the side of the

212

house to the front. Niall followed him quickly, his kilt flapping as he ran.

The young trees planted at the perimeter of the patio gave us some protection from the conference site and the property beyond. But with the patio lights blazing, we could probably be seen for a mile in any direction.

"Where did that shot come from?" I asked.

"Maybe someone hunting in the woods?" Lizzie said.

"At seven o'clock at night?"

"No, probably not," Lizzie admitted. "I'd just rather not think of the possibility that someone is out there shooting at one of us."

Two minutes later, Niall, Mac, and Rafe came walking back to the patio.

"Couldn't see anyone out there," Rafe said, "but I have a feeling whoever took the shot is long gone."

I was surprised, but also reassured to see Rafe carrying a shotgun. Now I figured out that that was why he had run inside. Because of course he had a shotgun somewhere in the house. After all, when there weren't a dozen construction workers and hundreds of conference goers milling around, it could get pretty solitary out here. And with his nearest neighbor at least a half mile away, there wasn't anyone he could call in an instant to help him protect his property except himself. And now Marigold.

I looked at Mac. "Did you see where the shot came from?"

"I have a feeling I know where it came from, but I'd rather check things out before I jump to any conclusions."

"I can't say where the bloody bullet came from," Niall griped. "But the damn thing took off a corner of my bloody hearth."

CHAPTER SEVEN

We were fairly certain that the shooter was gone, but in an abundance of caution, we quickly moved inside the house. Rafe whipped the steaks off the grill and brought them inside to the kitchen, where they would stay warm while we waited for the police to arrive. The potatoes were wrapped in foil and left in the oven, while the salad remained in the refrigerator.

Maybe it was silly that we were so focused on saving the food. But to be honest, that was more appealing than dwelling on the reality that someone had just taken a shot at one of us.

A few minutes ago, my mouth had been watering for a juicy steak, but now I couldn't stomach it. I knew the feeling wouldn't last long, but right now it looked as if none of us felt like eating until we had figured out what in the world was going on. Was one of us a target? Was Dillon only the first to die?

Chief Eric and Tommy arrived within twenty minutes of the attack and Leo Springer, the CSI guy, showed up five minutes later. Then a squad car raced up to the front of the house and two more officers poured out to begin searching the conference area, looking for anything suspicious. I recognized both of them and waved. Officer Mindy Payton was an old buddy from high school and I'd met Carlos Garcia when he worked on a murder case a few months ago while my sister was in town.

I wondered what sort of suspicious evidence they would find. Maybe a high-powered rifle stuffed inside someone's complimentary conference tote bag?

Eric stayed inside to question all of us and take notes, while Tommy and Leo worked the scene outside on the patio. They tracked down the bullet in the flower bed that lined the stone patio. They studied the damage done to the hearth, took pictures of it from every angle, and then tried to figure out the trajectory of the bullet. After a half hour, they came inside and warmed up.

"What's the verdict?" Eric asked Leo.

Leo packed his camera inside his steel briefcase. "The bullet struck the corner of the hearth at such an angle that there could only be one possible place the shot could've come from."

"Where is that?"

"The shooter had to have been standing on the rooftop of that tower out by the barn." Leo snapped his briefcase shut and glanced up. "Tommy tells me they call it an Ecosphere."

Frowning, I looked at Mac. I wasn't happy to hear that the Ecosphere had been used as a place to try and kill one of my friends, but I supposed it was good to know where the bullet might have come from. Maybe the killer had left some evidence up there, like fingerprints. Or a spent shell. Or hey, a greeting card. I didn't hold out a lot of hope for any of those clues to show up, but you never knew.

"When you're ready, I'll go with you and your officers to check out the Ecosphere," Leo said.

"I'll be a few more minutes here, Leo," Eric said. He was flipping through his notepad when I asked a question I hadn't heard anyone bring up yet.

"Who do you think the shooter was aiming at?" I wondered.

"Rafe, obviously," Marigold said immediately, and clutched her fiancé's arm. "He was standing right by the hearth while he was watching the steaks."

"You're the most likely target," Eric conceded, gazing at Rafe. He made another quick note in his pad. "Your business partner was just killed two days ago and now an attempt has been made on your life. Is there someone attending your conference who might be trying to destroy your company?"

"Yeah," Rafe said flatly. "Me."

Eric's eyes widened, then he frowned. "Explain. That is, if you don't mind talking about company business in front of everyone here."

"I don't mind at all. They are my friends." He squeezed Marigold's hand and they shared a private smile. And I felt a warm glow settle over my heart. Whatever happened next, I knew that Rafe and Marigold would be okay.

"After I left the company last year," Rafe began, "I held on to a majority interest. Dillon was in charge of the day-to-day running of the business, but I still had a say in the running of things, so to speak." He glanced around at the group. "That's confidential, by the way. We kept the arrangement quiet from the rest of the company because I wanted the staff to put their trust in Dillon and follow his leadership. But from the very beginning, it wasn't working. He was spending way too much money on stupid stuff, like a helicopter, for God's sake, and buying a hotel in Costa Rica. He was flying off to Vegas every weekend and losing a lot of money."

He shook his head. "A *lot* of money. When he told me he was going to borrow from one of the company accounts — but swore he would make it all back quickly — I knew I couldn't trust him with the finances anymore."

Or anything else, I thought. We already knew Dillon was a serious creep, but now, we were finding out he was fatally stupid, too.

"Some of you already know this," he continued as he began pacing back and forth. "But I've been thinking of cutting the cord completely for a while now. I want out. It's not like I need the money anymore. I've made enough for six lifetimes so I don't need to worry about that, but that's not the reason why I wanted to get out. Frankly, I just didn't need the hassle anymore." He glanced at Marigold. "I've got better things to focus on now."

"Can't blame you for that," Mac said.

"And by the way," Rafe said, scowling, "when I say *hassle,* I mean *Dillon.*"

"Think we got that," Eric said.

Hal gave a rueful laugh. "Yeah, we're hearing you."

Rafe went on, "He was getting more and more unreliable and he was scaring some of the staff with his erratic behavior. I'd been getting complaint calls from the office almost every day for the past year." He sighed. "And now he's gone. And there's no one else who can run the company."

"Sounds like it's way past time you cut that cord," Hal said.

"Yeah, it is. My life is here now, and I want to enjoy every day with Marigold. I've got my wacky experiments and inventions, and I'm fiddling with new ice cream flavors now that I've got the cows on a regular milking schedule."

"We're happy about that, too," Lizzie assured him with a grin.

"And most importantly, I'd like to try and save a little bit of the world through the foundation." He glanced around. "And I'm blathering. But I hope I answered your question."

"You did," Eric said, still jotting down details in his notepad. "But the person who shot at you tonight might not know about your plan to close down the company."

"Nobody knows," he said quietly, "since I

only made that decision final this afternoon."

"Is there someone next in line to take over?" Eric asked. "Or someone who *thinks* they're next in line?"

Rafe leaned back against the kitchen island. "We have a number of department heads that could handle different aspects of the business, but nobody can do it all, not like Dillon or I did."

Eric nodded, took another minute to catch up with his notes, and then glanced over at Rafe. "Any possible suspects come to mind? Who would have the most to gain with you and your partner both gone? To put it more bluntly, who would like to see you dead?"

Rafe mulled Eric's question, and at that moment I realized something important that nobody else had mentioned. I cautiously held up my hand. "Sorry to interrupt, but before you get too far into naming suspects and motives, there's one thing we should probably consider."

Eric turned and looked at me, and I could read exasperation in his expression. I couldn't blame him. He had been dragged out of the house at dinnertime to investigate a shooting. Besides knowing he would have to work late into the night, he was probably getting hungry. "What is it, Shannon?"

"Well, it makes sense that whoever killed Dillon might also want to kill Rafe. I mean, it's a horrible thought, but you know, that's how murdering psychopaths think, right?"

"What's your point, Shannon?" Eric said. His tone was scolding enough to make me wince.

"Getting there." I huffed out a breath. Nobody had any patience anymore. "My point is that barely two seconds before we heard the gunshot, it was *Marigold* who was sitting on the corner of the hearth where that bullet hit." I stopped pacing. "It was just lucky that she got up and headed for the kitchen at that exact moment."

"Oh my God, Shannon, you're right," Lizzie whispered. "Marigold was sitting right there talking to Rafe."

"That's right," I said. "So yeah, maybe Rafe could be the target, but I'm just asking you to consider the possibility that someone out there was actually aiming at *Marigold* instead."

Eric and Tommy wanted to go with Leo to check out the Ecosphere rooftop. Clearly, someone had used the spot for their kill site. They asked Mac and Rafe to go with them because of Mac's expertise with rifles and Rafe's connection to the conference.

"But aren't you all hungry?" Marigold wondered. "How about a bite to eat before you go out there?"

Eric gave our hostess a grateful look. "That's sweet of you, Marigold. But time is of the essence right now."

"I could fix you a mini-portion of steak and potato, just to tide you over for a little while."

Tommy gave Eric a soulful look and Eric rolled his eyes, but relented. "Fine. Let's do it. I'm starving. And Tommy will probably pass out in the dirt if he doesn't eat something."

"Thanks, Marigold," Tommy said gratefully. "Best offer I've had all week."

"I wouldn't turn down a few bites of steak," Leo said with a sweet smile.

Marigold beamed. "Then just have a seat and enjoy."

"We'll take ten minutes to wolf it down," Eric muttered to Tommy. "Then we're out of here."

"I can do this," Tommy said. He could, too. He was a speed-eater back in high school. Nothing much had changed there.

Twelve minutes later, they had their jackets on and were ready to go.

"Hold on, Chief," Mac said. "We're going to need to take Shannon with us."

Eric gave him a look that I interpreted as *Mac, you're out of your mind.* But Mac explained, "She's the only one of us who's been working on the Ecosphere from the very beginning. She would notice if anything inside there has been disturbed."

"I also know how to turn on the lights," I said helpfully.

Eric's lips twisted in frustration and he gave me a long gaze, then nodded. "Fine. Let's go."

I was grateful to Mac for including me, and despite Eric's grumpy words, I could tell that he was in a much better mood, thanks to Marigold. There was nothing quite like a rib eye and a baked potato to soothe the nerves of a couple of cranky cops.

I grabbed my jacket and we took off for the Ecosphere.

Ten minutes later I led the guys through the open doorway and into the Ecosphere.

"You don't lock it up at night?" Eric asked, staring at the plain cement block opening with no door attached.

"No," I said. "Rafe and Julian wanted to have the space available twenty-four hours a day because everything is so concentrated that there are changes happening every minute. It's cool. And it's educational.

That's the whole point of the display." I aimed my flashlight toward the left side of the space. "For instance, I can already see where much of that wall has been taken over by the clematis vine."

"Okay," he said slowly. He clearly had no idea what I was talking about.

"And some of the flowers only bloom at night or early in the morning," I added. "So it's nice to be able to check them out whenever you want to."

"Makes sense, I guess."

"Do you want me to turn the lights on?" I asked.

"No," he said. "I don't want to draw even more attention to us being here than we already have."

Mac chuckled. "We're not exactly fooling anyone with all six of us traipsing around, shining flashlights in every direction."

"Exactly what I was afraid of," Eric grumbled.

"Okay," I said, ignoring his gruffness. "We're about to walk up the ramp to the second level, so just follow me."

I was in the lead and my flashlight was trained on the ground in front of me. I was taking it slowly because I wanted to check whether the ground cover had been trampled or not. It was healthy enough that it usually sprang back quickly, but if someone had been inside here in the last hour, we might be able to see footprints.

I stepped onto the floor of the second level and moved along the pathway toward the next ramp up to the third level — and my foot jammed into something.

"Ow," I muttered, and started to fall forward. Mac grabbed the back of my jacket and pulled me up close to him.

"Thanks," I said, blowing out a breath.

"You okay?" he asked.

"Yeah."

"What happened?"

"I almost tripped over something."

"What is it?" Eric demanded from behind us. He stepped off the path and trampled over a pretty cluster of alyssum to get around to where Mac and I were standing.

"Be careful of the plants," I said.

"Not important right now," he said brusquely. "What's wrong?"

"Something on the path." I aimed the flashlight around the path and saw a pair of shoes. And felt my stomach drop. "Shoes."

"More than just shoes," Mac muttered.

I squinted to get a better look. "Oh my God. No."

Eric turned and flashed his light down and illuminated the obstacle in the path. "Damn it." He hissed out the words.

His body had fallen into the dark, leafy plants. Only his shoes were left blocking the pathway.

I would know those Hush Puppies anywhere, I thought, and wanted to scramble down the ramp and get the heck out of there. But I stayed where I was and forced myself to look at the face almost buried by the green leaves. I could just make out his polka-dot bow tie, slightly obscured by a thick green vine.

"I know him," I whispered. "It's Sherman."

The Ecosphere lights were turned up so brightly, the plants must have thought it was daylight.

Leo Springer got right down to it, examining the body and the surrounding area. Tommy and the same four cops from earlier were put to work combing over every inch of the Ecosphere, looking for any clues that might lead to the killer's identity.

"We'll check out the roof in just a minute," Eric said, "but first, Shannon, I need to ask you some questions. Then you can go back to Rafe's."

Eric, Mac, and I walked outside while Leo and his helpers started their investigation.

Eric leaned against the outer wall of the tower and peppered me with questions.

"How do you know that guy in there?" He checked his notes. "Sherman."

"I've met him a few times here at the conference. He's very odd, but harmless." I frowned. "At least I thought so. He's completely devoted to another conference goer, Wesley Mycroft."

"Do you have any idea why Sherman would be in here tonight?"

"Not really, except that he was probably trying to set up a meeting between Wesley and Julian."

Eric flipped a page and continued writing. Glancing up, he asked, "Who's Julian?"

"He's the ethnobotanist who created the Ecosphere."

He frowned. "Ethno . . ."

"Ethnobotanist. He's the plant guy."

"So why would Sherman be looking for Julian in here?"

"Because Julian is always in here. Well, not always, but this is his gig. So chances are good that you'll find him here. During the day, anyway."

"And who is Wesley?"

"Good question," I muttered. "He's weird. That's not nice." I shook my head. "Sorry. Wesley is an inventor, apparently. He's very nerdy. A Poindexter type, but dour. He dresses like a funeral director. Each time I've seen him, he's wearing a severe black suit. He's almost six feet tall and very thin, with stooped shoulders and hair plastered to his head. He wanted to meet with Julian because, according to Sherman, he had some complaints about the Ecosphere."

Eric glanced up at me. "Do you know what the complaints were?"

"Not really." I shrugged. "All Sherman said was that Wesley had some issues with the space. And before you ask, I have no idea what he meant by that. Frankly, both men are very strange. But that's not relevant. Sorry. You'd have to ask Wesley."

"And where do I find this Wesley character?"

Feeling a little frustrated, I glanced at Mac and shook my head. "Believe it or not, Eric, I don't have all the answers."

Eric suddenly grinned. "That's actually good to know."

I managed to refrain from rolling my eyes. "You could probably track Wesley down at one of the hotels. Or maybe just hang around the conference space. He's here every day, as far as I know. I could point him out to you."

I watched while Eric continued to jot

229

down his notes.

"Oh, hold on." I remembered something. "You might ask Rafe about Wesley. He's apparently applied for a foundation grant so he's probably got an appointment with Rafe sometime in the next day or two."

"Good idea," he said. "I'll talk to Rafe. Thanks, Shannon."

He turned to Mac. "Ready to check out the roof?"

"Yeah."

Mac glanced at me. I wanted to go sit in Rafe's kitchen and have a cup of tea — or better yet, a glass of wine — and not think about anything at all for a few minutes. But I wasn't about to leave the scene now.

"Let's go," I said.

An hour later, Mac, Rafe, and I returned to the house, where everyone wanted answers. "What did you find?"

"There were visible scrapes on the wood ledge up there," I said.

"They could've been made by a tripod," Mac added.

"Like a camera tripod?" Lizzie asked.

"Maybe," Mac said. "Or more likely, the kind that would hold a rifle."

"Although people do go up there and take pictures," Rafe allowed.

"The wood ledge is only a foot wide all the way around," I said. "Tripods are a lot bigger than that, aren't they?"

Mac shrugged. "You can get a tripod that'll shrink down as small as ten inches in diameter."

Rafe nodded as he poured more wine for his guests. "Depends on what you're shooting — and where."

What I knew about rifles and their accessories would fit on the head of a pin. Maybe a big pin, but still.

"So something that small" — I measured with my hands — "would fit on the ledge and be easy enough to fold up and slip into your jacket pocket."

"Yeah. Then you've just got to worry about hiding that big-ass rifle."

I thought about what might have happened in the Ecosphere tonight. "Do any of you know Sherman?"

"No," Jane said, and everyone else concurred.

"So what happened to Sherman?" Marigold asked. "Was he shot?"

"No," Mac said grimly. "He was strangled."

"Oh God." Lizzie grimaced.

"Strangled by Stephanie," I added.

Marigold's mouth dropped open in shock,

then she explained to the others. "That's a plant. A vine."

"Yeah," Mac said. "Sherman had the vine wrapped around his neck."

"So someone broke off a length of the vine and strangled him with it." I shuddered and immediately thought of an old science-fiction movie I'd seen once where plants walked down streets and randomly attacked people.

"That's just awful," Jane murmured.

"It is." I wrapped my arms around Mac's waist for comfort. "I mean, getting shot would be awful, too. But . . . ugh. Never mind. It's terrible, either way."

"Yeah, it is," he said.

Hal frowned. "So Sherman's death might have nothing to do with the fact that someone took a shot at Rafe or Marigold."

"Except that it all happened in the Ecosphere," Mac said. "And all within the last hour or two."

I glanced up at him. "Probably not a coincidence."

"Probably not."

"I think I've had enough excitement for today," I muttered, and finished my wine.

My hero said, "I'll take you home."

The next morning I fed Robbie and Tiger

and filled their water bowls for the day. I was checking my tote bag to make sure I had everything I needed, when the doorbell rang.

Robbie dashed for the door, barking joyfully at the prospect of meeting new friends who would scratch his back and rub his tummy. Tiger gracefully slipped in and out and around my ankles, trying to trip me up as I walked to the front door. We all had our priorities.

"Dad."

He wasn't alone. Belinda stood next to him, holding his hand. They were dressed casually in jeans, boots, and sweaters, and looked ridiculously healthy and happy, especially given the early hour.

"Hi, honey."

I swung the door open. "Come on in."

"Thanks. Sorry to drop by so early, but I wanted to catch you before you left for the day. You know Belinda?"

"We've met."

"Only talked for a minute or two," she explained to Dad. "But it was great meeting you the other night."

"You, too," I said. *Except for the part where you were flirting with my uncle and now you're here, holding hands with my father.* Was this awkward or what? Maybe it was just me.

233

I led the way into the living room and sat down in the comfy chair facing the couch. The two of them took the couch.

I started to stand, realizing what a bad hostess I was. "I can make coffee."

"No, sit down. We'll only stay a few minutes."

"Okay."

"So, you've met Belinda," Dad began, "but you haven't met her with me."

"No," I said, trying for a perky smile. "I met her with Uncle Pete."

Belinda shot a glance at Dad. "I told you she might've misunderstood."

"Did I?" Was that an understatement? Knowing how laid-back my father and my uncle could be, I turned to the woman at the center of everything. "What's going on, Belinda? You and Uncle Pete were so friendly, it looked like you might have a thing going on."

As euphemisms went, that was as good as I could manage.

"We don't have a thing going on," she said, "except that we're really good friends. The moment I met your uncle Pete, we clicked. As friends. He's like the brother I never had. We get along so well, it's eerie."

"You clicked," I repeated. "As friends. But are you sure Pete feels the same way?"

She grinned. "I'd only been working at the winery for a week and already felt like a part of his family. So when he told me he wanted to introduce me to your father, I thought, great. I'll have another brother to pal around with. And Pete says, I think you two could really make something happen."

"There's another euphemism," I muttered.

"Yeah, I'll say." She was still grinning. "I didn't think much about it, but then a few days later, Jack showed up."

She gazed at him and smiled. Dad smiled back.

I blinked and wished I'd made that extra pot of coffee. Because I hadn't seen that look in my father's eyes since I was eight years old and he was looking at my mother. "Oh my God."

They both laughed and Dad said, "That was our reaction, too."

"It was kind of a lightning flash," Belinda explained.

I sucked in a breath and held it for a second, then exhaled slowly. "And what about Uncle Pete?"

"He couldn't be happier," Dad said. "I'm serious, honey. I don't know why he didn't make a move on this one. I mean, look at her. She's gorgeous."

"All right now." Belinda slapped his knee. "Your daughter doesn't want to hear that stuff." She looked at me. "Please believe me when I tell you that I would never play your father and uncle against each other. Pete is happy for both of us. He gloats that he's responsible for us getting together."

"Yeah, he'll dine on that story for a long time," Dad said, chuckling. "And, honey, as soon as you finish with this conference, I want you to come and spend a few days at the winery and we'll just hang out, walk through the vineyards, pick grapes, and drink wine. It's almost harvest time. Oh, and Pete and Belinda can cook. It's amazing. They're a force of nature in the kitchen."

I looked at both of them and sniffled back another round of tears. "Can I bring a friend?"

After Dad and Belinda left, I drove out to the conference center. It was the day of the barn raising, take two. I didn't expect too many conference people to come out and watch us because at this point, with everything that had gone wrong, it was almost anticlimactic. But when I walked over to the new barn site, the bleachers were filled. I waved at a few familiar faces and the audience actually cheered me on.

Wade jogged over to meet me. "You ready for this?"

"Yeah. Are you?"

"You bet." He turned and walked with me toward the new barn's foundation. "Let's get this going before some new disaster strikes."

"So you heard about Sherman?"

He glanced at me sideways and frowned. "Who's Sherman?"

I almost laughed. "Sherman is the dead guy we found in the Ecosphere."

"What?" Wade stopped in his tracks and just stared at me. "You're kidding. Somebody died inside the Ecosphere? That's horrible."

"Yeah, it is." I scratched my head. "Isn't that what you were talking about?"

"No. I was talking about the food poisoning."

"Somebody got food poisoning?"

"Yeah. Last night at the slow food event. Jeez, Shannon, everybody's talking about it. They served a sautéed mushroom and zucchini roll that was apparently delicious, until an hour later when people started hurling in the parking lot."

"Oh, yuck." I didn't want that picture in my head. "Are they sure it was the mushroom roll?"

"Yeah. They interviewed everyone who got sick. Plus the chef who made the food got sick, too. So that kind of puts a cork in it."

We started walking again and headed toward the group of workers standing on the other side of the foundation slab.

"Maybe Sherman was right," I murmured.

"Sherman? You mean the dead guy?"

"Yeah." I frowned. "He said the conference was descending into chaos. I hate to give him any credit for being right about anything, but I'm starting to wonder." I reminded Wade of Dillon's death, the runaway mice, Sherman's death, and now the food poisoning. "And if that isn't enough, someone with a rifle took a shot at Rafe last night. From the top of the Ecosphere."

"Wait a minute," Wade said. "This is all besides finding the body of that guy Sherman?"

"Yeah. Add that to your list of coincidences."

He thought about it for a minute. "It could still be a lot of coincidences. But it kind of makes you wonder."

"Kind of." It was too much, though. Too many things had gone wrong in too short a time. What were the chances that the gunshot was unrelated to Sherman's death?

Slim to none. More likely, whoever had taken a shot at us last night had used the Stephanie vine to strangle poor Sherman. "Think about it," I said. "This conference is Rafe's brainchild and his foundation is at the heart of it. You don't think someone might be trying to destroy his reputation by causing havoc around here?"

He scowled. "I really hope not." He gazed out at the crowd in the bleachers. "But let's not tempt fate. We need to make sure this barn is standing strong and straight by the end of the day."

"That's the best idea you've had all day," I said with a determined grin, and patted him on the back. "Let's get to work."

Three hours later, all four side frames were standing straight and strong, and we were ready to start on the roof. Since Rafe wanted a classic, pitched-roof, stick-built barn with plywood sheathing, Wade, Sean, and I had designed the roof in an intricate crisscross configuration based on an Amish pattern.

Several dozen extension ladders were lined up against the frame and my workers were standing by, waiting for the signal to get started on the roof. I was feeling the good energy and couldn't wait to get up there myself, but I had one important thing to do first.

"Some of you have heard my safety speech," I began.

I heard a few groans, but they were mostly good-natured.

"I don't care if you think it's silly or makes you look weak or whatever. As long as you're working on this job, you'll wear the harness. I've seen someone fall off a roof and I still have nightmares. I don't ever want to see it happen again. So, enjoy the job, and wear the harness, and we'll all be happy workers. Deal?"

There were shouts of agreement and I gave a brisk nod in response.

"Let's do this," I said to Wade, and he gave the all clear for the guys to start climbing.

"Yeah," they shouted, and half the crew started scrambling up the ladders. The other half remained on the ground to pass the lumber up to the guys on top.

I watched the progress for about an hour, then handed the supervising over to Wade and Sean, who clearly knew exactly what they were doing. "Call or text me if you need anything."

"You got it, boss," Sean said. "Say hi to Mac."

"You bet." I checked my watch and realized I still had fifteen minutes before I had to meet Mac at the air dome. I took the long way around, by the old barn, just to see what was going on over there.

Along the edge of the barn, I spied a tiny speck of white and walked toward it. If it was litter, I would toss it away. But as I got closer, I realized the speck was alive. A small white fuzzy rodent nibbled on a piece of leaf.

"Oh God." I had to suck in a breath. "Mouse."

The tiny creature gazed up at me and its little eyes twinkled. It showed its teeth and I couldn't tell if it was smiling at me or ready to attack.

Shivers erupted over every square inch of my body and I hopped back, then ran in the opposite direction to the end of the barn and around the corner — and slammed into Julian Reedy.

"I'm sorry," he said, clutching my arms to slow my momentum.

"I'm sure it's my fault," I insisted breathlessly, still in the throes of my stupid mouse phobia. "I wasn't looking where I was going."

"It's okay."

I stared at his pale face and realized how tired he looked. "Are you all right?"

"Got food poisoning," he whispered. "I was up most of the night."

"Oh, Julian, that's awful. I heard about the food poisoning. Someone said it was the mushrooms, but that doesn't make sense. Chef Rhonda is a world-class chef, and she's vegetarian. She would've checked her produce. She would never use bad mushrooms."

"I had to cancel my private dinner with my ethnobotanist friends." He rubbed his stomach, looking ashen and miserable.

I hated to bring it up, but I had to make sure he knew. "Julian, did you hear what happened in the Ecosphere last night?"

"I just found out this minute. I was on my way to check on everything."

"I'll go with you." The way he looked, I wasn't sure he would even make it up to the second level, where we'd found Sherman's body.

We rounded the barn and I avoided walking anywhere near the site of that twinkle-eyed mouse. We headed across the field to the Ecosphere tower and found the area deserted. Yellow crime-scene tape was still wrapped around the doorway.

"I don't care if it's off-limits," Julian said, pulling the tape away. "I'm going inside."

"I'm right behind you." I figured as long

as he was the one doing the trespassing, I wouldn't get in trouble, right? Sure.

We hurried along the pathway across the ground-floor space to the first ramp and walked up to the second level.

Julian stopped suddenly, at about the same spot I had almost fallen last night. Thankfully, Sherman's body had been taken away, but a five-foot piece of Stephanie, Julian's beloved vine, lay like an old, frayed rope strewn across the leafy plants near the pathway.

"Stephanie," Julian moaned, and reached for the piece of vine. "What happened? She's tattered and torn in pieces. Who would do this to a helpless plant?"

Somebody looking for a quick way to strangle someone, I thought. I knew that CSI Leo had taken the part of the plant that had been wrapped around Sherman's neck into his lab to search for fibers and skin and whatever other evidence he could find. What was left of the plant was a distressed, stringy vine that had been thriving a day ago.

"She's so weak, so fragile," Julian crooned as he stroked the vine to find the points that were the frailest.

It occurred to me that the Stephanie vine couldn't have been all that fragile if she could be used for a murder weapon, but I didn't say anything.

"I rescued her, you know."

I nodded. "Yes, I know."

He looked dazed. "I already told you?"

"You did," I murmured. Months ago when I first worked with Julian in the Ecosphere, I had asked him how he became interested in plants and especially Stephanie.

I rescued her from a pharmaceutical laboratory, he had said.

"Rescued? That's right. You told me you rescue plants."

I'd remembered seeing a television show about actual cops who rescued animals, but I'd never heard of people who rescued plants.

Plant Police, I thought. It was an interesting concept.

"I hunt down abused and neglected plants," Julian said. "I have an anonymous tip line and I receive calls all the time from people who report plant abuse and any factories where plants are being subjected to violent or dangerous experiments, or treated with deadly chemicals or injected with viruses or diseases or radiation. I show up and rescue them."

"And Stephanie?"

"She had received megadoses of radiation and had grown so overly large that they had her hanging on hooks all around the laboratory and out into the hallways. She was so big, yet she was so damaged, so strung out, that she was dying a slow death."

Now he caressed Stephanie's limp leaves as if he were comforting a child. "I brought her back to life and she's really been thriving here. She's been happy. But now everything's changed. She's been abused again. She might not survive." He buried his face in his hands and I watched his shoulders shake as he cried.

I had the sudden thought that maybe the reason why Wesley had wanted to set up a meeting with Julian was because they were two of a kind.

But they weren't, I realized. While they were both definitely oddballs, Julian was a sweet guy. I wasn't so sure Wesley had a sweet bone in his body.

"I'm so sorry, Julian," I said. "But she will survive. You can bring her back to health again."

He gulped back tears. "I think I can, but I don't know if she'll ever trust me after I allowed her to be terrorized like this."

"She'll know it wasn't your fault." I put my arm around Julian's shoulders. "She knows you would never hurt her. She'll rally for you."

In that moment I realized that I needed to take a break from the conference. I was talking about a plant as though it were a human being.

Julian nudged me out of the way and began to crawl off the path and into the leafy green plants, crooning, "Stephanie, Stephanie."

"Julian, you need to come back to the pathway," I said in alarm. "You'll hurt the other plants and you're tearing up the crime scene. This is the spot where Sherman was killed last night."

He immediately straightened up. "Sherman?"

"Yes, Sherman. The man who was killed last night."

He scowled. "Short guy? Wears a bow tie?"

"That's him. Do you know him?"

"Of course I know him," he snapped. "He's the jerk who hurt Stephanie in the first place."

I felt my breath leave my lungs. "Sherman was working in the radiation lab?"

"Yes." Julian scowled. "The little worm. If he wasn't already dead, I'd kill him myself."

246

CHAPTER EIGHT

If he wasn't already dead, I'd kill him myself.

I'd been hearing that sentiment a lot lately. In fact, I'd uttered almost the exact same words when I'd been talking about Dillon Charles the other day.

Still, it was odd to hear Julian say it. He'd never been the most easygoing guy, but I knew that he loved his job, loved his plants, and had been pretty upbeat during the time I'd known him. Apparently, though, he also had a bit of a bloodthirsty streak.

I patted his shoulder. "You don't really mean that, do you, Julian?"

"Shannon!" Julian waved his hands for emphasis. "The man is a plant killer. Why should I care if he lived or died?"

I didn't know how to answer that. It just seemed so cold-blooded.

"But you didn't kill him," I stated, just for

247

the record.

"No." He sighed. "More's the pity."

I left the Ecosphere in Julian's somewhat shaky hands and raced across the field to meet Mac on time.

"There you are," he said. He stood near the doorway to the air dome and greeted me with a warm smile.

"Sorry I'm late." I was breathless and feeling foolish when I realized I must've done something to my ankle on the run.

"You're right on time." He frowned. "But what happened to you? You're limping."

"I was in the Ecosphere and realized I was going to be late so I jogged over here. And I thought I saw a mouse." I had wondered if it was the same mouse I'd spotted earlier or a different one. Naturally I had completely overreacted, jumping and flailing and hopping away. But I didn't need to mention that part to Mac. I shrugged casually. "I thought it might be one of the 'smart' mice. It caught me by surprise and I tweaked my ankle. It was stupid."

"Can you put any weight on it?" Still frowning, Mac looked down at my foot as if expecting it to give a report.

"Sure. It's not serious. I'll walk it off in a minute."

Running his hands down my arms, he cocked his head, puzzled. "I thought you were working on the new barn. How'd you end up in the Ecosphere?"

"Wade and Sean are doing a great job on the barn so I left them in charge and came over to meet you. But I ran into Julian on the way. He was determined to check out the damage in the Ecosphere, so I went with him."

"How'd that go?" He took a look at my expression. "Not so good?"

"He's flipped out about Stephanie."

He looked puzzled for one second, then nodded. "Right. That big crazy vine of his."

"Yeah. He was really shaken. Crying, patting the injured plant, trying to comfort it . . ." I shook my head. "The same vine that was used to strangle Sherman last night."

Mac shook his head. "That's really disturbing."

"It was definitely upsetting for Julian. I think he can save Stephanie, but it'll take some serious nurturing." I sighed. "He has this really strong connection to the plant. To all plants, actually. He rescues them, you know."

Mac glanced around, scratched his neck. "I guess it takes all kinds to save the world."

"Tell me about it," I muttered. "Anyway, when I told Julian that the dead guy was Sherman, he went a little nuts. Turns out, Sherman worked in the drug laboratory where the Stephanie vine was being used as a guinea pig for all kinds of experiments, including radiation therapies.

"And when he found out about the experiments, Julian actually broke into the lab and rescued Stephanie."

"Wait." Mac shook his head. "Come on. We're talking about a plant, right?"

"Yes," I said. "And I know what you're saying, but Julian is really radical about these things. He holds Sherman personally responsible for Stephanie almost dying. So when he heard that Sherman was dead, he was actually happy about it. I think he figured it was karma that Stephanie was used to kill her torturer. Said if Sherman wasn't already dead, he would've wanted to kill the guy himself."

"Almost sounds like a confession to murder."

"Julian is wound up a little tightly, but he's usually pretty nice. It was weird to see him so angry." I shook my head. "But he didn't kill Sherman."

"You sure? Sounds like he has a strong motive."

"You would think so, except he didn't even know Sherman was the victim until I told him just now." I sighed heavily. This was really turning into a very weird drama. "Still, I'd better call Eric before the workshop starts."

"Good idea."

I pulled out my phone and punched Eric's private number on speed dial. I chose not to consider what it said about me that I had the chief of police on my speed dial.

When Eric answered, I explained what Julian had said about Sherman and told him that Julian was still inside the Ecosphere.

"What? No," Eric protested. "The Ecosphere is off limits. It's a crime scene."

"Yes, I know. But Julian was desperate to check on his plants so he, well, he tore down the crime scene tape." I hated being a tattletale, but the police chief needed to know. I didn't add that I followed right behind Julian.

Eric huffed in disgust. "I'll be there shortly."

"See you soon." I ended the call and gazed at Mac. "Let's go watch Sketch Horn in action."

Mac made a face. "Seems to me we already caught him in action the other night."

"Oh, jeez. Don't remind me." I thought

251

back to that moment when we peeked into the barn. I still had to wonder how Midge and Sketch had found each other. Had they met before? At some other conference? Or were they suddenly struck with lust while standing on the conference stage the other night? And where were their respective spouses while the two of them were busy doing whatever they were doing in the barn?

I brushed aside those questions because I really didn't want to think about them, and we made our way into the air dome. The room wasn't filled up with people the way it had been with Mac's panel. We easily found two seats on the aisle near the back of the audience in case we wanted to leave before it was over. Mac assured me that it would be smart to plan our exit strategy in advance. He seemed pretty certain that we were going to want to leave early.

A few minutes later, the workshop participants walked out on stage and took their seats at the long table. Besides Sketch, there were three other speakers, all writers of various types of books, including a nonfiction war memoir and a volume of poetry.

Sketch Horn, looking admittedly handsome and groovy in a black sports coat over a white T-shirt with strategically bleached and torn blue jeans, picked up the microphone. "Good afternoon, everyone. Welcome to my workshop. I know you'll enjoy yourselves because I like to have a good time. And invariably everyone else does, too, when they come to hear me speak."

There were a few scattered laughs in the audience and Sketch looked taken aback. He hadn't been making a joke, apparently.

"I realize I need no introduction," he continued, "but let me take a few seconds to tell you who these other people are."

"Quite the ego," I whispered.

Mac's lips were twisted into a scowl. "It's only the beginning."

After the introductions, Sketch got right into it. "So let's start by talking about money. I think the public has a right to know how much we make on our books." He glanced at his fellow panel members. "What do you guys think?"

Basil the poet looked appalled. "I don't believe anyone should discuss —"

The audience began to boo and Sketch held up his hand. "Guys, guys, don't blame Basil. Not everybody wants to talk about money when they're on a panel with a bestselling millionaire author."

He continued to talk about money for a few more minutes, then thankfully allowed the other two panelists to talk about their latest book. Naturally, Sketch interrupted them at every opportunity. It was nerve-wracking.

Twenty minutes later, Basil the poet was halfway through his answer to a question from the audience when Sketch stopped him.

"Sorry to interrupt, Basil," he said, grinning at the crowd, "but I just have to tell you guys about this amazing plot twist I'm working on in my new manuscript."

The audience hooted and cheered. To our horror, we were surrounded by Sketch Horn fans.

"I'm featuring an absolutely awesome invention that, well . . ." He gave a manly chuckle. "Frankly, I invented it. It's a method for clearing up ocean garbage in a matter of months."

I glanced at Mac. "Is he an inventor?"

"Yeah, he invents lies."

"Okay," Sketch continued, "so the bad guys have set up camp on top of the garbage heap in the middle of the ocean. It's so thick with junk that you can literally walk across it without falling through and drowning. It's creepy."

There were boos and groans from the environmentally conscious crowd.

"So Blake, my hero —"

Now Sketch couldn't speak because of the screams and applause for his hero.

I looked at Mac. He rolled his eyes.

"Are you ready to go?" I asked.

He shook his head. "I just want to hear the magic of his latest plot twist."

Sketch continued. "So my guy Blake has invented this contraption he calls the Scoop-Monster."

Again he had to wait for the cheers to subside.

"He stole that idea," I muttered.

"Of course he did."

"No, he really did. I know the guy who invented it." Had Sketch overheard Wesley talking about it?

When the cheers died down, Sketch continued. "This crazy thing will scoop up all the garbage on the ocean floor in record time. So, spoiler alert! Blake steers the ship out to the garbage heap, activates the Scoop-Monster, and destroys the bad guys' garbage lair!"

And the crowd went wild.

"What do you guys think?" Sketch shouted. "Too goofy? Or totally Blake?"

"Blake! Blake!" the audience began to chant.

"Yeah!" Sketch bellowed. "And that's only one action-packed scene out of dozens you'll find in my latest book. Out next year in bookstores everywhere."

The audience screamed in approval.

"Let's get out of here," Mac grumbled.

I checked my watch. We had managed to make it halfway through the panel before we had to escape.

"He's astonishingly vain," I said, feeling shell-shocked. "He hogged the microphone and didn't stop talking."

"You don't have to tell me," Mac said, gazing up at the sky like a prisoner finally set free. "I was there. I saw it happening in real time. Now you get why I didn't want to be on a panel with him."

I frowned. "Do you ever mention how much money you made on your latest contract? I mean, in a public forum like he just did?"

"Never. And neither has any other writer I've ever met."

"Okay, good." I shook my head, still in shock. "The weirdest part was that the one time someone asked about the actual writing process, he didn't seem to know what he was talking about. Not that it kept him from blathering on and on anyway."

"I told you he doesn't write the books." Mac chuckled. "It was kind of interesting to watch the other panelists just staring at him."

"He never let them talk."

"That's his style. He can't take the chance that someone will call him out."

"There's one major thing that bothers me," I said.

"Only one?"

I chuckled. "It's what I told you in there. About that Scoop-Monster he was talking about?"

"Yeah." He smirked. "It sounded ridiculous."

"It *is* ridiculous. But I first heard about it from Wesley Mycroft. It's his idea. He dubbed it the Scoop-Monster, which is a silly name, but now Sketch is using the name and he's putting it in a book. He totally stole the idea from Wesley."

"That's not good," Mac mused.

"No, it's not."

"Maybe Wesley stole it from Sketch," Mac said, then quickly shook his head. "No, sorry. I misspoke. Sketch has never had an original thought in his life. He would've been the one to steal it from someone else."

Mac grabbed my hand and we started to walk away from the air dome.

"Everything you said about him is true," I said, still a little dazed. "You were so right."

He slid his arm around my shoulder and squeezed. "Hearing you say that? It never gets old."

I laughed. "Very funny."

He squeezed a little tighter. "It wasn't a joke."

"Hey, you two."

We turned and watched Rafe approaching quickly.

"I just ran into Eric Jensen," Rafe began, then glanced around and shook his head. "I can't talk here. Let's take a walk."

"Okay," Mac said, shooting me a curious glance.

We walked past the second air dome and out into the wide field beyond. Finally Rafe stopped and checked again to make sure he could speak freely.

"There's nobody out here," I assured him. There was only a light breeze and blue skies studded with puffs of white clouds for company. And it was quiet. Peaceful. So different from the hubbub going on a hundred yards away.

Rafe fisted his hands on his hips in frustration. "There's something going on around here, something bad. And I don't know what to do about it."

"You're right," I said. "A lot of odd occurrences along with a few truly tragic incidents."

Mac frowned. "And there's no way they can all be a coincidence."

I was well aware of Mac's longstanding belief that there was no such thing as coincidence.

"The thing is," Rafe said, "Eric doesn't have the time or the manpower to assign a bunch of cops to patrol the entire conference."

"So what do you want us to do?" Mac asked.

He gazed at Mac evenly. "You've worked plenty of covert ops in the past."

"Sure."

He glanced over at me. "And Marigold tells me that you've solved your share of murders around town."

"Uh, yeah. But that was just good luck." I frowned, remembering a few close calls. "Or bad luck, to be honest."

"Whatever it is, I need your help," Rafe said. "Ask yourself, how in the world did hundreds of people get food poisoning last night? It's crazy. And I really don't want to have someone taking another pot shot at Marigold. Or me."

"Don't forget the mice," I said with an involuntary shudder. "They're still running around loose."

"Not to mention, a killer or two," Mac added dryly.

"Oh, yeah. That." I felt a little foolish mentioning the mice before recalling that two people were dead. But hey, those missing mice were a sure sign of sabotage.

Mac folded his arms across his chest, all business. "You want us to do some looking around, maybe ask some questions?"

"I don't want to put you in danger," Rafe insisted. "But yeah, if you're willing to do it, find some answers, I'd be grateful."

I gave him an assuring pat on the shoulder. "We won't be in danger if we're just looking around, talking to people. I mean, that's what everyone's doing here. Meeting people, talking about stuff, checking out all the cool displays and events. We can do that."

"Sure can," Mac agreed.

"All right. Fantastic. Thanks." Rafe shoved his hands into his pants pockets. "So what do you need from me?"

Mac shrugged. "Depending on where we are and what we're doing, we might want to drop your name here and there."

"Do it." Frustrated, Rafe scraped his fingers through his dark hair. "Carte blanche. Whatever it takes. Seriously, I'm at my wit's end."

Now I gave him a hug. "Try not to worry, Rafe." It was easy for me to say. Nobody had aimed a rifle at me lately.

"Too late for that," he muttered.

"I hear you," Mac said. "We'll do what we can to find you some answers."

I stepped back and frowned. "Just don't expect too much, okay? Because if someone is deliberately trying to sabotage your conference, they're not going to come right out and confess. But we'll do what we can."

"That's all I can ask," Rafe said. "And don't forget, you're both on the foundation's board, so you can play that card if you think it'll help."

"We will."

He reached into his pocket and pulled out a business card. "And if you need to know about any of the attendees or where they're staying or what time some speaker is presenting their work, give my assistant a call."

He handed me the business card and I stared at it. "Hallie? Really?"

"Hallie?" Mac said, taken aback. He gave Rafe a sharp look. "Are you absolutely convinced that she had nothing to do with Dillon's death?"

Rafe's eyes went wide and then he started laughing. "Are you kidding?"

"No," Mac said slowly.

Rafe quickly sobered up. "Okay, I'll take that as a good sign that you're suspicious of everyone. But look, Hallie is one hundred percent loyal to me. But I appreciate you being cautious."

"That's how we roll," Mac said.

I chewed my lip nervously. "In the interests of caution, I just want to mention the possibility that being one hundred percent loyal to you could be a reason why Hallie might've killed Dillon."

Rafe stopped, thought about it, and waved it away. "Seriously, she's not involved in any of this."

I hesitated for a brief second, then nodded firmly. "Then that's the end of it." But it wasn't, of course. I would still be keeping my eye on Hallie along with everyone else on my suspect list.

"I'll text Hallie," Rafe said. "Let her know you might be calling her for some info."

"Good," I said, tucking the business card into my pocket. "That should help."

Rafe took another deep breath in and blew it out. "You can't know how much I appreciate this. And call me if you get any kind of a bad vibe from anyone. Or call Eric."

Mac gave him a salute. "You got it."

Rafe answered with another firm nod. "Thanks again. I owe you both."

We watched him turn and jog back to the conference area, then looked at each other.

"Any ideas on where to start?" Mac asked.

"Yeah," I said. "I want to find out how those mice escaped."

He bit back a grin. "It's good that you have your priorities in order."

"Hey, they may be smart but those mice didn't escape all on their own. And I also want to know how a world-famous vegetarian chef managed to feed some five hundred people a batch of poisoned mushrooms."

"Good question. Personally, I want to check out Sketch Horn and Midge Andersen."

"Really?" I said. "Do you think one of them could be the killer?"

"No." He had the good grace to look slightly abashed. "I just want to find out what she sees in him."

"Talk about priorities." I shook my head, chuckling. "After we check them out, I want to see if we can get into Dillon Charles's hotel room."

"Not a bad idea."

"And I should introduce you to Wesley."

We devised a plan of attack, but before leaving the conference center, Mac and I stopped off to check on my guys at the barn

263

raising. I was pleased with the progress they'd made, and after a quick talk with Sean and Wade, I congratulated them and calculated our timing over the next few days. "Looks like we'll have the framing done by the end of the day, and then have all day tomorrow to get the sheathing laid down."

"I'm sure we'll make it," Wade said. "We plan to start on the underlayment by the end of tomorrow."

The sheathing was a layer of material that went on top of the frame, and the underlayment was a protective covering that went over the sheathing. Basically, it would keep out the rain and snow and any other weather that threatened to invade the barn. After the underlayment, we would add the shingles.

"That's great news," I said. "We really made up for all the time we lost. I'm so proud of you guys."

Sean bowed. "We live to serve."

Wade grinned. "Yeah, right. And there's that little bonus that Rafe promised."

I smiled. "I figured that was the real enticement."

Rafe had added on the ten-thousand-dollar bonus after Dillon's body was found. Not only were we afraid that the murder would scare off some of our day workers, but it also had delayed our work, causing some of my guys to worry that we wouldn't be able to finish before the end of the conference. Nothing like a little extra cash to incentivize hard work.

It was four thirty by the time Mac and I left the conference center and drove into town. *The mice would have to wait until tomorrow,* I thought, as we headed for the Inn on Main Street. As the largest hotel in town, the Inn was where many of the board members and most of the conference speakers were staying. There were dozens of smaller hotels and motels around town to accommodate the rest of the conference attendees, not to mention some beautiful B and Bs, such as Jane's Hennessey Inn.

Since it was getting close to happy hour time, I hoped Midge Andersen would be easy enough to track down in the bar. And with any luck, Sketch Horn would be right there, too, as long as he had wrapped up his one-man workshop and chatted with his legions of fans.

"I have no idea where to find Wesley," I said. "Especially now that Sherman is gone."

"Give Hallie a call," Mac suggested.

I frowned as I pulled out my phone. "I'm not as convinced as Rafe is that she'll be helpful. But I guess it can't hurt to try."

Hallie answered on the first ring. "Hello?"

"Hallie, hi. It's Shannon Hammer."

"Hi, Shannon," she said, sounding so young and perky.

"Did Rafe tell you I might call?"

"He sure did, Shannon. How can I help you?"

I flashed Mac a look of encouragement. "Can you tell me where Wesley Mycroft is staying?"

"Wesley Mycroft," she repeated. "Just a second." It took her about ten seconds and she was back on the line. "He's staying at the Inn on Main Street, Room 230."

"That's really helpful, Hallie. Thanks."

"Anytime," she said.

"Oh, wait. Do you happen to know where Wesley works? You know, his day job?"

She hesitated, then said, "He doesn't have a job, as far as I know. I think he might be independently wealthy. I overheard Dillon talking to Rafe about Wesley sometime last year. He said that the guy was a trust fund baby and didn't need the money."

"So they know him pretty well?" I asked.

"I think they got to know him when he came in looking for advice on how to patent his inventions."

"Okay, thanks."

"You're welcome."

"Oh, and one more thing," I said. "Which room was Dillon staying in?"

There was silence on the line, then she whispered, "Oh God."

"Hallie? Are you okay?"

"I forgot I was supposed to clean out his room," she admitted. "The police chief told me that Dillon left a bunch of company documents lying around."

"Would you like us to collect everything and bring them to you?"

She let out a huge sigh of relief. "Would you mind?"

"Not at all." She gave us Dillon's room number and we ended the call just as Mac pulled into the parking lot behind the hotel.

"I wonder if Julian is staying here," I said.

"We can find out."

Mac parked. We got out of the car and headed for the hotel, holding hands.

"Prepare yourself," I said. "I want to try and find Wesley first."

"What should I be prepared for?"

"Well, for one thing, he's amazingly self-centered."

"We should introduce him to Sketch."

"Good idea," I said brightly. "Anyway, Wesley is also a very odd bird. He seemed to be good friends with Sherman, so I want to ask him about that. He introduced Sherman to me as his colleague, but Sherman came across more like a servant. Fetching his drinks, doing his bidding. You know?"

"Maybe the guy really was his servant."

"I don't think so. But then, I barely know either of them so I really shouldn't jump to conclusions. But I did get the feeling that they worked together somehow." I frowned and added, "Even though Hallie thinks that Wesley is independently wealthy and doesn't work."

"Maybe Wesley hired Sherman simply to take care of things for him at the conference."

"Maybe." I sighed. "Let's go find out."

We walked through the side entry and a minute later we had reached the end of the west hall. Turning a corner, we followed signs for Room 230 at the far end of the hall.

I glanced around. "I still have to wonder if Wesley had something to do with the pharmaceutical lab where Sherman worked."

"The lab where they kept Stephanie?"

"Yeah." I smiled. "You remembered."

He grimaced. "Hard to forget anything about Stephanie."

268

I batted my eyelashes. "She likes you."

"She — I mean, *it* — is a plant," he said through gritted teeth.

"And yet, she finds you very attractive."

"You are one sick puppy."

"I simply speak the truth," I said, laughing. "And speaking of sick puppies, let's go find Wesley."

The Inn was the largest and fanciest in town, with one hundred well-appointed rooms, two lovely restaurants, a fun bar, a beautiful pool, banquet rooms, and a decent-sized conference space. I couldn't count the number of parties and weddings I'd attended here over the years, including my senior prom.

The wide hallway was bright, thanks to big windows at each end of the hall. A deep scarlet carpet runner was stretched over the beautifully stained hardwood floors, muffling our footsteps.

As we walked toward Room 230, Mac asked for more information about the guy.

"I've mentioned that he's weird, but he's also annoying," I said. "Oh, and Sherman was trying to set up a meeting with you and Wesley."

"Why?"

"Sherman was elusive, although he did think you were a scholar."

"That's a laugh," he said easily.

"Wesley also wanted a meeting with Julian, by the way, because he had issues with the Ecosphere."

"Issues?" Mac frowned. "Did he say what they were?"

"No."

"I wonder if he has issues with me."

"He has issues with everyone, but I wouldn't worry about it."

"Not worried. Just curious."

I told him that Wesley thought the other conference goers weren't very smart.

"Seriously?"

"Yeah."

"Does he even know who's attending this conference?" Mac wondered. "There are three Nobel Prize–winning scientists here, two professors from MIT, one from Harvard, three from Princeton, and six or eight from Stanford. I lost track. And by the way, Rafe has an advanced law degree and a PhD in economics. And then there's you and me," he added.

"Well, duh," I said. "We're brilliant."

He grinned and pulled me close. "That's right, babe."

"Uh-oh," I whispered, staring over his shoulder at the woman exiting one of the rooms we'd already passed. "Is that Midge?"

"Yeah. Come here." He began to nuzzle my neck, causing goose bumps to skitter across my shoulders and down my arms.

"That feels so good." I gave a happy sigh, then counted to five. "Is she gone?"

He craned his neck to see farther down the hall. "She's gone. Headed off in the other direction."

"Did she see us?"

"She glanced this way," Mac said, "but I don't think she saw our faces."

"I wouldn't think so. We were pretty well hidden." I smiled at him. "You're very good at this."

"Anything for the job."

"Right." I looked over his shoulder. "I guess maybe it was dumb to hide. I want to talk to her, but not right here in the hall. She caught me by surprise."

"We'll catch up to her in the bar," Mac said.

"Did you see which room she came out of?"

"Yeah. Seven doors down on the right." He glanced both ways down the long hall, then said, "Be right back."

"Not so fast," I said. "I'm going with you."

"Okay. But be cool."

I grinned. "Always."

He grabbed my hand and we strolled

down the hall, the picture of easy nonchalance. He stopped and stared at the door we'd seen Midge exit. "Room 212."

I gazed up at Mac. "That's Dillon's room."

We spent way too long standing in the hallway trying to figure out what Midge Andersen had been doing inside a dead guy's room.

"How did she get in there?" I asked.

"And what was she doing in there?" Mac wondered. "I'm going to call Rafe."

"Why?"

"He'll be able to get us access to the room."

"It might take a while," I said, considering our options. "Let me call Jane first."

He raised his eyebrows, but didn't ask the question.

"Jane," I said, relieved that she had answered the phone. "Mac and I are at the Inn on Main Street. How can we get inside a room without having a key?"

"Which room?"

"Dillon Charles's room. We have Rafe's permission to get inside, but I'd rather avoid a hassle with the front desk." *And the police, too,* I thought, but didn't mention it.

She was silent for a moment. "Let me

make a phone call. I'll get right back to you."

"Okay," I said slowly, but she had already hung up.

Six minutes later, the assistant manager jogged down the hall and said, "Hi, Shannon."

"Hi, Trina."

She gave Mac a sultry smile, but didn't say anything. Her smile said it all. She pulled out a card key, swiped it in front of the door mechanism, waited for the green light, and then pushed the door open.

"Thanks, Trina."

"You can thank Jane," she said with a wink, and walked away, disappearing around the corner in seconds.

We stepped inside the room and closed the door quickly.

"Do you want to tell me what that was all about?" Mac asked.

"Jane was the general manager here for five years before she opened the Hennessey Inn." I shrugged. "She has connections."

He grinned. "Jane is quickly becoming my hero."

I smiled. "She's always been mine. But let's not mention this to Eric, okay?"

"Good plan."

I glanced around. The room was a junior

suite and it looked as if it had been kept in exactly the same condition as it had been before Dillon was killed. His suitcase sat open on the luggage rack. Some of his shirts were still folded while others were rumpled. I imagined that the police had searched through the suitcase, but had anyone else? Like maybe Midge?

"Speaking of Eric," I said, "why wasn't this room taped off by the police? Hallie said that all of Dillon's stuff is still here. Seems like they'd want to safeguard against having it stolen."

Mac considered. "Maybe the hotel itself removed the crime scene tape. Didn't want the other guests freaking out."

He opened the door to the closet and began to go through the pockets of Dillon's pants and jackets. I wandered over to the desk, where a thick, three-ring binder sat open. The rings were unclasped and I wondered if someone — Midge? — had removed something.

Since the binder was just sitting there, I began to browse through some of the papers. Frowning, I said, "These must be some of the company documents Hallie was talking about. They're mostly employment agreements. I suppose they're confidential."

"They probably are. You shouldn't look at them."

I stared at him. "Are you kidding?"

"Of course I'm kidding," he said, straight-faced. "Check them out."

I riffled through one section of documents, then checked out the tabs for each section. "The notebook is broken down into sections. So there's your basic employment agreements, nondisclosure agreements, noncompete agreements, patent applications."

"The noncompete agreements make perfect sense," Mac said. "A company that invents stuff would want their employees to sign a noncompete agreement so they couldn't take those ideas to another company. But as far as the nondisclosure one goes, hmm. That's a little trickier. I mean, I guess they'd want to guarantee confidentiality when it comes to their intellectual property and work product. But it gets tricky when the scope is too broad."

"You're sounding like a lawyer."

"I read a lot of contracts," he said with a shrug.

"I imagine you do," I said, staring at the next set of documents. "Okay, this could be what Midge was looking for."

Mac crossed the room and glanced over

my shoulder. "What is it?"

"Patent applications," I said. "They're just forms, not the actual application for the Patent Office. I guess they gather all the information from the applicant and then send in the actual form. Or type it up online." I kept turning pages, reading the handwritten information. "They ask all kinds of questions, but some of the answers probably don't get transferred to the actual application."

"Like what?"

"Well, like how long you've worked on the item and what the commercial potential might be. And whether you've done a patent search. I guess in case it's already been invented, right?"

"Right."

I flipped another page. "So here's a form that mentions sandcastle worms. But Midge's name isn't on it. Just Dillon's." I skipped a few pages. "And here's some kind of plant monitor that I'll bet Julian Reedy came up with. But his name isn't mentioned, either."

"Just Dillon's," Mac guessed.

My eyes narrowed. "Yeah." I found applications for gadgets related to smart mice. Turning the page, I blinked. "Uh-oh. Here's Wesley's Scoop-Monster."

"But let me guess. His name isn't listed."

"You're sensing a pattern."

"Sure am." He joined me at the desk and looked over my shoulder.

"This could be proof that Dillon was ripping off all of them."

"Maybe. Or maybe it doesn't mean anything."

"Do you think so?"

"No. I think he was totally ripping them off. I think he was a really bad guy. And now he's dead. Somebody found out what he was doing."

"I hope Rafe didn't know about this."

"He's about to find out."

"Yeah." He stared at the pages. "Why wouldn't Midge take her forms with her?"

"The binder was open to a completely different section," I said, "so maybe she didn't get this far. She might've been worried that she would be caught in here, so she didn't take the time to search through the entire binder."

"Maybe." Mac returned to his examination of the clothes in Dillon's closet, then studied the lock mechanism on the room safe. Turning, he said, "So an inventor comes to Rafe's company to get a loan or some kind of backing for an invention they've come up with. They fill out one of these forms and then, in theory, one of the company employees takes that information and applies for a patent through the U.S. Patent Office database. On behalf of the inventor."

I gazed up at him. "But they don't submit the application with the actual inventor's name. They submit it with Dillon Charles's name. Would you call that a problem?"

"No." Mac's eyes narrowed in on the form I was pointing to. "I would call that a crime."

I scanned a half dozen more patent application forms, and sure enough, Dillon's name was listed on every page. "I would call it grounds for murder."

CHAPTER NINE

I thumbed through more pages and made a quick calculation. There had to be at least a hundred patent application forms in Dillon's huge three-ring binder. But the binder had been left open in the employment agreement section, so I wondered if Midge had even seen all the patent applications with Dillon's name as owner/ inventor. There was no way of knowing the answer, unless we tracked her down and simply asked her.

According to Niall, though, Midge had known that Dillon had cheated her on at least one patent. She had accused him that night on the patio when Niall overheard them arguing. We just didn't know if she had seen all of these other different patents he had applied for that rightfully belonged to her, as well as all the other inventors at the conference.

Midge was a brilliant woman and probably could've applied for her own patents. But she must have gone to Rafe and Dillon for funding, and Dillon had offered to help her with the patent applications.

I looked around the suite. What else could Midge have been looking for in here? There was always the possibility that she hadn't even seen the binder. Maybe she'd been scrounging for money, although I couldn't picture Dillon Charles leaving even a dime lying around. And I couldn't picture Midge having to break into a hotel room in search of loose change.

Another weird thought occurred to me. Had she and Dillon been having an affair? Maybe he had taken something personal that belonged to her and she had been looking for that.

She was certainly having an affair with Sketch Horn. Why not Dillon as well?

I was grasping at straws again. I needed to apply Occam's razor to this dilemma: the simplest solution tended to be the best one.

On the other hand, who said that Occam's razor was always the way to go?

I shook my head. Why was I complicating things? We had seen Midge sneaking out of Dillon's room with our own eyes just a few minutes ago. And now here was this open binder. Chances were pretty good that

Midge had gone through it and removed a document or two.

But how had Midge known that these documents would be in Dillon's hotel room? Had someone told her that the binder was here? Someone who had snuck in here before Midge? The binder shouldn't have been in here. That much was for sure. It should have been kept in a locked file drawer in Dillon's office somewhere in Silicon Valley.

Had others been sneaking into Dillon's room to find their documents? Why not? I was perfectly willing to think the worst of Dillon, so I would bet that there was more than one set of fingerprints in here that didn't belong to that man. In fact, I wouldn't be surprised to learn that there were at least a dozen conference attendees who had a darn good motive for revenge, if not cold-blooded murder.

My mind was starting to take off on yet another tangent so I forced myself to shut it down and turned to Mac. "I think we should give Rafe a call."

"Maybe we should call Eric, too."

"Maybe," I agreed. "But Rafe needs to know that Dillon had these confidential documents in his hotel room and that some people are managing to get inside here "without benefit of a key."

"People like us, you mean?"

"Well, yes," I said with a smile. "And others."

"Like Midge," he added. "Who else might be tempted to break in?"

"Dr. Larsson, Julian Reedy, Wesley Mycroft, and anyone else whose name is in here." I let the notebook pages flutter down. "You know, I'll bet if we cross-checked the inventions on these patent applications with the names of the conference attendees who're applying for grants, we'd find a heck of a lot more names that match up."

"I'm not about to take that bet," Mac said. "Because I think you're right. And that's unfortunate for Rafe."

"Yeah." I pressed the rings together and closed the notebook. "The number of people who might be trying to sabotage the conference is growing by the minute. And one of those people took it even further and killed Dillon."

"Don't forget that Rafe is a target, too," he said. "That is, if you believe that the shooter in the tower was aiming at him."

"But what if they were aiming at Marigold?"

Mac scowled. "If they shot Marigold, they

would be hurting Rafe on a whole different level."

Just for a moment, I considered what might have happened if Marigold hadn't chosen just the right second to get up and go to the kitchen. She could have been killed. And that thought sent a shudder up my spine that had me pushing the whole idea out of my mind completely. I couldn't even fathom a world without Marigold in it.

"That would be awful," I murmured. "On any level."

"We should get out of here," Mac said. "We'll take the binder with us and give it to Rafe — and tell him he should hand it over to Eric."

"Right. Because even though it contains confidential company documents, it also contains some big fat motives for murder, which the police may not have realized when they searched the room before. They probably didn't know who truly came up with these inventions. As far as they knew, these patent applications were legit."

"Right. That binder shouldn't be sitting here in this room where anyone and their mother could sneak in."

"We're not *anyone,*" I said defensively.

He smiled. "I wasn't talking about us. But I'm wondering if someone else could get in by, you know, bribing the housekeeping staff."

I frowned. "The hotel staff here is probably a lot more honest than some of the guests."

"No doubt about that."

I picked up the unwieldy binder. "This thing is heavy."

"I'll carry it." He took it easily. "Let's go."

I started for the door.

"Are we going to Wesley's room now?" he asked.

I stopped. "Shoot. I forgot all about him. But yeah. Let's go find him."

"We can't go to his room holding this huge binder."

"You're right." I stared at the notebook. "Especially since some of those patent forms should have his name on them."

"Okay, we'll lock it up in the car. And then let's check out the bar before we try his hotel room."

I grabbed the door handle. "Maybe we'll get lucky and find him sitting there drinking a beer."

"Or maybe we'll run into Midge."

I nodded. "We know she's here somewhere."

"And if we can't find any of them in the hotel, I say we grab our own beers and figure out what to do next."

I smiled. "Best idea today."

After securely locking the binder in the trunk of Mac's car, we strolled back to the bar.

"Mac! Hey, buddy!"

We both whipped around and saw the grinning face of Sketch Horn. He was sitting in a booth, holding up a pilsner glass half filled with beer.

"Join me," he called out, loudly enough for everyone in the bar to hear.

Mac was mumbling under his breath. It wouldn't be nice to repeat the words I heard him say.

I slipped my arm through his and whispered, "We only have to stay for a minute. Come on."

But before we could take another step toward Sketch, I saw Midge walk into the bar from the lobby entrance.

"This could be interesting," Mac said.

I wasn't surprised when Midge headed straight for Sketch's booth. He wore a broad grin as he watched her approach and slide into the booth until she was squeezed up against him. She wrapped both arms around his neck and gave him a big, noisy kiss.

Ugh, I thought. There was just no accounting for taste. Or subtlety.

"Uh-oh." Mac nudged me. "Check this out."

From the door on the opposite side of the room, I saw another woman stalk into the bar.

"That's his wife," Mac explained.

"Are you serious?"

"Yeah." Mac tried to stifle a grin, but it didn't work.

"Oh dear."

Sketch's wife crossed the room and stood in front of his table. She wore impeccably tailored taupe trousers and a rich silk jacket that looked like haute couture, but what did I know? Her shoes were fabulous, if painful: five-inch heels with tiny little straps that looked like they could snap in a heartbeat. Her silky blond hair was brushed back in a ponytail. To put it bluntly, Sketch Horn's wife was drop-dead gorgeous.

Midge, on the other hand, was cute and lively. But Mrs. Sketch Horn was way out of everyone's league.

Mac and I moved a few feet to the left in order to get a front-row view of the drama that was unfolding before us.

Sketch's handsome face was drained of all color and his eyes were as big as bread plates. "Honey!" he exclaimed, his voice a little shaky.

"Her name is Honey, by the way," Mac whispered.

"What do you think you're doing here?" Honey asked, her fists resting on her hips.

"I was, uh, just interviewing Midge, you know, for the next book."

"Interviewing," his wife said sarcastically. She sent a slow, up-and-down look over Midge, then dismissed her. "Is that what the kids are calling it?"

"Honey, you sound angry," Sketch said gently. "Is your blood sugar dipping?"

Mac snorted quietly and I could not believe that Sketch was being so stupid. But then, I'd seen him in action on his panel, and maybe yes, he really was that clueless.

"No, you dolt. My blood sugar is fine. It's you who's dipping. And not for the first time. I've been coming with you to these conferences for years, and while I sit in the room and write, you play your little games with your little floozies."

"Honey! No way would I do that to you. I love you."

"You love me? How stupid do you think I am?" she asked dryly, then flicked her chin in Midge's direction. "Maybe you should explain to this floozy that you're married to me."

"That's Dr. Floozy to you," Midge said with a brazen smile.

"Well, *Doctor,*" the wife said, folding her arms across her chest. "You can give all the 'interviews' you want to this clown, but here's a clue for you. Sketch won't be quoting your golden thoughts in the next book and he won't be giving you any credit, either."

"Shows you what you know," Midge said haughtily. "He's promised to dedicate the next book to me."

"That's adorable," Honey crooned, with a smile letting Midge know that she was just as big a dolt as Sketch. "But it's just not going to happen because, to be frank, the man can barely read, let alone type."

"Now, Honey," Sketch started, glancing around nervously.

She ignored him and continued to glare at Midge. "I write the Sketch Horn books. Not him. He's nothing but a pretty face."

"Not that pretty," Mac grumbled.

I smothered a laugh.

Midge's mouth fell open. "What are you saying?"

"I think you heard me," Honey said.

Midge blinked so rapidly that I thought she might faint. "You . . . *you're* Sketch Horn?"

"You poor pathetic thing." There was no humor in Honey's rasping laugh. "There's no such person as Sketch Horn. The clown sitting next to you? His name is Marv Skolnick. And the rest of the bio is fake, too. We live in a suburb of Omaha, Nebraska, not on a sixty-foot sailboat in beautiful Gig Harbor, Washington. He's never been in the Army, either. He's a substitute teacher, but he just can't seem to keep a job because of his sick addiction to *Call of Duty.*"

"You're joking." Midge hissed the word. But clearly she believed Honey, because the looks she was shooting Sketch should have set him on fire.

"I wish I was." Honey turned to Sketch. "And you. I'm sick of keeping you afloat while you treat me like yesterday's garbage. Over and over again. You know, I can understand you're too much of an idiot to be faithful, but I just can't figure out what these bimbos see in you."

"But —"

"No more buts." She spat the words out. "The divorce papers will be served on you tomorrow morning. As far as the world knows, Sketch Horn will be devoting himself to writing and won't have any more time for conferences or interviews. Good luck making a living off of *Call of Duty.*"

"But, honey pie," he cried.

"You're making me nauseous, Marv." Honey wiggled her fingers in a wave. "Have fun, you two."

She swiveled on the toes of her elegant high-heeled shoes and walked out of the bar.

"Honey's got some moves," Mac murmured.

"I'll say." I really had to admire Honey's style. She'd taken care of a terrible husband and his floozy all in one smooth move. I watched Midge scoot out of the booth and slink out of the bar. Sketch — or Marv — looked as if he was ready to cry.

I turned to Mac. "Um, we need to go, too."

"Right-o."

We hurried out of the bar and sat down at a patio table near the pool.

A waiter hurried over and we ordered two beers on tap.

When he left, Mac sat back and beamed with pleasure. "Best day ever."

I chuckled. "That's sick."

"I know." But he laughed until he was holding his stomach. "Seeing old Marv brought low had to be the highlight of this conference. Marv. Seriously?" Shaking his head, he laughed even harder. After a few more seconds, his laughter faded. "It's about time he got his comeuppance. I wonder if Honey was just waiting for this one last straw or if something happened this week to cause her to strike out at him."

"You think she's always known?"

He frowned, thinking about it. "If she's like most working writers I know, she's buried in a book half the time and oblivious to everything else. But if she's been coming to conferences with him, she must have been seeing the way he carries on. These conferences are like a small town."

I could relate to that analogy. The gossip grapevine in Lighthouse Cove was legendary. "So even if Honey didn't see it with her own eyes, she would hear the rumors."

"There are always rumors."

The waiter was back with our drinks. He set them on the table with a small bowl of snack mix.

After the first sip, I sighed. "What's the story with Midge? I don't know her at all, but she seems too smart to have gotten involved with someone like Sketch slash Marv." I shook my head.

Mac stared into his beer. "She doesn't come out of this looking too good."

"Just now she sounded like a . . . well, to use Honey's word for it, a floozy." I frowned. "The first time he opened his mouth to talk, she should've been warned. He's such a blowhard."

Mac shook his head. "Sketch Horn strikes again." He paused, then added, "I mean *Marv.*"

Ten minutes later we finished our drinks and were about to stand up and leave. But at that very moment, Midge walked out to the patio.

"Hey, Midge." Mac waved. "Come join us."

"Are you kidding?" I muttered.

"I want to hear what she says," Mac whispered. "Let's get the story from the other side."

I couldn't blame him. I wanted to hear the floozy's side of the story, too.

Midge looked reluctant, but then finally relented and walked over to our table. "You were standing right there, so I don't have to tell you what happened."

"No, you don't have to tell us," I said, pushing out the extra chair. "Have a seat."

"Thanks." But she didn't sound grateful. She sounded suspicious.

"That was a pretty weird scene," I said lightly. "Who knew Sketch didn't really write his own books?"

"His name isn't even Sketch," Midge said,

annoyed, but also a little dazed. "What are you drinking?"

"Beer. And we were just going to order another round." Mac raised his hand to signal the waiter, who came running over. We ordered another round, plus a beer for Midge.

"Have you met Sketch before?" Mac asked in all innocence.

"No, this conference is the first time. He really pulled a number on me. I thought he was a famous author with years of experience as an Army Ranger. And he's so good-looking." She slumped against her seat. "Now I find out he's a total fake."

"Yeah, sounds like it."

"We were going to collaborate on his next book," she said wistfully. "I have this idea for a plot where sandcastle worms cause the infrastructure of the West Coast to collapse into the ocean. Sketch thought it was really cool."

"Sounds pretty cool to me," Mac said and I stared at him. I sincerely hoped he was just being nice.

She eyed him cautiously. "Would you be interested in collaborating on the story?"

"It's a fine offer, but no. I work alone."

Midge wasn't willing to let it go so easily. "It's my idea, but I would be willing to give you twenty percent if you'd do the writing."

"Wow, twenty percent," he mused, and shook his head. "It's tempting, but no. Sorry, Midge. But good luck with it."

I sat forward in my chair. "You should write it yourself, Midge."

Her shoulders drooped. "I'm not a writer."

"But you could be," Mac said, upbeat as usual. "You have a story to tell. Just sit down at the computer and go to it."

He was starting to sound like a motivational speaker. Frankly, I was beginning to think Midge didn't deserve his attention, but Mac couldn't help it. He was just a good guy.

"I could never do that," she protested.

"Sure you could. All you have to do is sit down and start typing," he said. "And then of course you'll need to send it to agents and editors and wait for a few hundred rejection letters and then you restructure the whole story and then start the process all over again. And if you don't give up, you might eventually publish the book."

Midge groaned. "I'll be dead by then."

"Or you could self-publish," he said. "That's a viable road to publication. Think about it."

She wiped a tear from the corner of her eye. "I was really hoping for Sketch's participation."

"He lied to you," I said flatly. "He's a liar and a cheat."

"Yes, but I didn't know that until just now," she insisted. She thought about it for a moment, though, and finally relented. "Okay, yeah, maybe he told me a few lies, but . . . oh God." She buried her face in her hands. "I just wanted so badly to believe him. Never mind. I'm an idiot. He's a total liar and a cheat."

"You'll get over it," I said. "But on another topic, what were you doing inside Dillon Charles's hotel room a little while ago?"

She stared at me in stunned silence.

"Were you looking for something?" I prompted. "It's okay. I won't tell anyone." *Except for five or six of my closest friends and the police,* I thought.

"I um, I wasn't, um . . ."

"We saw you coming out of his room, Midge," Mac said quietly.

"This is not my best moment," she whispered, and another tear fell from her eyes. "Heck. Not my best week."

"Just tell us, Midge," I urged.

Scowling now, she said, "I suppose there's no point in keeping it secret."

"Tell us what happened."

"Dillon stole my idea for harvesting sandcastle worms. I invented a process that would collect them and move them into prefabricated mounds, where they could perform their vital work without interruption."

"What is their vital work?" I asked.

Her eyes lit up. "The worms secrete an underwater adhesive that could be used to rebuild the Great Barrier Reef within five years. The adhesive forms a bond as strong as cement. I've also been experimenting with the adhesive in connection with tissue, skin, and bone repair."

The awful Sketch was forgotten for the moment as Midge warmed up to her subject. "The key factor is that many parts of our body contain fluids and that's why the sandcastle worm is so crucial. Because they produce their secretions underwater."

"Wow," I said. "That's fantastic."

"Dillon thought so, too," she said bitterly. "That's why he stole the idea and put his own name on the patent."

"He wasn't a very good person," I said lamely.

"That wasn't the only project he stole," she said.

"There's more?" Mac asked.

"Yes. I had an eco-fisheries project that was really promising. But Dillon told me that it was useless. I told him that if he wasn't interested, I would take it to Rafe and see about getting a foundation grant."

"That sounds like a good idea."

"I thought so, but Dillon threatened me. Said if I went over his head, I would never see a bloody cent from Rafe or any other investor in the country."

"Did you believe him?"

"Uh, yeah," she said sardonically. "Because when I said I was going to do that very thing, Dillon just smiled in that smarmy way he had."

"I know the smile you're talking about," I said.

"Everybody does, I guess." She sighed. "So anyway, he said that I couldn't get a grant for a project that he already held the patent for."

"So he admitted that he stole the patent."

"No, he didn't admit it. Not in so many words. But that's exactly what he did. I was so furious. I told him I would find a way to kill him. That probably wasn't very smart."

"So what did you hope to find in his hotel room?" I asked.

"I don't know." She shook her head, frustrated. "I just needed to try to find some kind of evidence that he stole my idea."

"In his hotel room?" Mac repeated.

"Well, yeah. He and Rafe were meeting with a bunch of people who'd applied for grants and I was one of them. So I thought he might have brought my patent information with him."

That made some sense, I thought. Knowing Dillon, he would want to have plenty of ammunition to shoot down applicants by claiming that their brilliant ideas had already been taken. By him.

"You need to talk to Rafe," Mac suggested. "He never would've let that happen, and I'm sure he'll be willing to remedy the problem."

Her face crumpled as she began to cry. "But they're partners. Why would he take my side?"

"Because they're *not* partners," I insisted. "Rafe was dissolving the company and he was in the process of completely cutting himself off from Dillon."

"And now Dillon's dead," she whispered.

"Yes, he is." I reached over and squeezed Midge's hand. "But that doesn't make what he did any less wrong. Talk to Rafe. He's a good guy. He'll make this right for you."

She pressed her lips together, blotted the tears with her cocktail napkin, and finally nodded. "I'll give it a try." She pushed her chair back. With a frown, she admitted, "I guess I'm glad I talked to you."

"I'm glad, too," I said.

"I felt like such a fool." She gave a self-deprecating laugh. "Well, I still feel like a fool, falling for that big fake Sketch Horn. But I'll get over it, which makes me think that there might be a light at the end of the tunnel."

"There is," I said cheerfully.

She took a deep breath and blew it out. "Just hope it's not a train."

Mac grinned, then stood and gave her a hug. "Good luck."

After Midge left, Mac and I stayed on the patio, enjoying the sunset and finishing our beers.

"She still could've killed Dillon," I said.

"I was just thinking the same thing," Mac said. "That could be precisely why she came to the conference.

"Maybe Sketch provided a distraction in between the hard work of killing Dillon and Sherman and attempting to kill Rafe."

"That sounds awfully cynical." I smiled at him. "It might be true, but still. Ouch."

He smiled back. "But look, there's a killer out there and he's starting to aim pretty close to home."

I rubbed my arms where shivers had

erupted. "The bullet that hit the hearth was way too close to home."

"And," he added, "Midge was really upset about Dillon stealing her work."

"I'd be furious if it happened to me. Anyone would be." The more I thought about it, the more I was actually sympathizing with Midge. Still, she could be a killer. "I wonder how good she is with a rifle."

"Speaking of rifles," Mac mused, "if I were Sketch Horn, or Marv, or whatever his name is, I would be hiding under the bed in my room right now. Because he just provided two determined women with a really strong motive to kill him."

"He sure did."

Mac paid the bar tab and we walked back inside. "Do you really think Midge could've killed Dillon?"

"I think she was angry enough to do it. But then, why would she kill Sherman?" Mac shrugged. "Someone else could've killed Sherman."

I glanced at him sideways. "What are the chances of having two killers show up at this conference?"

"It's a long shot," Mac said with a half smile.

"Okay, so Midge kills Dillon. Stabs him in the stomach." I pictured it happening as I

300

spoke. "She's petite, but strong. And motivated."

"I agree."

"Then she realizes — wrongly, of course — that Rafe is just as big an obstacle as Dillon was. She likes Rafe, but still, he's part of her big problem. So she sneaks out to the Ecosphere, climbs to the roof, takes the shot at Rafe, misses the shot, thank goodness."

"Thank goodness," Mac echoed.

"And on her way down from the roof," I continued, "she runs into Sherman. And in that moment she knows she has to kill him. But she's already got the rifle all packed up, so instead, she grabs the first thing she sees, namely the vine."

"Stephanie," Mac murmured.

I grinned. "Right. Midge grabs Stephanie and, without another thought, wraps it tightly around Sherman's neck."

"Quite the scenario," Mac said.

"It's outlandish at best," I admitted.

"Should be easy enough to find out if Midge has any experience with guns."

We stopped in the empty hallway near the elevator banks. For a moment, Mac pondered all the possibilities. "You know, it's really too bad that Rafe and I didn't race to the tower immediately after hearing that shot ring out. We might've caught the killer before Sherman was strangled."

"I've thought about that, too," I said. "But it would've been so dangerous. The killer had a gun. One of you could've been shot."

"Yeah, maybe. But Rafe had a gun, too."

"Great," I said, shivering again. "There could've been a shoot-out."

"Possibly." But he actually didn't look too bothered by the idea.

I was quiet for a minute. "I don't think Sherman was one of the killer's intended targets. I think he was just in the wrong place at the wrong time."

"Why was he there at all?" Mac wondered.

I glanced up at him. "Just enjoying some quiet time?"

"Yeah, right," he said dryly. "Maybe wanted to breathe in some of that clean air."

"Sherman worked at the laboratory where Stephanie was tormented, according to Julian. Who hated Sherman, as I've mentioned before."

"Answer honestly," he began. "Do you think Julian could have killed Sherman?"

"He sounded angry enough to kill when I told him that Sherman was the victim," I said. "But what hangs me up is Rafe. Why would Julian take a shot at Rafe? He and Rafe are friends. Or at least, they're friendly.

I mean, Rafe hired him to design the Ecosphere. He's making a lot of money on that job."

"Money's nice," Mac said, then added, "But didn't you mention Julian's name when you were going through those patent applications?"

"I did."

"So he was another target of Dillon's bottomless pit of greed."

"And therefore, highly motivated to kill. And he could have been convinced that since Rafe and Dillon were partners, Rafe was in on the patent stealing, too."

"If Julian's invention is on one of those applications," Mac said flatly, "then he had a motive to kill Dillon. And unlike most everyone else, he also had a motive to kill Sherman."

I started to speak, then snapped my jaw shut. Julian? Really? "I would have thought Julian was too mild-mannered to kill, but I saw how he reacted to the torn-up Stephanie vine. He hated Sherman and was happy to hear that he was dead."

Mac shrugged. "Just because he loves plants doesn't mean he loves people. Especially people who want to destroy plant life."

I sighed. "You're right."

"Okay, enough chitchat." He pushed

himself away from the wall. "Let's go hunt down Wesley."

As we headed for Room 230, I thought about Wesley Mycroft. Room 230 was a suite overlooking the pool, I recalled. I was beginning to believe that Wesley really was independently wealthy.

"Tell me more about this guy," Mac said.

"I only know what I read about him in his conference bio. It says that he's an innovator and an influencer."

"Really? He's got a social media following?"

"I have no idea."

Mac frowned. "We write our own bios so he could be lying through his teeth. Maybe he's an influencer in his own mind."

I made a face. "It's a stupid word anyway. Who even knows what it means?"

"You're just jealous."

I laughed out loud. "Wait 'til you meet Wesley. Then we'll talk."

I thought about that moment when I'd first met Wesley and how oddly he had behaved. Of course, at this conference, odd behavior was turning out to be the norm. No wonder Rafe wanted out of that world and into a simpler one with Marigold. On the other hand, he'd put on this conference and invited all of these people onto his land, so maybe he wasn't quite ready to turn his back on the business world.

"Hallie said he might be independently wealthy," I mused. "If that's true, I guess he can afford to call himself an eccentric influencer."

We walked halfway down the hall and stopped. "Here we are."

Mac knocked on the door to Room 230 and murmured, "Can't wait to meet this guy."

I could hear movement in the room. "He's in there."

"Yeah."

But we waited for another thirty seconds until Mac decided to knock again.

"All right, all right," Wesley shouted.

"Sounds like he's in a good mood," I muttered.

The door swung open and Wesley stood there glaring at us. He wore one of the thick white terrycloth hotel bathrobes tied tightly over his dress shirt, tie, and pants. He looked ridiculous, but that was just one woman's opinion.

No, wait a minute. It wasn't just me. Wesley was objectively weird.

But then, he was an *influencer*.

"Hello, Wesley," I said pleasantly. "I understand that you wanted to meet Mac

Sullivan."

He scowled. "That was yesterday."

"Mac was very busy yesterday," I explained with a patient smile, although it cost me. "But he has a few minutes to talk right now. Can we come in?"

His eyes widened and he shot a look from me to Mac and back again. "Why?"

"We could stand right here and talk," Mac said. "Loudly."

Wesley rolled his eyes. "All right. Fine. Come in."

Gracious as ever.

He pulled the door open all the way and stepped back to let us in.

I walked into the room. "Thank you so much."

"I don't have all day," he snapped.

"And neither do we," I said. "Wesley, this is MacKintyre Sullivan." I turned to Mac. "And, Mac, this is Wesley Mycroft."

"Hello," Mac said.

Wesley simply nodded. There was no shaking of hands. It was awkward.

But I had the feeling that any interaction with Wesley was awkward.

And right then I realized why Wesley might be upset. "I was very sorry to hear about Sherman."

"You're sorry?" he said, pressing two

306

fingers against his temple. "How do you think I feel? I've lost an important means of support."

"I'm sure that must be awful for you," I said, enunciating each word. "That's why I was offering my condolences."

"Condolences are of no use to me. I need more than . . . ugh." He stopped talking, pressed his fingers more tightly against his temples, and groaned.

"What's wrong, Wesley? Are you hearing the clicking?" I asked with a straight face.

"Of course I'm hearing the clicking. It means they've found me." He squeezed his eyes shut, then opened them warily. "It subsided for a while, but now it's back." And instantly suspicious, he gave Mac and me a thorough scanning up and down.

I took a step back from him. "It's a shame you don't have Sherman here to console you."

"Sherman's death is a great loss. He was my biggest acolyte and assisted me with many things."

"So he worked for you?" I asked.

"No." He swished his hand in the air, literally brushing away that statement. "He simply enjoyed being in my presence. As so many do. It was a comfort to have someone so compliant around. He was helpful. Useful. Sometimes."

Hmm. Somehow I wasn't quite feeling the love he felt for Sherman. Probably because he had no love for Sherman, except as a servant of some kind.

"I blame his death on the government," he said.

"Of course you do," I murmured.

"How dare you make light of my situation!" he cried. "Nobody seems to care that I could be the next to die!"

I exchanged a look with Mac, who quickly changed the subject. "How about if we sit outside on your balcony? It's a beautiful day."

Wesley's shoulders stiffened. "I don't go out there. The rays can kill."

"The ultraviolet rays?" I asked.

"Those, too." He glanced around the room. "I can say everything I need to say right here and now."

"Please do," Mac said evenly. I watched him subtly shift his position, moving his legs slightly apart so that he was equally balanced on both feet. It was a martial arts move that I'd seen him make a few times before, whenever someone nearby had threatened trouble.

Wesley wasn't the least bit physically threatening, but I was sensing an underlying rage. Where had that bubbled up from? Was it because of Sherman's death?

"What is it, Wesley?" I said, feeling a lot less pleasant and more demanding now.

He gave me a fleeting glance before turning to stare hard at Mac. "In your fifth book, the president is threatened by an army of androids led by a crazed scientist."

"Yeah," Mac said with a light grin. "I had a lot of fun with that book, and the whole artificial intelligence plotline was —"

"Fun?" Wesley fumed. "Fun? How dare you, sir."

Mac's eyes narrowed. "Beg your pardon?"

"You *should* beg my pardon!" Wesley said, shaking with fury. "How dare you make light of the fact that you stole that idea from me!"

CHAPTER TEN

"You're a liar," Mac said calmly, although his teeth were clenched. "I don't waste my time talking to liars." He turned and walked out of Wesley's hotel room.

Wesley stamped his foot. "I demand that you stay here and account for your actions."

But Mac was already gone.

I stared at the door and noticed that it hadn't closed all the way. Which meant that Mac had to be waiting right outside. I was relieved to know that he hadn't left me to fend for myself. Not that I couldn't handle this weasel on my own, but still, I was hopeful that Mac was nearby and probably listening in on our conversation.

I jabbed my finger against Wesley's chest. "You're lucky Mac walked out instead of punching you in the face. I wish he had done it, but he has too much dignity to stoop to your level."

His face was turning red. "How dare you!"

"Stop saying that," I insisted, furious all over again. "You sound like some kind of Victorian twit. Just FYI, 'how dare you' is not a real question or an answer to anything. It's just a snooty way to pretend you're better than someone else. And despite having your nose up in the air, you're definitely not better than anyone else."

As a punchline, it wasn't bad. But I knew I had to get out of there before I lost control, so I whipped around and stormed out to the hall, where Mac was waiting. He grabbed my hand and we ran down the hall to the elevator.

"You'll be sorry," Wesley shouted, holding the door open as he bellowed down the hall and shook his fist at me.

"No, *you'll* be sorry," I shouted. "You pathological, cliché-ridden bozo."

He stomped his foot. "I'll get you for that!"

I glanced up at Mac. "He meant to say, *I'll get you, my pretty.*"

"And your little dog, too." Mac laughed. "Come on."

I took one last peek over my shoulder. Wesley's face was still bright red. Good. I hoped his head would explode.

I was so angry, I wanted to hit something. The elevator door was open and Mac had to pull me inside.

"Wow, Red," he said, laughing. "You're on fire."

"He's such a fool." I felt like stomping my feet. "How dare he talk to you like that!"

"How dare he?" Mac laughed and drew me into his arms. "You said it. How dare he? Oh God, I love you."

"You know what I mean," I grumbled.

"Yeah, I know," he said, still laughing.

Despite his warm words and the feel of his muscular arms wrapped around me, I wasn't quite ready to calm down.

"I want to slap that supercilious attitude right out of his head. And then I'll yank his tongue out and wrap it around his skinny little neck."

"You're so ferocious," he said, gently rubbing my back. "I love it."

I tried not to smile. "How can you be so nice about it? He's awful."

Mac shrugged. "If he's truly determined to bring a case against me, I'll hear about it from my lawyer or my agent. They get paid a lot of money to handle lying idiots like him."

I gazed at him. "He's not the first to try it, I guess."

"No, and he won't be the last."

With that, I lost the last bit of my temper

312

and rested my head against his shoulder. "I'm exhausted. And we didn't even get to question him about Dillon. I'm sure that's who stole his ideas. Not the government."

"I'm sure you're right," he said, kissing the top of my head. "Let's go home."

On the short drive to my place, we stayed away from talk of Wesley and Midge and anything to do with the conference. Instead, we debated what to have for dinner. Mac had promised to cook.

"You can call for a pizza, if you want," I said, leaning back with my eyes closed.

"Nope. I'm going to grill that pork tenderloin I started marinating last night. We'll have it with wild rice and green beans. Very healthy and balanced."

"You marinated something last night?"

He grinned. "You've been distracted."

"I guess so."

He took one hand off the steering wheel, reached over, and stroked my hair. "I want you to go upstairs and relax, take a bath, drink a glass of wine, do that thing you do with your hair, and I'll take care of everything else."

I opened one eye to gaze at him. Touching his arm, I whispered, "My hero."

He smiled. "My warrior."

We walked into the kitchen and were immediately waylaid by a frisky little white dog and a slinky orange cat. After a few minutes of listening to their conversation — because Robbie and Tiger had plenty to tell us about their busy day — I took the glass of white wine Mac had poured for me, walked upstairs, and did exactly as he'd suggested.

I managed to make it back downstairs in less than an hour, a true miracle since I'd taken time to dry my mop of long curly red hair. And I did that thing Mac liked, where I pinned up half of my hair while letting the rest of it dangle and curl down around my neck and shoulders. It always looked a little messy to me, but Mac seemed to like it a lot. Or maybe he just liked what happened when he removed those few strategic hairpins.

Over dinner, we planned our tactics for tomorrow.

"I can't imagine Wesley will approach you again," I said, then dredged a tender piece of meat through the spectacular caramelized onion, mushroom, and cranberry-infused gravy Mac had prepared for the meat.

He started to speak, but I held my hand up to keep him from saying anything while

I closed my eyes and savored the intense, rich flavor of that bite.

Finally, I said, "This is the best thing I've ever tasted in my life."

He grinned. "I'm glad you're enjoying it."

"It's like tasting heaven." I sighed.

He reached over and took my hand. "Watching you right now is pretty close to heaven for me."

I stared at him for a few long seconds, and smiled. "And to think I suggested a pizza."

"Hey, pizza has its moments."

With a laugh, I reached for my wine. "Where were we?"

"I can't remember," he said, grinning. "Something about the conference."

"And Wesley."

"Oh, yeah," Mac said, grabbing a green bean off his plate. "I doubt he'll come anywhere near me tomorrow. You scared him senseless."

I scowled. "But he's unpredictable. Angry and unhinged. He could be our killer."

"But he wouldn't have killed Sherman," Mac reasoned. "Not that he cared one wit about him, but he was his biggest acolyte."

"That's the only reason Wesley isn't on the top of my suspect list."

He gazed at me. "Who's on the top?"

I took another bite of meat with some rice mixed in.

"I do have a list, but I wonder if it could be someone who's slipped off our radar."

"Like Hallie?"

My eyes widened. "Precisely. Hallie."

"She was awfully helpful this afternoon," he pointed out, using his fork for emphasis.

"That's because Rafe asked her to help us. She's probably in love with him."

Mac nodded. "If that's true, it gives her a motive to take a shot at Marigold."

I winced. "I hope she's not that crazy. But she clearly had a reason to kill Dillon. He was so rude to her, you have to believe that was just the tip of the iceberg." I played back my own words. "*Not* that there's ever a good reason to kill someone. But we're talking hypotheticals."

He smiled. "Understood."

"So let's focus on Hallie," I said. "She had a motive to kill Dillon because he treated her so badly. Ooh, maybe she was in love with Rafe, and after he left the company, Dillon started harassing her. Because he knew how she felt about Rafe. Maybe he was jealous. Or just mean."

"He's pretty mean, all right."

"I know, right?" I sipped my wine. "And if we assume her target was Marigold the

316

other night, she's got a motive there, too. A totally twisted motive, but somewhat logical from her standpoint."

He lifted his wineglass. "But then again, there's Sherman."

"I know." Frowning, I grabbed a green bean and popped it into my mouth. "Sherman screws up everything."

Mac shrugged. "Collateral damage."

"That's such a horrible term."

"I agree." He set down his wineglass and took another bite of the meat. "Sadly, in Sherman's case, I'm pretty sure that's exactly what he was."

Despite the grim subject matter, I had to smile. I recalled one of our first evenings together when we were trying to figure out who had killed someone very close to me. Mac had suggested that we make a list of suspects and motives and a timeline to figure out who the killer might be.

Mac called it the *Scooby-Doo* game, because in that old cartoon, all the kids — and the big dog — would sit around doing the same thing. They would try to figure out who the bad guy was. And even though Mac and I were trying to flesh out a vicious killer, the game had actually brought us closer together. And that could never be a bad thing.

■ ■ ■ ■

The next morning I rode with Mac to the conference site. I thought about Wesley. Remembering the way he had attacked Mac, it was hard for me to think about anything else.

"He's a nut job," Mac said, dismissing my fears. "Don't worry about him."

"I'm worried precisely because he's a nut job," I said. "The first time I spoke to him, he insisted that the government had stolen his invention for a device that could clean up the ocean in record time. You know, the one Sketch — or Marv, or whatever his name was — talked about putting in his next book. That was Wesley's idea. He also claimed that the government had stolen some kind of encryption thingie he'd invented. And now he claims that you stole his idea for your book. I think he might be a paranoid psycho-something-or-other."

"In other words, a nut job," Mac said.

"Yeah. Remember how freaked out he got when he said that he could be the next one to die?"

Mac thought about it. "Well, people do seem to be dying."

"So he's not as nutty as we thought?" I

rolled my eyes.

Mac smiled, reached over, and rubbed my shoulder. "He's plenty nutty, but he's also a really bad guy."

"You're right. You heard what he said about poor Sherman." I shook my head in disgust. "His 'biggest acolyte.' Ugh."

"He wouldn't make a good friend, that's for sure," Mac admitted. "Still, he did seem to have a relationship with Sherman. I mean, I can picture him killing Dillon for stealing his inventions, but I can't see him strangling his faithful manservant Sherman. He would no longer have someone catering to his every whim."

"Right. Sherman brought him cocktails and groveled incessantly." I was fuming all over again as Mac turned onto Olive Street and then drove another block to Sunset Hill Road. "I would so love to see him go to jail."

"Maybe we could ask Eric to do one small favor for us."

I chuckled. "I'm not sure he could put Wesley away for no reason, even for us."

Mac pulled into the conference parking lot and shut off the engine, then turned to me. "What's on your agenda this morning?"

"I get to go check out my tiny houses this morning."

"Cool," Mac said, grabbing his conference

satchel and slinging it over his shoulder. "I want to take a look at them, too. I'll walk with you."

"I'd like that."

Mac opened the trunk to check that Dillon's binder was still there and locked the car and pressed the alarm button. "That should keep it safe for now. We can take it to Rafe after we check out your tiny houses."

"Good," I said. "The sooner it's back in his hands, the easier I'll breathe."

"I'll call him and let him know we want to meet up with him in maybe an hour or so."

"We'll need to give him a full report of our findings yesterday. Tell him how we saw Midge coming out of Dillon's hotel room."

"Yeah," Mac said, nodding. "And he needs to hear the whole story about Dillon cheating those people out of their patents."

"Don't you think he knows?"

Mac thought for a moment. "No, I don't. If he knew, he would've remedied the situation immediately."

I nodded, knowing in my heart that he was right. Rafe was a good guy. He never would've gone along with Dillon to cheat people out of what was rightly theirs.

We walked along the edge of the gully where the creek ran. Rafe had set aside a full acre of space to park the ten houses I'd agreed to show. It was a short walk from the main conference area over to the tiny house park, but Rafe had wanted them to be placed closer to the woods so people could get a real feeling for the freedom of parking one's house anywhere they wanted. Preferably they would want to be surrounded by nature.

"Why weren't they here all week?" Mac asked.

"I asked him about that. Rafe said he didn't think the conference attendees would appreciate them enough if they were here all week. You know, they'd visit for a day or two and then stop coming."

"Makes sense."

"I think so, too. This way, they only have two days to take advantage of this golden opportunity."

"That's the way to sell it," he said with a grin.

"I think Rafe's got a bit of salesman mentality in him, too."

"It's funny, isn't it? In reality, he's the farthest thing from a salesman I know, but he played this one like he was standing on the showroom floor."

I smiled at the image.

We reached the edge of the tiny house park. "I can't tell if they're all here yet." I jogged around the perimeter of the temporary hedge border the landscapers had erected, then returned to Mac. "Yeah, looks like all ten houses are here."

"And so is the crowd," Mac remarked.

That's when I took a closer look between the houses and realized there were lines of people waiting to go inside each of the structures to check out the features.

"This is kind of exciting," I said. "Looks like our exhibit is a hit."

"Sure does. I hope you'll sell a few more."

"Me, too." I gave Mac a grateful smile, then quickly added, "Not that it matters, you understand. The idea wasn't to sell anything, but just to show people how they can live with a much smaller carbon footprint and still maintain a comfortable lifestyle. And most of the houses are pretty green, too."

"You don't have to explain it to me," he said, swallowing a laugh. "I know your heart is in the right place."

"Okay, fine." He knew me too well. So I shrugged and admitted, "I hope we sell a few dozen."

"That's more like it," he said, and laughed for real.

I moved toward the opening in the hedges. "I want to just walk through the crowd and listen to the comments."

"I'm with you," he said, and took my hand.

The ten houses varied in size from three hundred to five hundred square feet. Most of them contained a loft of some sort that was used for sleeping. This gave the owner some extra space on the ground floor to expand the living area.

Each house also came with some sort of outdoor element. On the bigger houses that usually consisted of a full-sized deck with patio furniture and space for a small grill. For the smaller homes, a front or back porch was all that would fit, but these could usually accommodate one or two small chairs, suitable for sitting and watching the world go by. Those smaller houses also had the option of a wraparound porch if they wanted to add to their square footage.

I had to marvel that I had managed to stumble onto such a ridiculously popular trend — and I didn't see an end in sight. Which was a very good thing. And according to the random comments I was hearing from the admiring crowd, it looked as though we'd be selling several more soon.

The best part of this project was that my crew and I could work on all different types of homes. Since I had lived in Lighthouse

Cove all my life, I had always been focused on Victorian style. But with the tiny houses, I was able to expand my scope to include contemporary modern and mid-century modern styles; an adorable clapboard cottage with French doors and a cupola that was accessible through the loft inside the house; several log cabins; and a charming California bungalow. The most popular design so far was the California Craftsman style with porches supported by thick square columns and low-pitched roofs. The interiors featured exposed oak beams and the kitchen cabinets featured clean, simple lines. I had built six of them so far and three were on display today at the conference.

I remembered taking the day off from the whirlwind job of refurbishing Rafe's house to go and finish the clapboard cottage. It had been relaxing to take up a paintbrush and add that second coat of pure white paint to the French doors, all the windows, the stair rail, and the cupola. The white was a wonderful contrast to the pretty dark blue of the rest of the house.

Mac and I strolled past a sleek mid-century modern home whose clever owner had parked their vintage pink Thunderbird next to the bright turquoise front door.

"It's fun to see the owners getting into the

act," I said, pointing to one of the log cabins where the owner was sitting on a window ledge holding a fishing pole.

"They're all fascinating, aren't they?" Mac said.

"I think so."

"I picture myself living in one of them," Mac said. "And then I think . . . no."

I laughed. We walked past a pretty wood deck filled with pots of cheery flowers and a comfy chaise longue. "So you don't think you could live in a four-hundred-square-foot space?"

"No way," he said with a self-deprecating laugh. "I hate to admit it, but my personal carbon footprint is a great big clodhopper."

I grinned and patted his arm. "Don't worry. I won't tell Rafe."

"Thanks. Wouldn't want to get drummed out of the survival conference."

An hour later, we walked into Rafe's house and handed him the binder.

"Don't take this the wrong way," I said, "but I'm really glad to be getting rid of this."

"I don't blame you." Rafe set it down on the dining room table and opened it to a random section.

"Look familiar?" Mac asked.

"Frankly, no," he admitted, turning pages.

"I've never seen this. But I appreciate you bringing it to me."

"We weren't about to leave it in Dillon's hotel room."

"No way," I said. "I'm afraid that a number of people have already seen it and have probably taken documents out of it."

Rafe frowned. "But you only saw Midge, right?"

"Yes," I said, "but someone else had to have told her it was in there."

"I'd suggest you call Eric about this," Mac said. "Those documents could provide a strong motive for Dillon's murder."

Rafe blew out a heavy breath. "This is bad. These are confidential personnel documents that nobody outside the company should see." He thumbed through a few pages, then looked up. "You said you had something specific to show me."

"Yeah, let me get to that." I stepped closer and pulled the tab labeled PATENT APPLICATIONS, and flipped to that section. "There are more than just confidential company documents in here. You'll see in this section that there are dozens, or maybe as many as one hundred, of these patent application forms. They've got all the information on the specific idea or invention or project or design. And they've got Dillon's name on the line for *Owner.*"

"Wait." He stared at the top page. "But that's not necessarily deceptive. He might've meant that he was the administrator. You know, the one who applies for the patent on behalf of the applicant."

"I wish that were true," I said, grimacing. "But we've heard from several people that Dillon basically ripped off their ideas. That he applied for the patents in his name and planned to take any and all royalties coming in for those ideas."

"Sorry, Rafe." Mac shook his head. "Like I said, we're pretty sure this is the reason why Dillon was killed."

Rafe turned the page and stared at the information listed, then turned to another page. "Why would he do this?"

Because he was a crook, I thought, but kept my mouth shut. I was pretty sure Rafe didn't actually want to hear the answer to his question. I felt so sorry for him right now. Of course he could remedy the situation. It would just take time and money, and he had plenty of both. But he had been cruelly betrayed by one of his oldest friends, someone he had trusted for years, and his business reputation would surely take a hit.

"What can we do?" I asked.

Rafe jolted, as if he had awakened from a

dream. Turning, he put his big arms around me and just held on for a long moment. Then he stepped back and gave Mac a quick hug, too.

"Just be a friend," he said softly. "That's the best thing you can do."

Mac patted him on the back. "We're already there, bud."

A half hour later, we left Rafe's house and returned to the conference. We had spent the last few minutes brainstorming with him, trying to figure out the best steps to take to fix this problem. Rafe decided that he couldn't go to the inventors yet. He would have to go to his company offices and investigate exactly what Dillon had done and why, and how much damage he had caused. Then Rafe would contact each of the inventors, including Midge and Wesley and Julian and all the others, and let them know that he was taking care of everything. After a quick check of the patent applications in the binder, Rafe had discovered that some of them had been applied for five years ago. So Dillon had been keeping this binder up to date even while Rafe was working at the company.

"This is ridiculous," Rafe said, shaking his head in disgust. "Dillon was committing fraud and theft under my very nose."

"You'll make it up to everyone," I said.

"You bet I will. I'll let everyone know that I intend to pay back any money owed in royalties and I'll reapply for the patents in their names."

"I hope that will be enough," I said to Mac as we crossed through the catering area.

"Yeah, me, too." Mac stopped and at the edge of the air dome. "I'm afraid some of these crazies will still want blood."

"Clearly, someone has already proven that to be true." I grabbed Mac's hand. "I'm glad Rafe called Eric. The two of them will be able to figure out the people who have the strongest motive to kill."

"I just hope they can pin down the killer in time." Mac shook his head. "I don't want any more rifles aimed at any of my friends." He glanced around the field. "I'm supposed to meet Brett Barlow to talk over some more worst-case scenarios. He was the guy on the panel with me."

I smiled up at him. "Are you two planning to take your show on the road? You were both pretty funny."

He grinned. "Not a bad idea. But no. Brett asked if I would sit down and help him plot out his new book."

"Sounds like fun," I said. "I'm on my way to the barn. I'll probably spend an hour or two helping the guys with the finishing touches."

"I'll try to get over there later." He looked past me then, at the milling crowd, as if trying to decide if there was danger close by. Seriously? I really did love him.

"Okay." I squeezed his arm. "I'll text you if anything changes."

"Good." He leaned down and kissed me, then touched my cheek with the back of his hand. "Beautiful."

I stared into his eyes. "I love you a lot."

He smiled and pressed his forehead to mine. "That doesn't get old."

"I know, right?"

He laughed. "I'll see you soon. Meanwhile, behave. And be careful."

I laughed, too, and grabbed hold of his jacket. "Same goes."

I was surprised to see that the bleachers were over half filled with people still watching the barn being built. I had been sure that the crowds would disappear after the first day, when everyone would've grown tired of seeing all those men — and a few women — continuing to work on that big old barn. But apparently it still held plenty of interest to some.

Or maybe the bleachers were simply the best place to eat a sandwich before heading off to some other event. And now I was hungry.

Didn't matter, I thought. I was just glad to see some of the attendees taking an interest in the activity.

And honestly, that beautiful new barn was glorious.

I stopped and stared at the clean shingled roof and the bright red siding, and felt a burst of pride. I knew I wore a silly grin, but I was so happy to see the work my crew had done, I wanted to shout about it. I wondered where that megaphone had disappeared to.

Crowing about the barn would probably be considered sort of weird. But then, being weird would help me fit right in with this crowd. As I considered it, I thought that in this bunch, I was actually pretty normal. I stared up at the sky, watched as the puffy white clouds scudded on the breeze. And realized that despite the strange goings-on all week, I felt a sense of relief that some things were working out with the conference. Rafe was making things right and I felt a renewed determination to find out who had tried to derail things.

I knew despite everything — the mice, the poisoning, the murders, the gunshots — the conference had been a huge success. And that was just about as weird as anything else that had happened this week.

No matter what else happened, I was just glad to know that Rafe would make good on all the pain and worry that his ex-partner had caused so many people.

I shook away those thoughts and walked over to the barn to find my guys.

"Hey, Shannon," Sean said when he saw me coming around the corner of the barn. "What do you think?"

I grabbed him in a big hug. "I'm so proud of you and Wade and all the guys. It just looks fantastic. You did an incredible job, and you did it right, and fast, and . . . wow."

His grin was so wide, it almost split his face in two. "Thanks, boss. We've really been kicking butt out here and we couldn't wait for you to see it."

"I'm just blown away," I said, and recalled Rafe's comment on the landscaping around his house. Was that only a week ago? Seemed like a year had passed since then.

"Well, come and look inside," Sean said. "We've really got things pretty well in hand, if I do say so myself."

"I can't wait to see it all." I followed him

over to the big, wide opening — otherwise known as the barn door, ha ha — and walked inside. It was cool and spacious and bright from the natural light that streamed in through the many windows we'd installed on all four sides.

"The guys are working on the electrical right now. The wires are being bundled up the walls and across the ceiling so we should have lights and fans working by tomorrow."

"Fantastic," I murmured, circling around to take in every possible inch of the space. "I should leave you alone more often."

"No, you shouldn't," he said. "No. Really. We like having you around."

"Right. I know that sentiment came straight from your heart."

He laughed. "You bet it did, boss."

Wade walked up just then and overheard the last bit of conversation. "What's this suck-up saying to you?"

I smiled sweetly. "He said he likes me the best."

Wade rolled his eyes and smacked Sean's arm. "Can't leave you alone for a minute."

"Seriously," I began, and circled around, looking at everything. "This is the most amazing, big, beautiful thing I've ever seen."

"Besides all the other big, beautiful projects we've been working on lately," Wade said, his mouth twisted in a grin.

"Well, yeah, of course," I admitted. "But this is the first barn ever, so it's extra special. You guys did a fabulous job. I couldn't be prouder."

"I'm going to accept that one," Wade said. "Thanks."

"Thank *you.*"

He bowed grandly, and we all guffawed.

"Okay, you knuckleheads," I said. "I'm going to go get a sandwich. Can I get you anything?"

"No thanks, boss," Sean said. "We'll take a break in about a half hour. Maybe we'll see you over at the catering table."

"I hope so," I said. "See you later." And I waved as I walked out of the big, beautiful barn.

CHAPTER ELEVEN

I stood in line at the catering tables and my mouth began to water just staring at all the delicious sandwiches available. Emily's Tea Shoppe made just about the best sandwiches in the world.

I was trying to decide between roast beef and chicken salad when I realized I was standing behind Hallie, Rafe's assistant. She wore a sleeveless canary-yellow jumpsuit so I wasn't sure how I had missed her until this moment.

"Hi, Hallie," I said.

She whipped around nervously, then relaxed. "Oh. Shannon. Hi. How are you doing?"

For a moment, I wondered who she had been expecting. "Good. How about you?"

"I'm fine," she said quickly, straightening her shoulders. The sleeveless jumpsuit suited her perfectly tanned, well-toned arms as well as her perky style. "Busy. And hungry."

"Yeah, me, too." I felt a little bland standing next to her in my blue jeans, work boots, and sage Henley. But then, I was also wearing my tool belt. That counted for chic, right?

The line moved forward and Hallie turned away from me to place her order. And I wondered all over again if she could have killed her boss. She was really jumpy for some reason. She had a strong motive, lest I forgot that scene the first night. Now I stared at Hallie's shoulders and arm muscles and wondered if she had enough upper-body strength to tote a high-powered rifle across the field and up three steep ramps to the roof of the Ecosphere.

But of course she could do it, I realized, remembering the time I went shooting with my uncle Pete and I used his hunting rifle. That big old thing didn't weigh more than seven pounds or so. Today, with all the latest materials, they probably weighed even less.

And if she had killed Dillon, then it followed that she had also tried to kill my friend Marigold. And Sherman, as well. I tried to picture Hallie running into him, randomly grabbing a thick green vine, and wrapping it around his neck so tightly that it cut off all the oxygen to his brain. The killer had run out, leaving Sherman dead and the Stephanie vine a tattered and shredded shadow of her formerly healthy self.

I flinched when Hallie suddenly whined, "What do you mean it won't take my card?"

"I'm sorry," the counter clerk said, "but it says that you've exceeded your credit limit. You need to call your card company."

The clerk looked beyond Hallie and smiled at me. "May I help you?"

I held up my finger. "Just a second." Feeling sorry for Hallie, I said, "Do you want to try it again? Maybe it didn't read the number right."

"This is impossible," she insisted. "I just paid my bill."

"Here," I said. "I'll pay for your lunch so we don't hold up the line."

"I don't have much cash to pay you back. I always carry my credit card."

"Do you have a debit card?"

She gave me a blank look. "I do, but it's not with me. I left everything in my hotel safe. I don't like carrying too much stuff with me while I'm here."

"I see," I said, although I didn't really. "Well, then, whenever you get around to it, you can pay me back. Or not. It's only a few bucks."

Her lower lip poofed out and quivered. Oh boy. Was she going to cry? The sandwich with chips and a soda was only eight dollars, nothing to cry about.

"I'm just going to call and make sure it's not a mistake."

I turned to the clerk. "I'll take a roast beef sandwich with chips and a bottle of water. And I'll take whatever she ordered, too."

I slipped my card into the reader, and a few seconds later, it beeped. I took the card and the receipt and two bags of food and grabbed Hallie's arm as I walked away from the counter. "Come over here."

She was a little disoriented until she saw that I was holding her lunch. I pointed to a group of tables nearby.

"Let's sit here."

"Okay," she said in a daze, and sat down, then abruptly jumped up when her phone beeped. "It's a text from my credit card company."

"That was fast," I said. "Did they rectify it?"

"No," she said, her voice quavering. "They're asking if I just paid twelve thousand dollars for a first-class ticket to Bali."

"Bali," I said. "That sounds like quite a vacation."

"It's not my vacation," she cried. "Someone stole my card."

I could see hysteria beginning to mount again and did what I could to cut it off at the pass. "You won't have to pay for it. Credit card companies are very good about this stuff. Right now you need to answer the text. Let them know you didn't make that purchase."

She shook out her hands and stretched her fingers, as though she were about to play a piano concerto or something. She nodded rapidly as she texted. "Okay. Okay. Done."

"Okay," I said cheerfully. "Now their fraud department is on the case. You don't have to worry anymore."

"Thanks." She smiled sheepishly. "I'm not very good in a crisis."

No kidding, I thought, but just smiled. "It's a traumatic thing when that happens. Did to me once. Someone charged three new computers on my card. But the card company took care of it and they'll take care of this, too. You handled it just fine."

I unwrapped her sandwich for her and set it down on one of the napkins. "Here you go."

She took a bite and chewed listlessly.

I wanted to get her talking. Maybe because she was so upset, she'd spill some information. "It's too bad you don't have that special encryption feature," I said. "The one that Wesley invented."

"Wesley?" She cocked her head and gave me a puzzled look. "I don't know about Wesley," she said, "but Dillon invented an amazing type of encryption software. He helped me apply it to my credit card."

"Oh," I said. "It doesn't seem to be working." And maybe the reason it didn't work was because it wasn't really his idea. Had he stolen the encryption idea from Wesley, too? I wondered if he knew he could use it to communicate with aliens. Or maybe that was just Wesley dreaming the big dreams.

She bared her teeth angrily. "Yeah. Big surprise. You can chalk up one more disaster for Dillon's column."

"Are there a lot of disasters in his column?" I asked quietly.

"A gazillion."

Probably an exaggeration, I thought. But she didn't sound like a happy employee.

Hallie stared at her sandwich and muttered, "I'm so glad he's dead. I mean, I didn't kill him or anything, but you know. Anyway."

My eyes widened at her words. I'd been looking for information and I guess she gave it to me. It wasn't quite a confession of

340

murder, though. Unfortunately.

Hallie must have realized she had said that out loud and clamped her lips together. Finally, she said lamely, "Sorry. You must think I'm awful."

"No. I think you're normal. Dillon wasn't well liked by anyone as far as I can tell."

She gave a quick, bad-tempered shrug. "Still shouldn't say stuff like that. Not to someone outside of the company."

"Did anyone like him?" I asked.

"Nobody I know."

I suddenly remembered what Tommy had said about Dillon's multiple stab wounds. Maybe everyone who hated Dillon had taken part in his murder. Sort of a *Murder on the Orient Express* thing.

So maybe Hallie had joined in the fun? I shook my head. I was letting my imagination go a little wild, but it was still an intriguing idea. And because I couldn't quite push it out of my mind, I no longer felt comfortable sharing a table with her. I checked my watch. "Oh, gosh. Look at the time."

I gathered up my lunch and stuffed it back into the bag, then flashed her a big happy smile. "I just realized I've got to meet someone over by the air dome in about five minutes. So, I'll see you around."

341

I took off at a brisk pace, then couldn't help but glance back at her. She was squinting in the bright sunlight, but I could tell she was watching me. Did she know that I thought she might be a cold-blooded killer?

I had to laugh. I really was seeing killers behind every bush. But why was Hallie watching me? Or was she?

Seriously, I needed to get some rest.

Whether or not Hallie had killed her boss, she had obviously hated him. I was practically a stranger to her, and she had admitted that she was glad he was dead.

I was clearly driving myself crazy. I glanced over my shoulder once more — and Hallie was gone. Disappeared. I stopped and turned around to scan the entire wide-open conference area. Where did she go? It would be hard to miss her in her canary-yellow jumpsuit, and yet she was nowhere to be seen. I couldn't spot even a blur of canary-yellow anywhere. I waited and watched, thinking maybe she was standing behind someone, but no. She was gone. I stood where I was and turned all the way around and finally had to admit that the woman had completely vanished.

The closest building was the old barn so maybe she had decided to check out the missing mice or the solar-powered farm tractor.

I started to walk. I needed to give myself a chance to breathe and think. I wanted to be somewhere quiet where there weren't too many people. I took another turn, glanced around in every direction, looking at Rafe's beautiful property. And that was when I saw the blades of the wind turbines moving.

I had seen them working the first time Mac and I had driven out to visit Rafe, but somewhere over the last eight months he had turned them off, saying he wanted to wait until he could operate them without making so much noise and without killing any birds.

Had he accomplished those goals? Was this some kind of new technology he was displaying for the first time at the conference?

I had always been fascinated by the wind farms of Altamont and Palm Springs, where hundreds of windmills and wind turbines were scattered over the hills for miles and miles. Rafe only had three of the wind turbines, but they were massive, standing on a rise beyond the barns and the Ecosphere tower.

I strolled in that direction and began to climb the hill, watching the blades circling quietly, catching the warm breeze that wafted over the rise.

Quietly?

I stopped and stared at the propeller blades spinning in the breeze. The last time I was out here, those turbines engines were loud. But now they were quiet. It was amazing to stand so close and not hear the noise. It was practically a miracle. A technological breakthrough, for sure.

So Rafe had done it. He had discovered a way to lessen the noise. *But what about the danger to the birds?* I wondered. But then I realized that Rafe would never turn the machines back on unless he had found a surefire way to make them safe for the birds.

I would have to ask him later, but for now I was proud of him. Maybe he was waiting to announce his success at the awards ceremony tomorrow night.

I stopped again and stared out at the view from the rise. I could see why Rafe had bought this property after so many years of living and working in Silicon Valley. It was just so peaceful and pretty here. Since it was so eerily quiet, I turned and kept walking toward the wind turbines, keeping my gaze on those huge, mesmerizing blades.

Stopping again, I whirled around to check out the beautiful new barn glistening red in the sunlight. Off to my right, the Ecosphere tower jutted up to the sky, momentarily blocking my view of Rafe's pretty house and all the landscaping we had added recently.

Rafe had done well for himself here, I thought. And I was proud to have been a part of it. I walked a few more yards and the hill grew steeper. Now I could see the house beyond the tower as well as a large part of the massive property of five hundred acres. There was pastureland and softly rolling hills that meandered up into the redwood forest. This time of year the woods lining the creek were beautiful with the trees starting to lose their leaves and the creek slowing down as the runoff became a trickle before winter. Next spring, the snow melt from the mountains to the east would make this creek run wide and fast.

And off to the north I could see the tip-top of the lighthouse three miles up the coast. It was lovely.

It was nice to take in all of the beauty and just breathe the clean air. I scanned the property from the woods over toward the new house.

And that was when I saw it.

I blinked rapidly to clear my vision and make sure I wasn't imagining things.

No, it wasn't my imagination.

"Oh no. Oh no," I whispered as I stared at the skinny barrel of a high-powered rifle peeking over the ledge of the roof of the Ecosphere tower.

I took off running toward the conference area a few hundred yards away. I had never been much of a runner, but I was moving pretty fast, even with the tool belt around my waist. After all, someone was up on that tower with a gun and they could pick off almost anyone in the conference area or beyond.

Halfway down the hill, I stopped. What was I thinking? The shooter could pick off *me*.

And why was I heading *toward* the conference site? Maybe I should've been heading toward the Ecosphere after all. But then, I couldn't go inside without a weapon or body armor or some kind of protection. I looked down at my tool belt and almost laughed. As if my hammer would protect me against someone with a high-powered rifle.

I needed to keep moving off the hill, needed to get out of harm's way. I couldn't stay out here and be the perfect target for a madman. Or madwoman.

Still running, I pulled out my phone and speed-dialed Mac.

"Hey, Red," he answered.

Just hearing his voice eased my mind despite the adrenaline racing around my system. "There's someone in the tower with a rifle."

"What?" he shouted. "Are you sure?"

"I saw the barrel sticking out over the ledge. Wait. I can't see it now."

"Where are you?"

"I'm on the hill out by the wind turbines."

"Get out of there," he ordered. "There's no cover."

I frowned, glanced around. "No kidding." I was stuck in the middle of the pretty grassland with no protection anywhere. That was why I was running. And why I had called him!

"I'm on my way," he added. "I love you."

My hero, I thought, rubbing my chest where I felt a warm glow. Now all I had to do was keep my heart beating. There was no way I was going to die today. Mac would be totally bummed.

I stared up at the roof of the tower. I couldn't see anything now and wondered if the shooter had gone over to the other side, which meant that he — or she — would have a clear shot at anyone attending the conference. Maybe I was in a better place than all those conference goers walking around by the air domes like ducks in a shooting gallery. Good grief, what a horrible thought.

Not being an idiot, I knew that if I didn't run faster, I would be one of those sitting ducks. I glanced over at the new barn, but it was too far away. I made an instant decision to head for the Ecosphere tower.

Yes, the shooter was perched up there, but the trick was that if I got close enough to the outer wall, the shooter wouldn't be able to see me. The roof's wooden ledge overlapped the edge of the structure by about six inches, effectively cutting off the view straight down. It was my only chance until Mac and the cavalry could get here.

I wondered if Mac had called Eric to come. Probably, but I decided to cover all the bases. I pressed Eric's speed dial number, but the call went straight to his voice mail. I tried Tommy, too, but got the same result. Voice mail.

Where was a cop when you needed one?

"Men," I muttered, and called Marigold.

"Hi, Shannon," she said cheerily.

"Marigold."

"Shannon? Why are you breathing so hard? Are you at the gym?"

"No, I'm at the conference. And I'm running. Marigold, there's a shooter on the roof

348

of the Ecosphere. Don't leave your house."

"I'm out on the patio. I wanted to plant more flowers along the —"

Oh God. She was the perfect target.

"Get inside," I shouted. "Tell Rafe and call Eric."

"Okay, okay." I could hear the sliding glass door open and then close. "Okay. I'm inside. Rafe isn't here right now, but I'll call him. Where are you, Shannon?"

"I'm heading toward the Ecosphere."

"Shannon, don't. It's too dangerous!" Thankfully, her voice wasn't shaking. She sounded cool and calm. Just what I needed at the moment.

"I'll be safe," I said.

"Oh God. Just be careful," she ordered. "I'm calling Rafe and Eric."

I was twenty yards from the Ecosphere when I looked up and saw the barrel sticking out over the ledge again. It wasn't pointing directly my way, but it didn't matter. Someone was up there with that rifle and they were ready to kill.

"I will," I said. "And tell them to hurry!"

I ended the call, then ran for my life.

I pressed myself against the wall near the doorway of the Ecosphere. I took a chance and leaned over to peek inside. I couldn't see anybody on the ground floor, but I could hear voices echoing through the interior.

Had the shooter found a hostage?

"I didn't do anything."

That was clearly a woman's voice, I thought.

"Stop pushing. You're hurting me."

It was Hallie, of course. Had she come here directly from the sandwich shop? Was she a hostage or a coconspirator? Hostage or criminal, I needed to know who was with her, but couldn't hear anyone else over her whine.

"You have him," Hallie said. "Why don't you let me go?"

"That's an excellent idea," a man said. "Wesley, I thought we had a deal. You don't need these two. I can get you whatever you want. I've already assured you that I'll pay back whatever royalties we've made on your behalf and I'll resubmit your patent applications as soon as I get out of here."

That was Rafe!

Oh my God. What was Rafe doing in here?

"Too little too late," Wesley growled.

And Wesley had the gun. He had killed Dillon. Which meant that he had killed Sherman. Why would he kill his only friend?

"He's bleeding," Hallie cried.

"Shut up," Wesley said. "Or you'll be the next to go."

Was Rafe bleeding? Who else was in there? I absolutely had to see what was going on. I stepped a few inches closer to the doorway and edged myself around until I could get a glimpse inside.

The ground floor was still deserted, but now I could hear the heavy footsteps as the trio, or foursome — I had no idea how many — began to descend from the roof.

I scanned the plant life on the ground floor. I knew almost every inch of this space and knew there were places I could hide if I had to.

If I could move fast enough, I could make it over to the corner where a large, leafy ficus tree covered half the wall. I figured my clothing was neutral enough to blend in with the green plants and the gray stone walls, so I could probably hide undetected.

It occurred to me that in that same corner were the controls for both the lights and the wide louvers that shaded the window openings. Light streamed in through the openings so I couldn't exactly switch the whole interior into darkness. But maybe I could use the louvers to distract the shooter just long enough to get his weapon away from him.

Not that I was delusional enough to think I could walk up to him and grab the rifle. But I had to do something. Rafe was in trouble.

It was now or never. I tiptoed all the way through the doorway and stepped into the cool interior. As I raced toward the corner where the lush, leafy ficus tree stood, I couldn't help but notice the clean air in here. But now wasn't the time to linger and breathe in the freshness.

"I don't know why you're so peeved about the Scoop-Monster," a man said.

Oh my God, that smarmy voice! Sketch Horn was in here, too.

"Shut up," Wesley snapped. "You're lucky I didn't shoot you in the head."

Part of me wanted to scream. I couldn't believe I was stuck inside this structure with two of the biggest blowhards I'd ever met. I hated to say it, but they deserved each other.

"I think you'd be better off staying on the roof," Sketch Horn said.

"Like you would know," Wesley countered. I could see him sneering, looking down his nose at the hapless faux writer.

"Hey, I write these kinds of scenes for a living," Sketch insisted.

His voice was sounding weaker. Was he the one who was bleeding? Or was it Rafe?

"No, you don't," Wesley snarled. "You were busted. Everyone knows your wife writes those books."

"Well, I make the revisions."

"You're straining my patience."

"Okay, fine," Sketch admitted irately. "But I live in the same house with my wife. I absorb the stories like osmosis."

Wesley actually sniffed. "You, sir, are a moron."

I winced at that since I couldn't disagree.

"Have a little sympathy, man," Sketch said. "You shot me in the leg."

"You should let me go," Hallie said in a tone of desperation. "I won't say anything to anybody."

"Yes, let her go," Rafe said. "I can get you out of here if you let Hallie and Sketch go. I'll get you to my car and give you all the money you need to make a safe getaway. You can be on a plane in an hour and fly off to another country."

Wesley sniffed. "It's just that simple, is it?"

"Yes," Rafe said. "I have the money to make it happen."

"Take the deal," Sketch said, sounding desperate. "I need to go to the hospital."

"You're not going anywhere," Wesley said. "I heard you talking to that handywoman about the encryption device that Dillon Charles stole from me."

I frowned. Did he just call me a handywoman? Like a slur? Was that supposed to be a dig? What was wrong with being a handywoman? I hired a few of them on a regular basis and they worked their butts off for me.

I really wanted to smack his smart mouth, just as I'd told Mac yesterday. I itched to throttle Wesley until that supercilious attitude drained right out of him.

"Hey, I read you loud and clear, man," Sketch said. "Look, I confess I overheard you telling that girl about the Scoop-Monster idea so I took it and ran with it. What's the big deal?" Sketch managed to sound like the most egotistical jerk ever, and that was becoming a crowded field. "It's a great idea. We could split the profits. I could have my wife write up some great ad copy. She's quite the little writer, you know."

Did he just call me *that girl*? I suppose I was getting off easy, since he had referred to his wife as *quite the little writer.* I couldn't wait to track down Honey and tell her.

"You can stick your ad copy where the sun don't shine," Wesley said, then sniffed again. "I just might write the story myself. I couldn't do worse than the hatchet jobs you turn out on a regular basis."

"Hey. That's my wife you're talking about."

I shook my head. Mac had always told me that narcissistic male authors had one thing in common: they never stopped talking about themselves. Apparently the only person Wesley could match wits with was Sketch Horn. *They really should collaborate,* I thought. They thoroughly deserved each other.

"Look, just think about the collaboration idea," Sketch said. "We're both well known in our fields. We could cash in."

Wesley inhaled so deeply, I thought he might pass out. "I'm tempted to shoot you in the head right here and now."

"Hey, come on now." Sketch's voice was growing thin with fear and weakness. "Calm down, dude."

I caught a glimpse of canary yellow through the leaves and watched as Hallie traipsed down the ramp to the ground floor. *Now what?* I thought. I had to do something. Or not. I could wait for Mac and Eric to show up. But I didn't know if they would get here in time before Wesley had a complete meltdown. He was sounding more and more deranged by the minute. If he shot Rafe, I would have to find a way to kill him.

I blamed Sketch. Blabbing about the Scoop-Monster and calling it his own idea in front of the entire conference had taken a lot of brass. I had a feeling it was the straw that broke the camel's back for old Wesley.

Sketch came down the ramp next, limping badly. He looked paler than he had when his wife confronted him in the bar the day before. Of course, she hadn't been pointing a rifle at his head. Not at that moment, anyway.

And then I saw Rafe. I could tell his teeth were clenched and he was angry. But he looked strong and determined. And unharmed. He paused halfway down the ramp and it made me wonder if he had a plan to get them all out of here.

Finally Wesley appeared at the top of the ramp. I stared and watched in horror as he readjusted the position of the rifle to aim it directly at me.

Could he see me? There was no way. The tree was six feet tall and thick with leaves. But then, we had already seen that Wesley had no problem killing plants. Maybe he had a thing against ficus trees.

My clever thoughts were doing nothing to take away the feeling of abject terror racing through me. I stood perfectly still and barely dared to breathe.

Then he shifted, adjusting the rifle in his hands so that it pointed down at his three hostages. I hated to admit that I was relieved that it was no longer aimed in my direction.

He remained at the top of the ramp as if that gave him more stature.

I suppose it did, though. I scowled at the thought.

"I know why you killed Dillon," Hallie said. "Because he stole your idea, right?"

"That's right. And when I confronted him, he denied it." Wesley's voice hitched a little higher. "He lied. People keep lying to me. He was taking full credit for it and had no intention of paying me back, even though I had proof, full documentation of everything I'd worked on for the past five years."

"I'm glad he's dead," Hallie said.

Wesley studied her for a moment. "Maybe you have some saving grace after all."

"I do," she said eagerly. "If you'll let me go, I'll —"

"Enough!" Wesley shouted. "Stop groveling. It's unseemly."

"Now you sound like Dillon," she said crossly. "Always telling me what to do like I'm stupid or something. I hate that."

"Has it occurred to you, miss, that you *are* stupid?" Wesley huffed out a breath. "This conference has simply been exhausting, and I don't even have Sherman here to fetch me some tea."

"Because you killed him," Hallie said belligerently. "Who's stupid now?"

"Dearest," Wesley said dryly. "You're not making any friends here."

"Hallie, I'm sorry," Rafe said, ignoring Wesley. "I didn't know what Dillon was doing behind my back, but that's no excuse. I'll make it up to you and to everyone at the company."

"It's not your fault," Hallie insisted.

"Yes, it is," Wesley said. "Ignorance is no excuse."

"I agree," Rafe said, his voice strong and firm. "That's why I plan to make it up to everyone who was hurt by Dillon's actions."

"Don't blame Rafe," Hallie said defensively.

"I'm sick of stupid people," Wesley said, and pointing his rifle toward the ceiling, he pulled the trigger.

Hallie screamed.

So did I. I couldn't help it. I just hoped and prayed that the sound of Hallie's screams covered up my own.

Sketch crumpled to the ground.

Rafe dashed over to help him.

"I'm okay," Sketch said. "I'm okay."

"Nobody cares, Mr. Horn," Wesley said.

He laughed as he reloaded the rifle.

"You're the one who's stupid," Hallie cried. "It was Dillon who caused all the problems, not Rafe. And Rafe said he'd give you everything you wanted. If you kill us, you won't get anything."

She had a point. And I had to give her credit for being loyal to Rafe.

"Dillon wouldn't be in charge if Rafe had stayed," Wesley reasoned. "And Rafe will be collecting just as much money on my ideas as Dillon. So I blame him just as much."

"Doesn't seem fair," Hallie mumbled.

Wesley sniffed once again. "I don't recall asking your opinion."

My eyes rolled so hard it was a wonder they didn't hear them rattling around in my head. He was so freaking snooty!

I was going crazy hiding behind this tree. I needed to take some action. I knew I would only get one chance, so I had to wait for my moment and make it good. While they were talking, I ran through half a dozen scenarios in my head. *I could start shaking the tree,* I thought, *creating a diversion for Wesley and giving Rafe a chance to grab the rifle.* But he might be just as distracted and not act quickly enough.

I wondered if Wesley had an endgame. Was he going to kill all of them? And if so, why did he bring them down to the ground floor rather than kill them all on the rooftop? And why had he shot Sketch? Maybe the man had tried to sneak up on him.

Ideas and questions were spinning around in my head and I had to make them stop. I had to think clearly. Had to do something to help.

"Why'd you kill that other guy?" Sketch asked.

Despite the dire circumstances, I was pleased to hear them peppering Wesley with questions. They must have figured out that the more they kept him talking, the more it would keep him from hurting them.

"You mean Sherman?" Wesley said, staring at his fingernails.

"Yeah. What did he ever do to you?"

"He followed me out here and threatened to turn me in. I was stunned. He thought he could talk me out of shooting anyone. He actually believed that he could hold sway over me. Pitiful. I was sick of his attitude so I got rid of him."

"I heard you strangled him with a vine," Sketch said, struggling to sit up. "That's a big ten on the weird meter."

"It was a crime of passion. That hideous vine was handy. One must be open to innovation."

360

"You almost killed that plant. Julian was pissed off."

"I kill people and don't care. Do I look like I'd be concerned over a plant?" Wesley yawned.

His show of ennui made me want to strangle him myself.

He leaned indolently against the window shade and stretched his neck and shoulders.

I tensed up. This was my only chance, the perfect moment to make my move. If it worked, it might allow Rafe to get the rifle away from Wesley. Slowing turning my upper body, trying not to move my feet or make noise, I reached out, opened the control box, and switched the louver mechanism to manual operation. Then I turned up the dial to increase the speed, and holding my breath, I flipped the switch.

The groaning sound of swiftly moving louvers at every window echoed through the entire Ecosphere. I watched Wesley quickly jerk away from the window, throwing off his balance. He rotated his arms to try and regain some control, but he was standing at the edge of the ramp and there was nowhere for him to go but down.

Rafe pushed him the rest of the way down the ramp and grabbed the rifle.

Hallie screamed and jumped out of the way.

Sketch covered his head with both arms. "Are we going to die?"

I came rushing out from behind the tree and jumped over the plants to the walkway, then raced over and yanked Wesley's hands behind his back. He squealed in pain, much to my delight. I pulled the roll of duct tape from my tool belt and wrapped his wrists together.

"What are you doing here?" Hallie cried.

"Saving your butts," I said, giving Wesley a quick look. I ran up the ramp and wrapped my arms around Rafe. "Are you all right?"

"Couldn't be better," he said with a grin. "Thanks for saving our butts."

"You were doing pretty well on your own." I turned to the rest of them. "Hallie, help Sketch up and get the two of you out of here. But don't go too far. The police are on their way and they're going to want to talk to you."

Sketch managed to get on his feet. His shoulders were pulled in close. The man was scared of his own shadow at this point.

"Hey, Sketch," I called. "Don't even think about sneaking off to avoid the police. They're going to want to talk to you, too."

"I had no intention of sneaking anywhere,

young lady. I am looking forward to telling my story to law enforcement."

"Young lady? Really? I just saved your life. Can you get any more patronizing?"

He looked befuddled. "I thought I was being nice."

"You thought wrong. Ask your wife."

"I don't have to stand here and be insulted."

"No, you can probably stand anywhere and be insulted."

He actually looked hurt. I heard Rafe laughing behind me.

I rolled my eyes. "Just go."

Wesley moaned and tried to push himself up from the ground. It was an almost impossible job with both hands tied behind his back.

Rafe pointed the rifle at Wesley and said quietly, "You're not going anywhere. Don't even think about moving."

He moaned again and I nudged his leg with the toe of my boot. "Hey, Wesley. Are you nuts?"

"What?"

I realized that we had just caught a murderer, but I still had a few bones to pick with him. "Seriously, I went to all the trouble to introduce you to Mac Sullivan, and you go and accuse him of stealing a story idea. What's wrong with you?"

"I . . . I had an android in my short story."

I just stared at him for a second. "You wrote a story? I thought you were an inventor."

He sniffed. "I'm multifaceted."

"Well, whoop-dee-do. You must be really special because nobody ever thought of putting an android in a story before." Sarcasm dripped off every syllable. "Welcome to the wonderful world of science fiction, Wes. There's only a few bazillion authors writing about androids."

"But I'm the only —"

"Really. How dare you?" I said, and then laughed out loud at my own words. "How dare you accuse Mac Sullivan of stealing from you? He doesn't even know you. Mac has been writing these books for years. What have you been doing?"

"I'm important," he shrilled. "An influencer."

"No, you're not." As comebacks went, it wasn't one of my finest. But I was irate and upset on Mac's behalf.

"One more thing," I said. "Did you poison the mushrooms the night of the slow food event?"

"Certainly not!" Even though he was down on the ground, he managed to look down his nose at me. "I would never stoop that low."

"Really?"

He sniffed. "I made Sherman do it."

I shook my head. "You're a real piece of work."

And then I heard the tiny shrieks and squeaks and cackles.

"No," I whispered. "No, no, no."

"What's that?" Wesley asked, clearly worried.

I knew what it was and I couldn't breathe. The chills started at my feet and worked their way up to my neck and shoulders.

They came out of the greenery, skittering across the walkways and down the ramps like an army of tiny fuzzy white soldiers.

"Smart mice!" I shouted, and started hopping up and down to keep them from jumping on my boots and running up my legs and biting my face and chewing on my eyeballs. Oh, my dear sweet lord. This was not going to be pretty.

"You okay, Shannon?" Rafe asked.

"Not really." My legs were shaking and I needed to get out of there before I completely humiliated myself.

Mac chose that moment to storm through the doorway, followed by Eric, Tommy, and four other officers. They all had their guns drawn.

And here I was, hopping and squealing like a moron instead of hanging tough like the warrior queen of my imagination. Breathing heavily, I managed to point out the bad guy. "Wesley. He's the one who shot at Rafe. He killed Dillon and Sherman. He shot Sketch, er, Marv, in the leg and he was going to kill Hallie and Rafe."

"Shannon pretty much saved the day here," Rafe said.

Smiling with relief, I said, "You guys kept him talking."

Tommy reached for Wesley's arm, but pulled back when he saw that the killer was incapacitated. "Did you duct tape his wrists, Shannon?"

"Sure did. You know it's good for everything."

Mac moved right up to me. He wasn't smiling.

"M-m-mice," I whispered. I was trying not to hop like a fool but I was still jerking my feet up every time I saw movement. "Mac."

"I'll get you out of here," Mac said, and picked me up and held me in his arms.

"Oh, thank you," I whispered, wrapping my arms around his neck. "You are my hero.

The ultimate savior of my dreams. The man of my —"

"They're just mice, Shannon."

"No. They're *smart* mice."

"True." He buried his face in my hair and just held on for a few seconds. "Babe, you sound out of breath."

"Did you see all of them?" I glanced around uneasily. They could still climb up Mac and get to me. "There's thousands of them. They were running in a herd. And they're smart, remember. They came right for me."

He turned to look away from me and I felt him shaking. Was he laughing at me? I didn't care. "Could you, like, get me out of here?"

"Shannon, you just stopped a violent homicidal maniac from killing three more people and now you're scared by a few tiny rodents."

"It doesn't have to make sense," I grumbled.

"Right." He kissed my head. "Absolutely right. Let's get you out of here."

"Best idea yet."

He stared at me, then whispered, "God, you scared me."

"I'm sorry."

But when we got close to the doorway, I

changed my mind. "You can put me down now. I want to see what's going on."

Eric and Tommy had pulled Wesley up to his feet and were dragging him out of the Ecosphere. Rafe handed the rifle to one of the officers, who used a clean white cloth to take hold of it.

"Hold it right there!"

I turned and saw Julian Reedy standing at the doorway and holding out his arm like a traffic cop. He glared at Wesley Mycroft and pointed an accusing finger at him. "Are you the psychotic animal who tried to kill Stephanie?"

Wesley cringed. "Who's Stephanie?"

"I'll kill you myself." And Julian charged forward, hands extended in hopes of strangling Wesley in Stephanie's honor. He was angry enough to take Wesley down right then and there, but Rafe stepped in and grabbed the ethnobotanist in a fierce hug. Julian tried to wrestle him, but Rafe was clearly more powerful and was able to subdue his plant-loving pal.

"Easy there," Rafe said when Julian stopping fighting him. "They're taking him into custody. He'll be in jail for the rest of his life."

Julian swallowed uneasily, then turned to stare at Wesley. "Look at me, Mycroft."

Wesley lifted his head and sneered at Julian.

"I hope you spend every single day in a dirty, stinking prison cell, thinking about what you did to that innocent creature."

Wesley, expressionless now, just shrugged, and the two officers walked him out of the Ecosphere.

"Julian?" I said.

He glanced up at me.

"Wesley will be charged with two counts of murder, at least three counts of attempted murder, and a few counts of destruction of private property. He'll spend the rest of his life in prison. He's going to pay for hurting Stephanie."

"I'll make sure of it," Rafe insisted. "Don't worry."

Julian stared at Rafe for a long moment. "It's still not good enough, but okay. Thank you."

Rafe walked him outside.

I stared into Mac's eyes. "What took you so long to get here?"

"It's only been a few minutes since I talked to you," he said. "I raced like a madman to get here."

"It felt like hours," I admitted. "And the gun wasn't even pointed at me. Well, except for once when I thought Wesley might shoot up the ficus tree." I told him about my hiding place and the cool trick with the louvers.

His eyes narrowed dangerously. "If he had seen you behind that tree, he would've killed you."

"Yeah, probably." I shivered at his words. "You know, I never could picture him killing anyone. I thought he was too wimpy. But then I heard him confess to killing Dillon and Sherman and shooting at Rafe. And causing all those people to be poisoned. He shot Sketch in the leg. And all the time his voice was completely dry and emotionless."

"He's psycho."

"You're right." I leaned against him. "He wrote a short story with an android, so naturally he wanted to blame you for stealing it. He blames everyone for stealing all of his ideas."

"Well, turns out he was right about Sketch and Dillon. Dillon actually did steal Wesley's ideas, and Sketch talked about the Scoop-Monster as though it were his own."

Mac gazed at me. "The Scoop-Monster idea is so ridiculous, for a minute I believed it was Sketch's."

I laughed. "Yeah."

He shook his head and absently kissed my temple.

Someone else dashed by. "Where are my

370

babies?"

I leaned over and caught a glimpse of Dr. Larsson and his flapping lab coat entering the Ecosphere.

"Your mice are in there, Doctor," I said helpfully. "Hope you find them all."

He stopped and gazed around the space. "I'm just happy they found such a pleasant habitat. Unlike the woods, there are no natural enemies in here."

"Except for that psycho with the rifle," Mac muttered.

"I wonder if Wesley's the one who released the mice?" I rested my head against his chest and closed my eyes. "I could kill him for that alone."

He was shaking again. Laughing? Probably. "You look a little tired."

"I guess I am."

"Rounding up murderers and escaping smart mice makes for a hell of a day."

"I'd rather not do any of that again."

"If you want to go home, I'll take you."

"Okay. If you want to go."

He stared at me and slowly shook his head. "I'm not going anywhere."

I heard a different tone in his voice so I looked up into his eyes and saw the intensity he'd put behind those words. I touched his cheek and he turned to plant a soft kiss on the palm of my hand.

Despite facing off with a liar, a killer, and a knucklehead only minutes ago, I couldn't help but smile brightly.

"I think I'll stick around, too," I said. "Things are getting interesting."

He set me down on the ground and slung his strong arm across my shoulders. I wrapped my arm around his waist. And together we walked out of the Ecosphere and into the sunlight.

EPILOGUE

An hour later we were ensconced in Rafe and Marigold's comfortable living room. Marigold handed me a glass of iced tea and placed a platter of homemade cookies on the coffee table. I could've used a stiff drink, but it would have to wait. "I can't believe you faced another killer, Shannon. You must have nine lives."

"Rafe and the others were the ones who faced him. I just hid in the bushes and pushed a few buttons." *And squealed at a bunch of mice,* I thought. But I would keep that to myself.

Rafe sat in the big leather chair across from me. "That was smart thinking, Shannon." Rafe's expression was stark and he shook his head, remembering. "He was going to kill us."

"I believe that," I said. "He was out of his mind."

"I was about to rush him," Rafe said. "I

373

didn't have any choice. And then those louvers started moving. He freaked out and fell."

Marigold walked out of the kitchen, handed Mac a beer, and then sat on the arm of Rafe's chair. She smiled softly. "You scared the life out of me with that phone call, Shannon."

"I'm just glad you answered. I felt so much better after hearing your calm and clear voice."

"She's good in a crisis," Rafe said with a fond smile for his fiancée.

"Unlike Hallie," I said, "who kept arguing with the maniac holding the gun."

"She gets a little overwrought sometimes," Rafe said.

"She could've gotten you killed," I muttered.

"Are you still planning to shut down the company completely?" Mac asked.

"Yes," Rafe said. "Dillon caused too much damage to our reputation with all of the patents he stole."

"It was his reputation that tanked, not yours," I insisted.

Rafe nodded. "In any case, I'll keep my employees on for another six months while we clean things up and work on restitution for everyone who suffered."

"And you'll give them all bonuses," Marigold said, rubbing his arm. "And extra compensation and all the perks they need to keep them going until they all find jobs again."

"It's only fair," he said, gazing up at her. "I left them alone to deal with a monster."

It was the closing night of the conference. The massive air dome held one thousand seats and every one of them was taken. Latecomers were perfectly happy to stand against the walls to get a glimpse of the man of the hour. Rafe did not disappoint.

When he finally walked into the dome, the crowd began to chant his name, and as he approached the stage, he smiled and waved. He wore his now-trademark white linen shirt, sleeves rolled to the elbows and tucked into lightly pressed khakis, and sturdy recycled plastic flip-flops on his feet. A man of the people. Especially these people.

As he walked toward the front stage, row after row of attendees stood as he passed by, cheering and applauding.

"He looks happy," I said to Mac. "I wonder what he's thinking."

"He's probably dreaming of going home and grilling a big fat steak right about now."

"That is so *not* environmentally responsible," I said with tongue in cheek. I refused to feel guilty for joking about the subject. After a week of dealing with people like crazy Wesley Mycroft and lying Sketch Horn, mice experts, and sandcastle worm women, I needed to blow off a little steam. That didn't mean I wouldn't continue to run my business using the safest products and following the best practices possible, but we all needed to be able to crack a joke once in a while. Besides, I was not about to give up cheeseburgers. Or big fat steaks.

Glancing around, I noticed there were plenty of local people here tonight who had not registered for the conference, but who wanted to hear Rafe's closing remarks and see whose names came up at the awards ceremony. Our local newspaper, the *Light-house Standard,* was represented, and I'd heard a rumor that there was even a reporter from one of the big Bay Area newspapers in attendance.

It wasn't the first time I'd been impressed with what Rafe had accomplished. He had managed to turn this first-time conference into a major groundbreaking event for the entire technological industry and beyond. And he did all that despite having attendees who ran the gamut from earnest do-gooders to wing nut murdering whack-a-doodles.

And in spite of the aforementioned whack-a-doodles, I was truly thrilled to have participated. Yes, it was horrific that two people had been murdered in cold blood and Rafe and others had been violently threatened. Never mind that a legion of smart mice had escaped their cages, or that food poisoning had felled a quarter of the crowd, or that plants had been seriously injured, or that at least one marriage had been destroyed.

Never mind all that. The Future Global Survival Con had been a real E-ticket ride. Or to put it another way, absolute chaos had been achieved. And with that thought, I gave a mental tip of the hat to poor old weird Sherman.

But chaos or not, people were psyched to be here. Reporters, industry leaders, and technology experts would be talking about this conference for years to come. In fact, Rafe had confided earlier that next year's conference was already booked to capacity. Rafe, more than anyone, had been blown away by the news.

I smiled at Marigold sitting behind me. She squeezed my shoulder and then sat back to enjoy Rafe's speech.

He finally reached the podium and the

crowd cheered all over again.

"I'd like to thank everyone who attended the first annual Future Global Survival Con," Rafe began. "We had a few glitches, but otherwise, it was fantastic. So many people contributed to help bring this massive event together and I want to thank every one of them, including all of our speakers and special guests, our caterers, booksellers, event coordinators, and vendors. Without each one of you, we wouldn't be here. So thank you."

The audience applause was deafening since we were all basically cheering for ourselves. Everyone had obviously forgotten all about those little glitches Rafe had mentioned.

"I would especially like to mention a few people by name," Rafe continued. "These three went above and beyond the call of duty this week. Your efforts, your good counsel, and your courage will never be forgotten. They are MacKintyre Sullivan, Shannon Hammer, and Marigold Starling. Please stand up so everyone can see you."

I stood in a daze as the audience erupted in frenetic applause. I could feel the ground vibrating under my feet and it was starting to concern me. I squeezed Mac's hand the whole time until he finally had to laugh and slip his hand out of mine.

"I think you've cut off my circulation," he murmured, flexing his fingers.

"Sorry," I said as we took our seats again. "That was a little intense."

Mac glanced around. "We've got an enthusiastic crowd tonight."

"There's a fine line between that and a frenzied mob," I muttered.

"Now, I'd like to announce the winners of the foundation grants."

For the next few minutes, Rafe called up the grant winners and listed their amazing ideas for saving the world. The crowd, as expected, went wild.

"Next year," Rafe began speaking again, "I will give a fifty-thousand-dollar award to any participant who comes up with the perfect solution to save the birds from being hurt by my wind turbines."

Everyone cheered that news.

"Some of you commented that the wind turbines were operating again last night. I've successfully overcome the noise pollution issue, but the bird protection measures are an ongoing experiment. Last night I tried a new technique after learning that birds are apparently repelled by the aroma of grapes."

The crowd reacted with quizzical looks and some laughter.

"With the help of the good folks at Hammer Winery, we kept a continuous fine mist created from grape-seed extract spraying on and around the turbines. If it works, I'll be ecstatic. But if not, I'll try something else. So help me out, people. If your idea works, it could win you fifty thousand dollars."

And yet more applause greeted that line.

Rafe grinned as he walked back and forth on the stage, carrying the microphone.

"Whatever the results, you'll hear all about it at the *second* annual Future Global Survival Con! Now go enjoy the party and we'll see you next year!"

The cocktail party was in full swing when Jane came up and joined Mac and me.

"I love having a full house at the hotel, but I'll be glad to see everyone leave." She smiled and shook her head. "I'm ready for things to get back to normal."

"Do you have new people coming in?"

"Not until Tuesday, thank heaven."

"So you get one day off."

She smiled. "Not really, since we've got to spend all day tomorrow cleaning out all the rooms to get them ready for the next group."

"It's a good thing your housekeeping staff is so fabulous."

Jane nodded. "I pay lots of money to keep

them happy."

"Good practice," Mac said.

"Oh, there's Niall," I said, and waved.

"So what?" Jane said quickly. "I mean . . . who needs another drink?"

I stared at her and watched her cheeks redden. There was something going on here. But Jane still wasn't talking.

I shrugged and glanced back at Niall. "He looks busy. I guess he's helping Emily right now. He's a really good brother. A really good guy."

Jane let out a deep breath and looked pointedly in the opposite direction. "Shannon, I thought that woman Belinda was dating your uncle."

I followed her gaze, and frowned. "I thought so, too, but apparently she's dating my father."

"Awkward."

"No." I had thought so, but it was no longer awkward at all. I still wasn't so sure how I felt about my dad with a girlfriend, and I had to admit that a part of me was going to keep an eye on Belinda for a while. But I wanted to see my dad happy.

"Seriously, Shannon?" Lizzie asked. "No ugly triangles? How does Pete really feel?"

I shrugged. "He insists that Belinda is like a sister to him."

"Hmm." Jane gave another glance at the three people being discussed. "I didn't get the sister-brother vibe from those two that night at the wine bar."

Neither had I. And I still wondered if Belinda had switched her affections from Uncle Pete to my dad. But she and Dad were so sure of everything, so who was I to disagree? I would try to take the time in the next week or so to drive out to the winery and get the full scoop from Uncle Pete.

"There's a mystery wrapped up in there," I said thoughtfully. And I would get to the bottom of it eventually.

"But your dad looks really happy," Jane said.

"He sure does."

Marigold joined our little group, and after we all clinked glasses, she leaned against me. "I'm exhausted," she admitted.

"Right there with you."

"And all I did was talk about quilting one afternoon," she said. "You unmasked a vicious killer and plant strangler."

"And poisoner," Lizzie added. "And mouse liberator, and . . . what else?"

"I don't even want to think about it," Marigold said, giving me a quick one-armed hug. "But you did it."

"All in a day's work," I said, and they all

laughed.

"I know you, Shannon." Jane gazed at me perceptively. "You had to have been scared to death. I mean, there were mice."

Everyone laughed again. They all knew about my little phobia now that word had gotten out about the attack of the smart mice.

"But there was also the aforementioned vicious killer," Lizzie added, bringing them all back to reality.

I exhaled heavily. "Yeah, well. Wesley Mycroft is just plain evil. And creepy, too. And then, okay, all those mice pouring out of the greenery just freaked me out."

I was trying my best to make light of it, but talk about creepy. I rubbed my arms all over again.

My friends were quiet for a moment while I shook off the memory of staring down that rifle barrel and then confronting the army of fuzzy rodents.

"Hey, there's Midge," Mac said, changing the subject while subtly squeezing my hand.

I gave him a grateful smile for moving the attention away from me, then turned to see what everyone else was looking at. The petite woman was standing at the bar, deep in conversation with Dr. Larsson.

"That's an interesting pair," I said.

Marigold turned to see. "That's the mouse doctor. But isn't she still involved with Sketch Horn?"

"Oh no," Mac said dryly. "Actually, I understand that Midge and the mouse doctor are collaborating on ways to get smart mice to live underwater."

"Smart mice," Lizzie said, shaking her head. "That's just weird."

"You don't know the half of it," I muttered. The shivers hit again without warning and I didn't even try to be subtle as I rubbed my arms briskly again.

"There's Honey," Lizzie said, pointing out Sketch Horn's wife as she moved with cat-like elegance over to the bar.

"You know her?" I asked.

"She came into the store for the book signing the first day of the conference. She's really sweet. And smart."

I wouldn't have called Honey *sweet,* but I liked her. Mac and I gave the girls an abbreviated recap of the scene with Honey raking her husband over the coals the other day. Not that he hadn't deserved it.

Lizzie frowned as a thought occurred. "Do you think she calls herself Honey Horn?"

I spluttered my wine, looked up at Mac, and we both laughed out loud.

Mac managed to say, "I don't think she'll

be using her husband's name much longer."

"And that's not even his real name," Jane said.

"And even if it was," I added. "Honey Horn? That name probably won't work for her."

Lizzie nodded soberly. "You're probably right."

Rafe joined our group and wrapped his arm around Marigold's waist. "I hope you're all having fun."

"The best," Jane said. "You throw a good party, Rafe."

"Thanks. I had a little help." He glanced at Mac and me. "I'd like the board to meet in a few days for some post-conference discussions, but I want to get your first impressions while they're still fresh."

"First impressions of what?" I asked.

"Of the conference," he said, grinning. "What did you think of it overall?"

I started to answer, but then saw something that distracted me completely. "Wait. Sorry, Rafe. But isn't that Julian Reedy putting his arm around Sketch Horn's wife?"

"Ooh," Jane said. "Julian and Honey make a pretty couple, don't they?"

I stared at her. My friend Jane had a romantic soul, but she was getting carried away with the twisted dream of a Julian-

Honey hookup. "Seriously?"

Her smile was dreamy. "I just want everyone to be happy."

"Honey's probably just gathering research for her next book," Lizzie said. "But they are awfully cute together."

"That settles it," Mac said, patting Rafe on the back. "You want my opinion? This conference is so much better than any writers' conference I've ever been to, simply for the amount of crazy whacked-out coupling going on."

Rafe threw his head back and laughed. "I guess that's one way to gauge its effectiveness."

"I give it a big thumbs-up," I said. "For world-class thrills and chills."

"Oh, Shannon." He gave me a warm hug. "You saved some lives this week and I appreciate it. I especially appreciate you keeping Marigold safe."

"My absolute pleasure, believe me," I said, sharing a secret smile with Marigold. "She kept me safe, too."

"Then I'd say it was a real success," Rafe said.

"Hmm, let's see," I mused. "Two murders, rampaging mice, a barn raising, couples uncoupling, and a shot through the hearth."

I raised my arms in a victory salute. "Best conference ever!"

ABOUT THE AUTHOR

A native Californian, *New York Times* best-selling author **Kate Carlisle** worked in television for many years before turning to writing. Inspired by the northern seaside towns of her native California, where Victorian mansions grace the craggy cliffs and historic lighthouses warn fishermen and smugglers alike, Kate was drawn to create the Fixer-Upper Mysteries, featuring small-town girl Shannon Hammer, a building contractor specializing in home restoration. Kate also writes the *New York Times* best-selling Bibliophile Mysteries featuring Brooklyn Wainwright.

ABOUT THE AUTHOR

A native Californian, New York Times best-selling author Kate Carlisle worked in television for many years before turning to writing. Inspired by the northern seaside towns of her native California, where Victorian mansions grace the craggy cliffs and historic lighthouses warn fishermen and smugglers alike, Kate was drawn to create the Fixer-Upper Mysteries, featuring small-town girl Shannon Hammer, a building contractor specializing in home restoration. Kate also writes the New York Times best-selling Bibliophile Mysteries featuring Brooklyn Wainwright.